"Why do you think Brandon asked you to marry him?" Alex asked.

Highly miffed, Kari said, "What? You don't think he's madly, passionately in love with me?"

She *knew* Brandon wasn't in love with her, but she was offended that Alex obviously hadn't considered it a possibility. Just because *he* didn't care about her was no reason to assume another man wouldn't.

"I didn't say that," Alex replied. "I was just wondering if you thought he had some ulterior motive." He winced, as if aware he was only making bad matters worse. "I'm sorry. I didn't mean to imply—"

"That I'm not a desirable woman in my own right?" Pleased to see him so discomfited, she eyed him with a slight smile.

He met her gaze steadily. "You're the most desirable woman I've ever known."

Dear Reader,

We've got six great books for you this month, and three of them are part of miniseries you've grown to love. Dallas Schulze continues A FAMILY CIRCLE with *Addie and the Renegade*. Dallas is known to readers worldwide as an author whose mastery of emotion is unparalleled, and this book will only enhance her well-deserved reputation. For Cole Walker, love seems like an impossibility—until he's stranded with Addie Smith, and suddenly... Well, maybe I'd better let you read for yourself. In *Leader of the Pack*, Justine Davis keeps us located on TRINITY STREET WEST. You met Ryan Buckhart in *Lover Under Cover;* now meet Lacey Buckhart, the one woman—the one wife!—he's never been able to forget. Then finish off Laura Parker's ROGUES' GALLERY with *Found: One Marriage*. Amnesia, exes who still share a love they've never been able to equal anywhere else...this one has it all.

Of course, our other three books are equally special. Nikki Benjamin's *The Lady and Alex Payton* is the follow-up to *The Wedding Venture*, and it features a kidnapped almost-bride. Barbara Faith brings you *Long-Lost Wife?* For Annabel the past is a mystery—and the appearance of a man claiming to be her husband doesn't make things any clearer, irresistible though he may be. Finally, try Beverly Bird's *The Marrying Kind*. Hero John Gunner thinks that's just the kind of man he's *not*, but meeting Tessa Hadley-Bryant proves to him just how wrong a man can be.

And be sure to come back next month for more of the best romantic reading around—here in Silhouette Intimate Moments.

Yours,

Leslie Wainger

Leslie Wainger
Senior Editor and Editorial Coordinator

Please address questions and book requests to:
Silhouette Reader Service
U.S.: 3010 Walden Ave., P.O. Box 1325, Buffalo, NY 14269
Canadian: P.O. Box 609, Fort Erie, Ont. L2A 5X3

THE LADY AND ALEX PAYTON

NIKKI BENJAMIN

Silhouette®

INTIMATE™MOMENTS®

Published by Silhouette Books

America's Publisher of Contemporary Romance

 SILHOUETTE BOOKS

ISBN 0-373-07729-7

THE LADY AND ALEX PAYTON

Copyright © 1996 by Barbara Vosbein

Printed in U.S.A.

Books by Nikki Benjamin

Silhouette Intimate Moments

A Man to Believe In #359
Restless Wind #519
The Wedding Venture #645
The Lady and Alex Payton #729

Silhouette Special Edition

Emily's House #539
On the Whispering Wind #663
The Best Medicine #716
It Must Have Been the Mistletoe #782
My Baby, Your Child #880
Only St. Nick Knew #928

NIKKI BENJAMIN

was born and raised in the Midwest, but after years in the Houston area she considers herself a true Texan. Nikki says she's always been an avid reader. (Her earliest literary heroines were Nancy Drew, Trixie Belden and Beany Malone.) Her writing experience was limited, however, until a friend started penning a novel and encouraged Nikki to do the same. One scene led to another, and soon she was hooked.

When not reading or writing, the author enjoys spending time with her husband and son, needlepoint, hiking, biking, horseback riding and sailing.

For my very special circle of
hometown friends and fellow writers:
Francyne Anderson, Christie Craig, Mica Kelch,
Dawn Mulholland and Linda Jenkins-Nutting.
You're the best!

Special thanks to Francyne Anderson for
THE ARTIST'S WAY.

Chapter 1

"Going somewhere?"

Halfway across the darkened living room, Alexander Payton paused, then turned and scanned the shadows. He had hoped to get away without a confrontation, but obviously he wasn't going to be that lucky.

Should have waited awhile longer to make his exit, he thought, his gaze falling on his friend Devlin Gray. Devlin was sitting in the rocking chair near the side window with his infant son—and now, officially, Alex's godson—cradled in his arms.

Alex had heard the baby crying over an hour ago. However, when he'd quieted almost immediately, Alex had assumed that either Laura or Devlin had tended to him, then tucked him into his crib again. Wanting to leave as planned, he had finished packing, called a cab and slipped downstairs. Only to be caught in midflight.

He supposed he ought to be grateful Laura wasn't the one eyeing him reproachfully while rocking gently. He'd stayed as long as he had only because he hadn't wanted to hurt her feelings. Had *she* caught him sneaking off, he would have been mortified.

But Devlin... Devlin he would like to string up by the thumbs.

"What do you think?" Alex countered, making no effort to hide his sarcasm, though he kept his voice low in deference to the baby.

"That you're making a big mistake," Devlin replied, his tone matter-of-fact.

"By getting out of here as fast as I can?" Alex snorted. "The way I see it, if I'd had any sense at all I wouldn't have waited thirty-six hours. I'd have left as soon as I laid eyes on your little sister."

"So, why didn't you?"

"I promised Laura I'd be here for Andrew's christening, and I always keep my word."

True enough. But it was not the only reason he had come to Virginia or stayed longer than he should have.

Contrary to what he had once teasingly told Laura, he wasn't psychic. However, on occasion, he *was* highly intuitive. Not that he had needed more than simple common sense to know, with undeniable certainty, that Kari Gray would be there for her nephew's christening.

Besides Laura's six-year-old son, Timmy, and baby Andrew, Kari was the only family Laura and Devlin had. So naturally she'd be the one they would ask to serve as Andrew's godmother. And since she was the type to take such a responsibility seriously, she wouldn't willingly miss the ceremony.

Though neither Laura nor Devlin had said anything to confirm his suspicion, Alex hadn't been the least bit surprised by her arrival early Saturday afternoon. In fact, he'd actually been looking forward to it. Until the moment she met his gaze and he realized what a fool he'd been.

He should have known better than to believe that after almost six years she might finally be able to forgive him for the unconscionable way he'd treated her. Talk about wishing for the moon.

She'd paused just inside the doorway and stared at him as if he were something nasty smeared on a sidewalk. And though she had never been anything but excruciatingly polite the rest of the weekend, she had let him know he'd done a better job of burning his bridges than he had ever imagined.

"Yeah, sure. Because you gave your word. Tell me another one," Devlin growled, bringing Alex back to the present.

"All right, I admit I came here expecting to see your sister. And I had hoped she'd be able to let bygones be bygones so we could be friends again...for Andrew's sake. Unfortunately, she wasn't ready to forgive me yet. So..." Feigning indifference, Alex shifted his backpack from one shoulder to the other and turned away.

He couldn't blame her. Not after what he'd done to her. When you walked out on a woman in the midst of making love to her—when you rolled away from her, gathered your clothes and left her without explanation or apology—then suddenly came face-to-face with her six years later, you could hardly expect her to greet you with open arms. That she had simply stared at him wordlessly until he'd had sense enough to leave the room, and had not flown into a murderous rage, was actually more than he had deserved.

Later, walking the quiet, shaded streets of Devlin's suburban neighborhood, Alex had admitted they were better off remaining estranged. He knew he could never think of Kari as just a friend. Yet he was no more able to give her now what she had needed from him six years ago.

Back then he had seen the longing in her eyes as she'd reached for him and held him close. A longing for marriage and a family that had torn at his heart. And he had known that by finishing what he'd started, by claiming her in the most intimate way a man could claim a woman, he would be making a promise he couldn't allow himself to keep.

Not tainted as he was by the monstrous acts of the two seemingly normal people who had been his parents. And certainly not believing—as he always had—that somewhere beneath the surface of his own civility there might very well lurk a similar streak of sadism.

Instead he had done what he'd deemed best for her. He had ended their relationship... unequivocally.

"So you're going to let her go back to Brandon Selby, huh?" Devlin queried, drawing Alex from his reverie yet again.

Less than pleased by the new tack Devlin had taken, Alex hesitated a moment. Then, refusing to be baited, he continued toward the door.

"The trainer she works with in San Antonio? Sure, why not? From the little she said yesterday, I gather she's learned a lot from him, and he's finally going to let her show a couple of his horses on the regional circuit later this summer."

"He's also asked her to marry him," Devlin stated softly.

Feeling as if he'd been punched in the gut, Alex spun around and stared at his friend. That she worked for the man was one thing. But Kari *married* to Brandon Selby? Over *his* dead body.

From all accounts, the former United States Olympic equestrian team member who owned the exclusive stable where Kari worked was highly regarded among his associ ates. And Devlin, having met the man on two or three occasions, had pronounced him quite personable.

Until last summer, Alex hadn't had any reason to question his friend's judgment. But then, on his way to Mexico—where he'd been ordered to recuperate under Devlin's watchful eye—Alex had made a side trip to San Antonio. Having barely survived a terrorist attack in the Middle East, he had wanted, *needed,* to see Kari again. Not up close and personal. Just at a distance. And while he'd been lurking around Selby Stables, he'd caught more than a glimpse of the owner in action.

To say he hadn't liked what he'd seen would be an understatement. Granted, Selby was a topflight trainer capable of getting the very best out of his clients' horses. But Alex had also discovered that the man had a mean streak.

Standing in the shadows, Alex had had to fight to remain still and silent while Selby tore a strip off Kari for what he deemed her coddling of a nervous young gelding. His cruel, abusive language had left her in tears. Then, not more than five minutes later, he'd returned to the barn full of sweet talk. He had teased her playfully as if nothing had happened, throwing her utterly off balance in a way that made his blood run cold.

"Has she accepted his proposal?" Alex forced himself to ask at last.

"Not yet."

"But you think she will eventually?"

"Actually, no, I don't."

"Well, then—" Alex began, more relieved than he wanted to admit.

"Unfortunately, *that* is what's worrying me," Devlin hastened to add. "Not too long ago she thought Selby hung the moon. She should be thrilled he's proposed to her, but she's not. And although she hasn't said anything specific, I get the feeling she's upset about something."

"Something to do with Selby?"

Recalling the scene he'd witnessed last summer, Alex understood how that could be possible. But why would Kari continue to work for the man if he upset her?

"I'm not sure," Devlin replied. "She always seemed to be in awe of him. Yet when she mentioned his marriage proposal last night, she was anything but happy about it. In fact, I got the impression Selby's amorous interest in her was making her more than a little uneasy."

"So, why doesn't she just quit?" Alex asked, voicing his thoughts. "Whether or not Selby gives her a reference, she shouldn't have any trouble finding another job."

"She told Laura she's been thinking about moving on, but not just yet. In fact, Laura said she seemed really leery about leaving Selby Stables. When she tried to find out why, Kari put her off. Said she had some loose ends to tie up, and she could deal with Selby for as long as it took. But I'm not so sure."

Alex wasn't, either. Not after seeing the way Selby had treated her on at least one occasion. But Kari had always had a mind of her own. Convincing her that she needed help would be no easy task.

"Since she's managed to work with him successfully for several years, she must know how to handle him," he offered, trying to reassure himself as well as his friend. "And although they've obviously had a parting of the ways, she must feel reasonably safe staying on at the stable. She's too smart to do anything to purposely endanger herself."

"I wish I could agree with you. But something more than a simple parting of the ways has come between her and Brandon Selby. Something that seems to be scaring the hell out of her. Yet she can't walk away."

"Or won't," Alex muttered, aware just how obstinate Kari Gray could be.

Once committed to a course of action, she wouldn't back down willingly. Nor would she ask for assistance. She'd simply forge ahead on her own as long as possible.

"Or won't," Devlin acknowledged. Hesitating a moment, he met Alex's gaze, then continued quietly, "Either way, I want you to find out why. And I don't want you to let her go back there until you do."

"Oh, really?" Alex drawled, trying to mask his sudden dismay.

He understood Devlin's concern for Kari. And he knew that with Laura, the children and a demanding job, Devlin couldn't possibly look after her himself. But surely he could find someone better suited to the task than Alex was. Kari hated his guts, and not without good reason. She'd never allow him to help her. Never in a million years.

"Yes, really," Devlin stated simply, shifting in the rocking chair as Andrew began to fuss again. "You mentioned you were heading out to your ranch in the Hill Country north of San Antonio. You could take her with you and keep an eye on her while you find out what's going on with Brandon Selby."

"Just like that, huh?" His tone derogatory, Alex snapped his fingers. "I'm supposed to take her to my little hideaway and get her to tell me all her troubles? Get real, Devlin. You know as well as I do that she wouldn't spit on me if I was on fire, and you know why—"

"Please, Alex, you're the only one we can trust to look out for her," Laura cut in quietly.

Whirling around, Alex saw her standing in the doorway, wearing a long, white cotton robe, her dark hair curling around her shoulders, and instantly realized he was fighting a lost cause. Laura Burke Buschetti Gray was like a sister to him. There wasn't much he'd refuse to do for her.

"Laura is right. You're part of the family now. And we really need your help," Devlin added.

As Laura crossed the room, he stood, then handed her the baby. Settling into the rocking chair, she shifted the bodice of her robe discreetly and began to nurse her son.

Feeling as if he were caught in a bad dream, Alex watched as Devlin and Laura shared a smile, then shifted their attention to the baby. They *had* made him a part of their family, and for that he was more grateful than he could say. He had no one else. No one at all. And he really would do anything for them.

But the thought of spending several days alone with Devlin's sister, trying to talk her into letting him help her, filled him with a sickening sense of dread. She'd already made it clear she wanted nothing to do with him. To think she'd go with him willingly, much less *stay* with him, was downright silly.

"I wish I could," he hedged as he glanced out the front window. *Where the hell was that taxicab?* "But you know as well as I do Kari is not going to cooperate."

"Probably not at first," Devlin admitted, tucking his hands in the pockets of his sweatpants. Beside him, Laura murmured soothingly at Andrew.

"So what am I supposed to do? Kidnap her?" Alex demanded.

"I imagine that would be the easiest thing to do," Laura replied, regarding him gravely.

"Oh, you do, huh?" Shifting his gaze from Laura to Devlin, he willed his friend to disagree.

"You said yourself she's not going to go along with you of her own accord, so..." Devlin shrugged dispassionately.

"So I kidnap her." Shoving a hand through his shaggy curls, Alex bent his head and stared at the floor, then eyed Devlin again. "Here and now?"

"You'd have to transport her halfway across the country to get her to your place, but if you're game..." Devlin smiled slightly. "I say go for it."

"Why do I have to take her *there?*" Alex retorted. Then, referring to the head of the government agency that employed them both, he added, "Surely McConnell has a safe house somewhere around here I could use for a few days."

"Because you'll have better luck finding out what Selby is up to if you're reasonably close to his base of operation. And your place is nice and secluded. Kari won't have much choice but to stay there."

"Well, I can guarantee I'm not driving cross-country with a woman who's more than likely going to fight me every inch of the way."

He wasn't that crazy. At least not yet.

"I can't say I blame you," Devlin admitted, his voice tinged with laughter. "But there is an alternative."

"And what, pray tell, would that be?" Alex asked, not nearly as amused as his friend.

"Waylay her at the San Antonio airport," Laura replied, rejoining their conversation.

"Come on, give me a break. She'll scream bloody murder and I'll end up in jail. Or worse, she'll haul off and knock me senseless. I've seen the way she handles those horses she rides. She may look like a fragile little thing, but she's not."

"So knock *her* out," Devlin advised.

"Are you nuts?" Alex growled. "We're talking about your *sister*. And surely you haven't forgotten how I feel about using violence against a defenseless woman."

"I didn't mean for you to hit her over the head."

"Well, then, what *did* you have in mind?"

Alex stared at his friends dubiously as Devlin outlined several alternatives. They eyed him in return, their expressions intent, as if they weren't quite sure what he would say or do next.

Instinctively, he wanted to run—far and fast. Yet he was caught by the bonds of their friendship. He had a duty to honor those bonds in whatever way he could, regardless of the emotional toll doing so might take.

They had asked very little of him in return for all they'd given him. To turn his back on them when they so obviously needed his help would be unconscionable.

Much as he would like to believe they'd simply concocted some sort of scheme to throw him and Kari together, he knew better. Having seen Brandon Selby in action, he had no doubt crossing the man could prove dangerous. And that might be just what Selby would assume Kari was doing by declining his proposal.

With an inner sigh of resignation, Alex shifted his backpack again. "Sounds like you two have given this a lot of thought."

"We were going to talk to you about it earlier, but we were afraid Kari might overhear us," Laura acknowledged. "Devlin figured you'd try to leave before morning, so we decided to wait and catch you on your way out."

"So this was a setup?"

"Sort of," Devlin admitted with a sheepish smile.

"Sort of, my butt," Alex retorted, aware he'd been well and truly had. All for a good cause, of course. But that didn't make him any happier about what was in store for him in the days ahead.

"You know I'd handle this myself if I could," Devlin said, resting a hand on Laura's shoulder.

"Yeah, I know."

Alex bent his head and tried to order his thoughts. Devlin had enough to worry about, and he did have a month's vacation coming to him. Might as well use a few days of it doing a good deed. How much would it cost him in the long run? Not much provided he kept Kari at a distance. And that certainly shouldn't be a problem. Not considering what she thought of him.

"So, what's the plan?" he asked. "Because I'm sure you've got one."

"She's booked on a five o'clock flight nonstop to San Antonio. We'll make sure she's on the plane," Devlin said. "Since you're leaving on an early-morning flight, you should have time to make whatever preparations you consider necessary and be waiting for her when she arrives, right?"

"Right," Alex agreed. "What about Selby? He's expecting her back at work Tuesday morning, isn't he? Surely he'll raise some sort of hue and cry if she doesn't show up as scheduled."

"I'm going to call him as soon as Kari is on the plane and tell him she's ill. Too ill to talk to him herself," Laura said. "That should buy you three or four days, and maybe that will be all you'll need."

"Maybe," Alex muttered, somehow doubting he would be that lucky.

Out of the corner of his eye, he saw a pair of headlights cut through the darkness beyond the front window, then heard the muted hum of the taxi's engine as the vehicle drew to a halt in the circular driveway. *Finally*. The dispatcher had told Alex he'd have a thirty-minute wait, but he felt as if he'd been standing in Devlin's living room much longer than that.

"You'll let us know she's all right?" Laura asked.

"I'll call just as soon as we get to my place," he promised.

"We know you'll take good care of her."

"Yeah, sure."

"And you'll keep us apprised of the situation, too," Devlin urged.

Suddenly eager to be on his way, Alex nodded as he edged toward the door. He had a lot to do in the hours ahead. Without careful planning, Kari could slip by him. And he simply couldn't allow her to go back to Selby until he was absolutely sure she had nothing to fear from the man.

"Have a safe trip," Devlin said.

"And remember you're supposed to be staying with us when you come back to see McConnell next month," Laura added. "We'll be expecting you."

"I'll be here," Alex promised her. "As long as I'm still welcome."

"You'll always be welcome in our home, Alex. Always," Laura assured him.

He nodded again, then slipped out the door. He could only hope that would still be true four weeks from now. But he couldn't guarantee it.

Though neither Devlin nor Laura would ever admit it, *he* could be as much a danger to Kari as Brandon Selby. And while he would never intentionally do anything to hurt her, physically or emotionally, there was no telling what might happen between them in the coming days.

They would be thrown together in such a way that he would have to keep his own emotions deeply buried. He'd have to think of her as his best friend's sister, nothing more, nothing less. And he'd stay as far away from her as he could in the little house they'd be sharing. Not only for her good, but his, as well.

In an upstairs bedroom overlooking the driveway of her brother's house, Kari Gray pressed her forehead against the cool glass and watched as Alexander Payton climbed into the waiting taxicab. He did so swiftly, without a backward glance, evidently anxious to be on his way.

She should be glad to see him go. Instead she was filled with a sudden, bewildering sense of loss.

How silly, she thought, brushing at the single tear sliding down her cheek. You couldn't lose someone who had never really been a part of your life. Someone who had also made sure you understood—in no uncertain terms—that he never would be.

But she had fallen in love with Alexander Payton the first time she had laid eyes on him. And though she had tried hard to put him out of her mind and heart since the night he'd so rudely walked out on her six years ago, the just-stepped-off-a-cliff sensation she'd experienced upon seeing him again Saturday afternoon had been a cruel reminder of just how futile her attempts had been.

She had read somewhere that your first love was often your true love, and that people who were reunited after years of separation often rekindled their romance, became permanent partners and experienced the most intense emotional satisfaction of their lives. And she had hoped that maybe, just maybe, one day that would happen to her and Alex.

But then, she had never been able to accept the probability that he hadn't ever cared for her in quite the same way she had cared for him.

The first time Devlin had brought Alex home to San Antonio she had been only sixteen, a late-in-life second child, twelve years younger than her brother, shy and somewhat sheltered. Alex had been twenty-two, a cool and aloof second lieutenant recently graduated from West Point, a loner without any family according to her brother, who had been his commanding officer.

He had obviously felt out of place in the laid-back atmosphere of the Gray household. But once he'd learned to relax a little, Alex had treated her much as Devlin did, with the teasing fondness of an elder brother. She had wanted so much more from him, yet she had schooled herself to be patient. Because she had believed that one day he would see her as a woman and claim her as his own.

He had come home with Devlin several times over the next five years, and with each subsequent visit, he had spent more and more time with her. And then, when he'd visited just after her parents had died, one after the other within a few weeks, Kari had sensed a definite change in their relationship.

Alex had stayed a week, then two, helping her deal with her grief. Devlin, now married with a young daughter of his own and assigned to the American embassy in El Norte, hadn't been able to be there for her. But Alex had stepped in and filled the void, not so much as a brother but as a very dear friend.

He had helped her sort through her parents' belongings and get the old house ready to put up for sale. And when he had found her crying alone in the dark, he had held her and kissed away her tears.

Though he had done nothing but kiss her that night, Kari had begun to believe he loved her as much as she loved him. And when he put off leaving for another week, she had been sure that their time had finally come.

Over the next few days, she had told him about her dream of raising horses and children on a ranch in the Texas Hill Country. When he'd agreed that would be a wonderful life, a life he wouldn't mind living himself, she had assumed he meant with her, and she had been elated.

Throwing caution to the wind, she had gone to him with her heart on her sleeve that last night. Lying down beside him, she had offered him all she had to give, and after some moments' hesitation, he had responded as she'd always hoped he would. But in the midst of making slow, sweet love to her, he'd suddenly rolled away, gathered his clothes and fled as if he had the hounds of hell at his heels.

To say she had been devastated would be putting it lightly. For days she'd agonized over what she'd said or done to chase him away. Then anger at herself as well as him had taken hold of her. Gradually she began to realize she'd done nothing to warrant such crass treatment. Nothing but love him with all her heart, then make the mistake of letting him know it.

Her fury at his unconscionable behavior had enabled her to shake off the vestiges of the painful humiliation he'd caused her, and she'd finally pulled herself together. She had gone back to work at the small stable where she kept the books and gave riding lessons. And she had ridden for every owner who offered her the opportunity, winning at show after show, attracting the attention of Brandon Selby, who had eventually invited her to join his staff.

Deeply flattered, she had accepted, only to realize all too soon that she'd made a big mistake, one that left her convinced she had no savvy at all where men were concerned.

But at least with Alex only her ego had been hurt. Unless she was very careful, her relationship with Brandon Selby might end up costing her life. If he was doing what she was almost certain he was doing, and realized she was onto him, he wouldn't have any qualms about getting rid of her permanently. And the longer she stayed at Selby Stables, the greater that possibility became.

Yet she couldn't just walk away. Not until she had enough evidence to put the bastard behind bars.

Unfortunately, Brandon Selby was among the most highly regarded trainers in the equestrian world. He was also a celebrated member of San Antonio society. Without some verification that her suspicions were valid, who would give credence to her claim that he was killing million-dollar show horses for the insurance money? Certainly no one in the business, and more than likely, no one involved in local law enforcement, either. Why, she hadn't even considered the possibility herself until Moonwalker was put down.

Turning away from the window, Kari crossed to the bed, sat down amid the rumpled sheets and stared into the waning darkness.

She dreaded going back to San Antonio. Dreaded it deeply. But she couldn't see that she had any other choice if she hoped to catch Selby in the act.

Yet how could she go on as if nothing had changed between them? And how long could she dither over his marriage proposal before he demanded an answer? In order to stay on at the stable she'd have to say yes, and then she'd have no good reason to keep him at bay.

At the mere thought of having to submit to him sexually, she shuddered.

Looking back, she had no idea what she had seen in the man. She had never loved him. Not in the same way she had loved Alex. But for a time she had thought that with their shared interest in training horses they could have a future together. Until she began to see the cruel side of him he usually managed to hide so well, and realized he wasn't half the man she had wanted him to be.

Recalling how she had made excuses for him, telling herself he was just slightly eccentric or perhaps a tad temperamental, Kari shook her head in disgust. She had enabled him to go on fooling others even as she'd allowed herself to be fooled. Now she found herself between a rock and a hard place. And she was there all alone.

She had come close to telling Devlin and Laura about her predicament. But seeing them together with Timmy and the baby, she hadn't had the heart to involve them.

And she had learned to fend for herself long ago. With Devlin out of the country until recently, she hadn't much choice.

Leaning back against the headboard, she shoved her hand through her short, dark hair, suddenly aware how desperately weary she was. Her head ached, her eyes felt hot and gritty and she was starting to feel rather sorry for herself.

She had hoped that in the relative safety of her brother's house she would find a little peace. She hadn't expected Alex to be there, too, stirring up old memories that taunted her mercilessly through the night.

Well, he was gone now. Hopefully, gone for good. And she still had a few hours to go before she'd be expected to put in an appearance at breakfast.

Sliding under the bedcovers, she turned and pressed her face into her pillow, closed her eyes and willed herself to think soothing thoughts. But all she saw in her mind's eye was Alex, still and silent, watching her with his bright-blue eyes as she had caught him doing off and on all weekend, his expression one of utter disinterest.

"Damn you, Alexander Payton," she said with a sigh. "Damn you for still being able to hurt me."

Chapter 2

Following the crowd of newly arrived passengers shuffling through the main corridor of the San Antonio airport on their way to baggage claim, Kari shifted the strap of her garment bag from one shoulder to the other. She'd wanted to carry on her overnight bag, as well, but Devlin had insisted on checking it, saying he hated seeing her so weighed down. She had been too tired to argue with him then. Now, thinking of the added wait she was going to have, she wished she had.

All she really wanted at the moment was to find her car in the parking lot, drive home and go straight to bed. She had dozed a bit before dawn and a bit more on the plane, but that had barely taken the edge off her exhaustion. What she needed was about twelve or fifteen hours of deep, dreamless sleep. Then she might feel like a human being again instead of a muzzy-minded robot running on automatic pilot.

Unfortunately, with the wait for her bag and the drive to her little cottage on the stable grounds, she'd be lucky to make it home by ten. And Brandon would expect her to be ready for her first training session at seven o'clock in the morning.

Just the thought of having to face him again made her want to weep. But she couldn't afford to waste her energy on such self-indulgence.

Recognizing several people from her flight among those clustered around one of the baggage carousels off to the left, Kari moved to join them. As she tried to wedge herself between a harried woman with two small children and an elderly man, she gazed at the revolving, yet still-empty conveyor belt, willing her bag to appear.

Within moments, a huge suitcase tumbled out of the opening, followed closely by several smaller bags. Around her, other passengers crowded closer, angling for a better position. Someone jostled her elbow and she drew her arms against her sides, annoyed. She wanted out of there as much as anybody else, but pushing and shoving wouldn't—

From behind, someone bumped into her hard. At the same instant, she felt a sting in her left hip. As if someone had jabbed her with a needle. Angry now, she whirled around, prepared to give the person a piece of her mind. But as she lifted her chin and eyed the stranger hovering less than two feet from her, she bit back her words.

Talk about a real weirdo. Dressed in black jeans and a black T-shirt, he had a black baseball cap pulled low on his forehead. Long, greasy black hair hung straight to his shoulders, a scraggly black beard covered his cheeks and chin, and thick-lensed, black-framed glasses obscured his eyes.

He looked back at her leeringly, as if given half a chance he'd gladly eat her alive, then muttered an apology, his speech slurred.

Probably drunk, she thought as she acknowledged his words with a nod. Still, a shiver of fear slid down her spine as she turned away.

She couldn't remember seeing him on the plane, but that didn't mean anything. She didn't remember seeing half the people standing around her. Yet there was something vaguely familiar about him.

She was fairly sure she'd never met him. His face wasn't one she would have easily forgotten. Maybe he worked at one of the other stables in the area. Or maybe she'd seen him at a distance at one of the horse shows. Maybe with Brandon—

No, she assured herself. Not with Brandon. Although the possibility that the two men knew each other wasn't completely out of the question. She had seen Brandon talking to several shady characters at horse shows as well as at the stable over the past year or so. And if he had somehow realized she was onto him, and wanted to be rid of her—

Aware she was jumping to some pretty wild conclusions on the basis of a little bump at the baggage-claim area, Kari gave herself a firm mental shake.

She'd been very, very careful not to say or do anything to put Brandon on the alert. And she certainly hadn't shared her suspicions about him with anyone. He shouldn't have any reason to be worried about her. Which meant she had no reason to be worried about some stranger at the airport. Except in the way any normal, intelligent woman ought to be worried about some odd man who happened to cross her path.

Rubbing her sore hip with her hand, Kari finally saw her overnight bag on the far side of the carousel. When it rolled around in front of her at last, she grabbed it gratefully and with a swift, sidelong glance at the man she hurried toward the exit.

Because she was going to be away only a few days, she had opted to park in the lot just outside the terminal rather than in one of the less costly remote parking areas. Despite the added expense, she was very glad she had. She would have probably fallen asleep on her feet if she'd had to stand and wait for a shuttle bus. As it was, she hoped the short walk through the cool evening air would revive her enough so she could drive home without running off the road.

Pausing just outside the doorway, she glanced over her shoulder cautiously. Much to her relief, the stranger was nowhere to be seen. She dug her car keys out of her purse, along with the parking receipt on which she'd wisely jotted down the section where she'd left her car. M-12, she noted. Off to the right and about halfway back.

After juggling her bags so she had one hand free to hold her keys and receipt, she started toward the lot along with a couple of other returning travelers. She glanced back again, but saw no one out of the ordinary following her in the growing darkness.

Reassured, she faced forward once more, then stopped short as a wave of dizziness washed over her. Weaving slightly, she put a hand to her forehead and closed her eyes.

Maybe she was too tired to drive home. Maybe she ought to go back to the terminal and take a taxi. But no, she really needed her car. And Brandon wouldn't be pleased if she had to take off again tomorrow to fetch it. As he'd reminded her Friday night while watching her pack, summer was their busiest time of year.

Opening her eyes again, Kari saw that her car was parked just a few rows away. Surely she would feel better once she was sitting down. And she could stop for a cup of coffee at one of the fast-food restaurants on the highway. A little caffeine ought to wake her up.

Though she felt as if she were trudging through a foot of mud rather than traversing a patch of tarmac, she forced herself to continue to her car. But by the time she halted next to the driver's side of the aging compact car she'd inherited from her parents, the dizziness had returned with a vengeance.

She dropped her bags on the ground, wondering how she would ever manage to pick them up again, much less heave them onto the back seat of the car. Then, fumbling slightly, she tried to fit the key in the door lock.

Out of the corner of her eye, she caught a glimpse of sudden movement. Fearfully, she spun around as the stranger from baggage claim stepped out of the shadows.

Her dizziness intensified a hundredfold. Unable to fight it off, she closed her eyes, then felt herself begin to fall. With a muttered curse, the man caught her arms and stood her upright. Jerked awake again, she stared up at him.

Vaguely, she realized she was more than just overtired. She'd been drugged, more than likely by the man towering over her. But why? Hazy thoughts of Brandon and all he had to lose flickered through her mind once more.

Her head spun, her legs trembled and her arms hung uselessly at her sides. More than anything, she wished she could let the darkness swallow her up. But surely that would mean certain death. She had to at least try to get away.

Drawing in a breath, Kari opened her mouth to scream, but all she could manage was a whimper. Frantic, she dredged up what had to be her last bit of strength, took a wild swing and smashed her fist against the side of the man's face, knocking his glasses slightly askew.

Cursing anew, he grabbed her wrists before she could flail out at him again. The last of her resistance gone, she sagged against him helplessly.

"I told your brother you'd knock me senseless if you had half a chance," he muttered.

The all-too-familiar voice was laced with admiration as well as amusement. Sure that she must be dreaming, Kari tilted her head back and stared at the stranger in confusion. He didn't look like Alexander Payton, but—

"Alex?" she murmured.

"Yes, love." He let go of her wrists and slipped his arms around her, holding her close.

Utterly at a loss, she leaned against him, rubbing her cheek against his chest, the warm, solid feel of him somehow grounding her. She should be furious with him. She should be demanding explanations and extracting apologies. But she was finding it harder and harder to think. Putting angry, outraged words together in a sentence and saying them was simply beyond her. Because . . . because—

"I don't feel so good," she said, then sighed softly, nestling closer to him, savoring the safety, the security of his gentle embrace.

"I know. It's the drug. Try not to fight it."

"The drug?"

Not so stupid after all. She *had* been drugged. By Alex. Alex dressed up like some weirdo. But why?

"To help you sleep," he said, as if in answer to her unspoken question.

Of course. To help her sleep. She'd been so tired, and he'd known it. Just like magic.

"Mmm, I want to sleep," she admitted. "But I haven't been able to. Been too scared."

"No need to be anymore. I'm here now. I'll watch over you."

Somewhere in the back of her mind, Kari knew she shouldn't trust him. Not after the way he'd once betrayed her. But she did. With all her heart.

Silly girl, she thought. *Will you ever learn?*

A wry smile tugging at the corners of her mouth, she sighed again, closed her eyes and let the darkness drag her away.

Sensing that Kari had finally succumbed to the drug, Alex lifted her into his arms.

"Well done, Payton," he muttered, his voice edged with sarcasm.

He hadn't had to sedate someone surreptitiously for quite some time. Obviously he hadn't lost his touch. But the drug had worked faster than he'd anticipated, probably because Kari weighed at least fifteen pounds less than he'd estimated when he had measured the dose.

Along with not sleeping, apparently she hadn't been eating, either. Not good. Not good at all when you worked with high-strung horses on a daily basis the way she did.

Still, woozy as she'd been, she'd had strength enough to knock him a good one upside his head.

With a rueful smile, Alex shifted slightly, freeing one hand, and straightened his glasses. Then he reached for the key Kari had somehow managed to insert in the door lock just before he'd startled her.

Although he'd done all right with the drugging, he had to admit he'd gone a bit over the top with his disguise. He hadn't meant to scare the wits out of her. But he'd had to make sure she didn't recognize him and he hadn't had a lot of time. Since he hadn't had all his gear with him, either, he'd had to make do with the few things he'd found at a costume shop in the mall near the airport.

When he had studied himself in the mirror, he'd been amazed at how vile he appeared with the hair, the beard and the glasses in place. However, without one or the other, he would have looked too much like himself to attempt to get close to her.

Yet he'd hated having to frighten her. And he had definitely done that. To a much greater degree than the situation had seemed to warrant. Either she had instinctively known that "he" posed a threat to her, or she had connected him in some way to whatever was scaring her so much she couldn't sleep.

Probably a combination of the two, he thought. In any case, he would find out soon enough. If she would talk to him once the effects of the drug wore off. Unfortunately, all things considered, that was one hell of a big *if*.

Oh, well. At least he'd cleared the first hurdle, he reminded himself, glancing around to make sure no one was taking undue notice of them. Now all he had to do was get them out of the airport parking lot without incident. From there, the going would be all downhill.

Until she woke up sometime tomorrow and realized what he had done.

He knew better than to be fooled by her earlier acquiescence. Compared with whoever she'd been afraid he might be, *he* wouldn't have seemed that bad. And even if she'd wanted to get away from him, she had been too doped up to offer more than token resistance. But once she had her wits about her again, there was going to be hell to pay.

Which was probably a good thing. Just standing there in the dimly lit parking lot, holding her in his arms, he was aroused. Forced into proximity with her over an extended period of time, he couldn't tell what he might be tempted to do.

At least once she was fully conscious again, she wouldn't let him near enough to touch her. Otherwise...

Otherwise he'd probably end up trying to finish what he'd started all those years ago.

With a groan, Alex swung the car door open, set Kari on the wide bench seat and slid her across to the passenger side. He slipped her purse off her shoulder and set it on the floor, then arranged her as comfortably as he could, leaning her up against the door and fastening the seat belt around her.

He shouldn't be thinking such thoughts. Not if he wanted to get through the next few days without hurting her more than he already had. Better to keep in mind that she was his best friend's little sister, he reminded himself. Just as he had when she was sixteen and strictly off-limits.

"Yeah, sure, and the moon is made of green cheese," he groused, all too aware that some mental gyrations weren't quite as easy to perform as others.

Kari Gray wasn't a sixteen-year-old girl anymore. She was a lovely young woman who still owned a bigger piece of his heart than he would ever willingly admit.

Still grumbling, Alex eased out of the car, grabbed Kari's bags and stowed them in the trunk along with his backpack. As he walked around to the open car door, he spotted what appeared to be a parking receipt lying on the ground. A glance at the date led him to believe it was more than likely Kari's.

To guarantee he wouldn't have any hassle getting out of the parking lot, he'd rented a car that afternoon, then parked it in the lot after his trip to the costume shop. He'd planned to use the receipt he'd gotten if he couldn't find Kari's, mail the car keys back to the rental agency and let them retrieve their vehicle. Now that wouldn't be necessary. He could come back for it himself just as soon as he was done with Kari. Maybe by the end of week. If he was lucky.

He'd also contacted Estella and Felipe, the couple who took care of his place while he was away, and asked them to open up the house. Estella had assured him the beds would be freshly made and the refrigerator and pantry well stocked with a variety of food and drinks. Felipe had added that he'd have the hot tub running, as well.

Settling into the driver's seat, Alex couldn't think of anything he'd enjoy more than a good, long soak. Well, almost anything, he amended, then slammed the car door shut, disgusted with himself. Talk about a one-track mind.

Switching on the overhead light, he glanced at Kari. Still out cold. He reached across the wide seat, took her wrist in his hand and measured her pulse. Slow, but steady. As weary as she'd seemed to be, she would probably sleep well into tomorrow.

And that would be just as well, he mused, brushing a wisp of her short, dark hair off her pale cheek. He was going to need all the time he could get to consider just how to go about convincing her he had only her best interests at heart.

Honesty would be the best policy. And honesty would be possible. Up to a point. As long as she didn't question him too closely about his reasons for walking out on her, he wouldn't lie to her.

But there were some truths he had no intention of telling. Better to have her go on hating him than horrify her with the revelation of what he could become. An abusive monster... Just like the man and woman who'd brought him into the world, then tormented him for eight years, leaving their invisible, yet indelible mark upon him.

Drawing his hand from her face, Alex sat for a moment, staring into the shadows. He'd put the past behind him in so many ways. But the scars on his soul would always be with him. And all he could do was live with them . . . alone.

Reminding himself that he still had a lot to do before he'd be home free, he tossed aside the glasses, jerked the hat and wig from his head and, wincing slightly, peeled off the scraggly black beard.

He'd cause much less attention leaving the parking lot with a sleeping woman slouched beside him if he looked like the all-American boy he had learned, long ago, he could easily pretend to be.

Slanting the rearview mirror, he gazed at his image dispassionately, rubbed a bit of glue from his chin and another from his cheek, then combed his fingers through his shaggy blond curls. Satisfied he wouldn't cause the parking-lot attendant any undue concern, he adjusted the mirror, switched off the light and turned the key in the ignition.

At the exit booth, he offered the middle-aged woman a slight smile as he handed her the parking receipt and a fifty-dollar bill. Her gaze swept over him indifferently as she turned to ring up her register, then she handed him his change and waved him on his way.

From the airport, Alex headed west on the loop that circled San Antonio, then cut north on the four-lane highway that would take them deep into the Texas Hill Country. Traffic wasn't bad at that time of night, and it wasn't long before he left the bright lights of the city and the suburban sprawl behind them.

Since the gas tank was full, he didn't have to make any stops along the way, and not quite two hours later, he came to the first turnoff, a narrow two-lane road. About three miles farther on, he turned onto a gravel lane that wound through a dense overgrowth of trees and bushes for almost a mile to where a padlocked metal gate barred the way.

He shifted into neutral, climbed out of the car, unlocked the gate with his key, drove through, then stopped and locked the gate again.

Around a curve a short distance ahead, he glimpsed a flicker of illumination. Then the small, secluded, ranch-style house, set in a wide, neatly kept clearing, came into view.

Much to his relief, Estella and Felipe had left both the inside and outside lights burning as he'd asked. He hated coming home to a dark house. Had for as far back as he could remember, and with good cause. But he wasn't afraid anymore. Not as he'd been as a young boy. He knew how to defend himself now.

Yet he still avoided dark, closed-up houses whenever he could. Just as he still slept little and lightly, snatching a few hours whenever he could.

He pulled up near the side door and, leaving Kari in the car, went to open the house. A quick survey assured him everything was in order. Even the hot tub bubbled invitingly on the deck out back.

Promising himself he would indulge later, Alex returned to the car, lifted Kari into his arms and carried her to the master bedroom. As quickly and efficiently as he could, he stripped off her shoes and socks, her tailored khaki pants and plain white T-shirt. Underneath her clothes, she wore serviceable white cotton briefs and a gauzy white cotton camisole. Comfortable enough for her to sleep in, he thought, relieved he wouldn't have to undress her any further.

Though he knew he shouldn't, Alex sat on the side of the bed and allowed himself one long, lingering look at her. While she was slimmer than she should be, she seemed quite fit, yet feminine. Very, very feminine.

His gaze drifted over the gentle swell of her breasts, then down to the juncture of her thighs, to the darkness there, a darkness barely concealed by her briefs. And suddenly he wanted to howl. Wanted to throw his head back and *howl*. And then, *then,* he wanted to bury himself so deep inside her—

With a muttered curse, he stood abruptly, averting his eyes. Reaching out, he drew the top sheet and woven cotton blanket up over her. He crossed to the windows, opened them an inch or two to let in a little of the cool night air, then turned the ceiling fan on low. At the bedroom doorway, he allowed himself a last glance around the room, assuring himself that Kari would be all right on her own, at least for the time being. Leaving the small lamp on the dresser lit, he headed out to the car to collect her bags and his backpack.

In the house again, Alex dropped their things on the kitchen floor and crossed to the refrigerator, the gnawing in his belly a reminder that he hadn't eaten all day. He grabbed a carton of orange juice, a plastic-wrapped package of sliced ham, a chunk of Swiss cheese and a jar of mustard. With the bread he found in the bread box he made a sandwich, then poured juice into a tall glass. Food and drink in front of him, he sat on a stool at the kitchen counter, reached for the telephone and dialed Devlin's number.

They had talked twice already, once after Alex got to San Antonio—he'd called for more details about Kari's arrival as well as the location of her car—and again just before Kari's plane was due to land.

Devlin answered on the first ring.

"So far, so good," Alex muttered by way of a greeting.

"You've got her?" Devlin asked.

"Right here with me. She's safe and sound and sleeping like a baby." In the background he heard Andrew crying, and amended laughingly, "Well, like *some* babies."

"Laura assures me he's going to start sleeping through the night anytime now, but I'm beginning to have my doubts," Devlin admitted wryly. Then, more seriously, he asked, "Any problems?"

"Not a one. I clipped her at baggage claim and she was looped by the time she got out to her car. Slept all the way here, and unless I'm mistaken, she should sleep most of tomorrow, too."

"Did she say anything?"

"Something about being too scared to sleep. Looks like you're right. She's in some kind of trouble. But whether she'll tell me about it remains to be seen."

"Use your charm. She won't be able to resist."

"Yeah, sure," Alex retorted sarcastically. "A boyish grin, maybe a little foot shuffling coupled with a humble apology, and she'll be putty in my hands, won't she?"

"I wish," Devlin replied, his tone implying he was as aware as Alex that Kari could give new meaning to the word *recalcitrant* when she put her mind to it. "So, what do you plan to do?"

"Let her sleep off the drug, then try, as kindly as I can, to convince her to talk to me."

"Well, good luck."

"Thanks a lot."

"You'll let me know how it goes?"

"Will daily reports do, sir?"

"Daily reports will do just fine," Devlin assured him with a hint of laughter.

"You know, I'm supposed to be on vacation," Alex stated, making no effort to hide his annoyance. "A long-overdue, well-deserved vacation."

Just over a year ago, Alex had taken Devlin's place in Mexico. On McConnell's orders, he'd moved Uncle Sam's listening post from San Pedro to a small town farther south.

Over the past few months, he had made innumerable forays into Central America, keeping tabs on the social and political climates of various countries, both friendly and unfriendly toward the United States.

But that part of the world wasn't Alex's forte—his experience had been mainly in the Middle East—and McConnell had finally found a permanent replacement for him. Alex had been given four weeks' leave, after which he would be reassigned to the field. If that was what he wanted.

More and more lately, he'd been thinking about leaving the agency. Since he'd come close to dying eighteen months ago, he'd realized that risking his life would never be as easy for him as it had been. Sometime during the past twenty-five years, he'd done what he'd never believed he could do: he'd begun to enjoy being alive. Yet he had no desire to follow in Devlin's footsteps and end up sitting behind a desk.

Nor was he sure that he would be able to maintain his sanity living alone in the quiet of the Texas Hill Country. At least working for McConnell he rarely had time to dwell on the horrors of his past or contemplate the long hours of loneliness that would comprise his future.

"Hey, there's no reason you can't enjoy yourself," Devlin teased, drawing Alex's attention back to their conversation.

"Fat chance," Alex growled.

"But you two used to get along so well," Devlin insisted.

"Yeah, well, that was a long time ago."

"You never did tell me exactly what happened between the two of—"

"And I never will," Alex cut in. Then, refusing to go where Devlin was so obviously leading, he added hastily, "Tell your lovely wife hello for me."

"You know, Alex—"

"Talk to you tomorrow," he interrupted again, and cradled the receiver.

Still sitting at the counter, Alex finished his sandwich and drank the last of his juice as he noted the homey touches Estella had added to the cozy kitchen in his year-long absence. There were pots of herbs on the windowsill above the sink and new curtains in a simple blue-and-white-striped fabric framing the window itself. Matching place mats and napkins graced the old oak table along with a basket of blue, rose and white silk flowers and an odd assortment of brass candlesticks topped with blue candles.

Though she and Felipe had a home of their own in the small town of Mason ten miles away, and Alex was rarely there himself, Estella had been adamant about making his house look like a real home. Otherwise, she'd advised him, coming there to clean would make her too sad. Valuing her services as he did, Alex had told her to do what she wanted with the place, within reason, and charge any purchases to the household account. And she had.

He had no doubt he would find additional evidence of her decorating throughout the rest of the house. But that could wait until tomorrow. Right now, what he had in mind was that soak in the hot tub he'd promised himself earlier.

Although he had been awake for almost twenty hours, Alex knew it would be a while yet before he would be able to sleep. And, he acknowledged as he crossed to the sink to rinse his plate and glass, his leg had begun to ache, a sure sign he'd pushed himself far enough for one day.

Telling himself he needed a pair of swim trunks, he returned to the master bedroom, dug them out of a dresser drawer, allowed himself all of ten seconds at Kari's bedside to make sure she was still resting comfortably, then retreated to the hall bathroom to change.

Out on the deck, the wood smooth and warm beneath his feet and the night air cool against his bare skin, Alex paused and took a deep breath, giving his eyes time to adjust to the darkness. Around him the silence was broken by nothing more than a whisper of wind through the branches of the tall oak trees, the croak of a frog in the pond in the pasture, the chirrup of a cricket in the grass and, occasionally, the hoot of an owl in the distance.

Here was peace, he thought as he slid into the steaming water, settled onto one of the bench seats and gazed up at the starlit sky. Real peace.

Maybe spending the rest of his life here wouldn't be that bad after all. He had fought one kind of war or another all his life. Surely he had earned the right to some serenity.

But for him that would also mean solitude.

There was only one person he wanted with him here. Not just for a few days, but forever. And that was just as impossible now as it had ever been.

Yet sitting there alone in the black of night, with the heat of the bubbling water seeping into his bones as he stared up at the stars, Alex couldn't help but wish all kinds of wishes. Even knowing, as he did, that they would never come true.

Chapter 3

With a sigh of utter contentment, Kari nuzzled against the downy pillow, savoring the feel of the crisp, sun-scented linen against her cheek. Lying on her tummy, she stretched luxuriantly, then shifted slightly onto her left side.

She couldn't remember the last time she had awakened feeling so rested. But then, lately she had spent most nights tossing and turning. And when she *had* fallen asleep, she'd been plagued by horrible nightmares.

To have slept so deeply, so dreamlessly, she must have been even more exhausted than she'd thought. She could only hope she had remembered to set her alarm. There would be hell to pay if she arrived at the stable late. Although she doubted Brandon would wait more than fifteen minutes before stalking down to her cottage to rouse her himself.

The realization that she'd have to face her employer sooner rather than later was enough to make her want to pull her pillow over her head. Unfortunately, hiding out wouldn't help her in the long run. Eventually, she was going to have to deal with Brandon Selby...one way or another.

Reluctantly, Kari opened her eyes at last, started to push up on one elbow, then froze, her breath catching in her throat. Where in the world was she?

Her mind still muzzy, she surveyed what she could of the room with growing bewilderment. She was facing what must be the far wall. An antique oak armoire stood between two lace-curtained windows open just enough to let in a cool breeze that smelled of summer flowers and trilled with bird song. She seemed to be somewhere in the country. And it was daytime, she mused, eyeing the smattering of sunlight that slipped beneath the partially drawn shades to play across the hardwood floor.

Shifting her gaze to the connecting wall, she spotted an open doorway that led into what appeared to be a bathroom. Next to the doorway was an oak dresser topped by an oval mirror. Both pieces of furniture seemed to match the old armoire, as did the footboard and—she tipped her head up slightly—the headboard of the bed. But there was nothing atop the dresser except a small brass lamp. Nothing personal at all.

The bed itself had been made up with white cotton sheets, a lightweight white woven blanket and an old-fashioned patchwork quilt that lay neatly folded at the foot.

All in all, the room was quite nice, she thought, easing onto her back and staring up at the slowly spinning ceiling fan. But totally, completely, unfamiliar. Definitely not her bedroom, or the bedroom she'd slept in at her brother's house in Virginia. Or Brandon's bedroom, for that matter. Though she'd never actually spent any time *there*.

Vaguely, Kari realized she should be concerned, deeply concerned. She'd awakened in a strange bedroom, lying in a strange bed, dressed only in underpants and a camisole, with absolutely no idea how she'd gotten there.

But as she watched the ceiling fan whirl and listened to the chirp and chatter of the birds just outside, she felt oddly safe and incredibly... secure. As if she had finally come to the place she'd been searching for all her life.

But how had she made the journey from Devlin's house to here? She remembered Laura and Devlin taking her to the airport and waiting, despite her protests, until it was time for her to board the plane. And she remembered her arrival in San Antonio, as well as her long, weary walk to the baggage-claim area. But after that...

Frowning, she conjured up a picture of herself waiting for her bag to tumble onto the carousel. She'd been standing patiently and—

With startling clarity, Kari recalled the unsettling encounter she'd had there. A weird man with stringy black hair, thick black glasses and a scraggly black beard had bumped into her and—

Increasingly aware of the ache in her left hip, she closed her eyes and willed her head to clear.

He'd bumped into her and she'd felt a sharp stab in her hip. By the time she'd collected her bags and walked out to her car she'd been literally asleep on her feet. And suddenly he'd been there, holding her in his arms, soothing her in a voice she'd recognized. Alex's voice.

Alex—

Had her mind been playing tricks on her? Had the stranger who'd caught her as she'd collapsed really been Alexander Payton? Or had she only imagined he'd come to her rescue?

Frightened and confused, Kari slowly shifted to her right side and saw him slouched in an easy chair in the corner nearest the nightstand, sound asleep. With a momentary sense of relief, she gazed at him silently, taking in his familiar features. His face was clean-shaven, his shaggy blond curls falling over his forehead. And, as he had done one day at Devlin's house, he wore khaki shorts and a navy blue knit shirt.

Thank God, she thought, her panic subsiding. She hadn't been drugged and kidnapped by some pervert after all. Rather, she'd been drugged and kidnapped by her brother's best friend.

But why?

He'd spent two days acting as if she were invisible. Surely, if he'd had something to say to her, he could have done so at Devlin's house. Why knock her out and carry her off to what she assumed was his lair?

He had made it known six years ago that she meant nothing to him. And he certainly hadn't given any indication he'd had a change of heart over the weekend. He'd barely even looked at her, as if the very sight of her made him sick. So why waylay her halfway across the country? And why do it in such a drastic manner?

Had he gone over some mental edge as, according to Devlin, government agents sometimes did? Alex had seemed sane enough in Virginia. But this was the same man who had turned himself into the embodiment of every woman's worst nightmare, drugged her and dragged her off God only knows where.

If she had any sense at all, she'd be scared to death. But as she lay there, watching him sleep, she was more furious than frightened. What in the world was he up to?

She didn't honestly think he meant her any physical harm. Of course, she could be wrong. Especially if he'd had some sort of emotional breakdown.

However, as she thought back to those last moments before she'd passed out in the airport parking lot, she remembered his promising to keep her safe. And somewhere deep in her heart she couldn't help but believe that he would.

Still, after the way he'd treated her six years ago, he just happened to be the last man on earth she wanted to have looking after her. She'd had no choice but to learn to take care of herself, and she preferred to continue that way.

Granted, dealing with Brandon on her own could prove dangerous. But she'd much rather take her chances with him than end up having her heart broken again.

She'd never gotten over Alexander Payton, and she probably never would. For some reason unknown to her, he'd hurt her badly. She should hate him. Really she should. But along with the anger welling inside her was a longing so intense she literally ached with it.

What a fool she was. What a sad, sad fool, she thought, blinking back the tears stinging her eyes. The man had made it clear he wanted nothing to do with her. Yet here she was, hoping against hope that maybe he'd changed his mind.

She had to get away from him. Had to get away *now*. She had no idea what kind of game he was playing, but she simply couldn't afford to stay around long enough to find out. He'd hurt her once, and unfortunately, he had the power to hurt her again. But only as long as they were in close proximity. Once she was back at Selby Stables, she would have other things to occupy her mind. A lot of other things. Eventually, Alex would be no more than a distant memory.

As she pushed herself into a sitting position, Kari wished she could slip away without disturbing him. But she knew better than to count on that happening. He had always been a light sleeper, and though he hadn't awakened yet, she had no doubt he would any minute now.

At least if she was out of bed she'd have some chance of standing up to him. She'd really like to have her clothes on, too. However, the pants and shirt she'd been wearing when he'd abducted her were nowhere to be seen. She was also going to have to use the bathroom. And then there was the small matter of transportation back to San Antonio.

Yes, making a fast getaway was definitely out of the question. But she had to at least try to put some distance between them. She would find her clothes, dress quickly and, ignoring any protest he might make, leave.

Just as soon as she used the bathroom.

Her need growing more urgent, Kari shoved the top sheet and blanket out of the way and swung her legs over the side of the bed, then paused a moment to glance at the clock on the nightstand.

Almost ten. She'd been out for about twelve hours. That, along with the remnants of whatever drug Alex had pumped into her, probably accounted for the grogginess she couldn't seem to shake.

Although she felt more rested than she had for a while, she was having an awfully hard time getting herself moving. Sitting up had been an effort. Standing was something she found herself contemplating with hesitation. Had she not been desperate to get away from Alex, she could have been easily tempted to curl up under the covers for what remained of the day.

Realizing he had yet to stir, she glanced at him and wished, once again, that she was wearing more than underpants and a cotton camisole.

Maybe her things were in the bathroom. If she could make it there without waking him, she could take care of her needs, dress, then face him, at least somewhat fortified.

Kari stood slowly, her head bent, her eyes on the polished hardwood floor beneath her feet. So far, so good, she thought, then made the mistake of turning too quickly toward the bathroom.

A wave of dizziness washed over her and she swayed precariously. She reached out to steady herself on the bed, but her hand met only air. She felt herself start to fall and moaned as the room spun around her.

As if from a great distance, she heard Alex swear. An instant later, he caught her in his arms and lifted her gently, holding her close. Shutting her eyes, she sagged against him gratefully. But then, as her head began to clear, she stiffened angrily.

She refused to thank him for coming to her rescue. Absolutely *refused*. Had he not drugged her, she wouldn't have had to be saved from falling on her face.

"Put me down," she snapped.

Arms folded primly over her chest, she stared across the room, determined not to look at him. She was all too aware that he had her at his mercy. But she wasn't about to let him know how impotent she felt as a result.

"Whatever you say," he murmured, his voice laced with laughter.

He set her on the bed, took a cautious step back and, propping his hands on his hips, waited for her next move. As if she were a loaded gun about to go off. The rat. *He* was the one who'd drugged her, then carried her off wherever.

Furious, Kari stood up again. Another, milder, wave of dizziness assailed her. But this time she managed to catch herself, bracing a hand on the mattress until her head stopped spinning.

"Maybe you ought to get back into bed," Alex suggested solicitously. "You look like you're still feeling kind of woozy."

"I'm fine. Just fine," she rasped, shrugging away from him when he reached out to take her arm.

"I don't think so," he retorted, sliding an arm around her waist as she stumbled against the side of the bed. "Now, get back into—"

"No." She tried, unsuccessfully, to pull away, then glared at him miserably, her face burning with embarrassment as she admitted heatedly, "I have to...have to use the bathroom."

"Well, why didn't you just say so?" Alex asked.

That hint of amusement in his voice again as he helped her across the room infuriated her.

She hated him. Hated him with all her heart and soul. He was a no-good, dirty, rotten son of a bitch, and he had no right, *no right at all,* to laugh at her.

"Can you manage on your own or would you like some help?"

"I can manage on my own."

Freeing herself from him at last, Kari slipped into the bathroom and slammed the door in his face. She would have shot the lock, as well, but not at all to her surprise, there wasn't one.

"Well, just holler if you need me."

"Fat chance," she muttered, sure that she'd rather die first.

In the relative privacy of the little bathroom, Kari took care of her most urgent need, then washed her hands and face. Using what appeared to be a new toothbrush and tube of toothpaste she found in the otherwise empty medicine cabinet, she also cleaned her teeth.

She would have liked to take a long, hot shower, but she was still too unsteady to trust that she wouldn't end up falling on her fanny. And she wasn't about to give Alex an excuse to come in after her.

Warily, she eyed her reflection in the mirror. There was nothing she could do about the dark circles under her eyes.

Nor could she neaten her short, straight hair without a comb or brush. Not that she thought for a minute her appearance mattered to Alex. Granted, he'd seen her looking much better. But he'd also seen her looking a lot worse.

With a quiet sigh, she turned away from the mirror and glanced around the bathroom, hoping to see her slacks and shirt. All she found was a long, white terry-cloth robe hanging on a hook on the back of the door. Alex's, she imagined. But it would do for the time being. Especially since it hung down to her ankles.

Feeling slightly better with the robe wrapped around her, Kari opened the door and walked into Alex. Instead of leaving her in peace, he'd chosen to lounge negligently against the doorjamb. She stumbled to a halt, hands clenched at her sides, and gazed at him wordlessly.

The look on her face must have revealed the vile thoughts she was thinking, because he straightened quickly and moved out of her way.

She'd had every intention of searching for her clothes so she could dress. But as she stepped out of the bathroom, all she really felt like doing was hobbling back to bed. Whatever Alex had given her still had her reeling, and probably would for a while longer.

Much as she hated to admit it, she wasn't going anywhere anytime soon. Even if she found her clothes and managed to dress, she knew she wouldn't be able to get away from Alex unless he chose to let her go. Considering all he'd done to bring her there, she seriously doubted that was on his agenda.

Knowing there was little she could do until the effects of the drug had worn off completely, Kari crawled back into bed. Doing her best to ignore Alex, she plumped the pillows against the oak headboard and slumped against them.

Apparently satisfied that she wasn't going to cause any commotion, Alex moved back to the easy chair and perched on one arm. She would have preferred to be left alone, but since he didn't appear inclined to leave the room, she thought maybe she ought to at least try to find out what he was up to.

He didn't seem irrational. And his manner toward her wasn't threatening. Actually, he'd treated her with great solicitude. Yet what he'd done to her—drugging her, then abducting her—was *criminal*. Had she the chance to press charges against him, he would most certainly end up in jail.

Had she the chance...

Bracing herself for the confrontation she seemed to have no choice but to initiate, Kari lifted her chin and forced herself to meet his gaze. Across the short distance that separated them, he regarded her with such obvious concern that for a moment she could almost believe he cared for her, *really* cared for her the way she had once thought he did.

Talk about clutching at straws, she chided herself.

"Are you feeling ill?" he asked, his voice sounding a little rough around the edges.

"No," she replied as she glanced away again.

She wished he would go back to looking at her with the same disinterest he had when they'd been together at her brother's house. Otherwise she was going to find it hard to remain as dispassionate as she knew she should. Any softening toward him would be disastrous in the long run.

Yet she couldn't seem to quell the ache in her heart as her gaze rested on the rigid patch of scar tissue slicing across his left kneecap and trailing halfway down his shin.

She'd first seen the scar Sunday morning when she'd come upon him as he and her brother were returning from a jog around the neighborhood. That he could walk, much less run, after such a devastating injury was a testament to his willpower and determination.

Eighteen months ago he'd come close to dying. So close Kari had almost gone to him after Devlin called to tell her Alex was fighting for life in the intensive care unit at a military hospital in Virginia. But pride, coupled with a sense of self-preservation, had kept her from making a fool of herself.

Realizing she had allowed her thoughts to wander in an unavailing way, Kari raised her head again. Alex still sat on the arm of the chair, watching her and waiting with irksome equanimity.

He had to know she was confused and upset by his behavior. Yet he didn't seem ready to offer any explanations on his own. Well, fine. She'd just badger him mercilessly with one question after another until she managed to pry some information out of him.

"You dressed up like some weirdo and drugged me at the airport, didn't you?" she asked, her voice surprisingly steady.

"Yes," he admitted.

"And brought me where?"

"To the house I own in the Hill Country about thirty miles northwest of Fredricksburg."

To the house he owned in the Hill Country. Of course. Why hadn't she guessed?

Because her beloved brother had never told her that Alexander Payton had bought a house in her part of the country, she answered herself angrily. But then, why would he? Every time Devlin had mentioned Alex's name over the past few years, she had cut him off.

Aware her mind was wandering again, Kari gave herself a firm mental shake. She would never find out what kind of game Alex was playing if she kept allowing herself to be so easily distracted.

"So you drugged and abducted me," she reiterated. Then she demanded disconcertingly, *"Why?"*

"Because your brother asked me to," he replied casually.

"My brother?" Kari repeated, unable to hide her bewilderment.

She had been wrong about Alex. He was crazy after all. Devlin would never—

"He's worried about you. He believes you're in some kind of trouble. Trouble involving Brandon Selby. He wanted to investigate on his own, but he didn't want to leave Laura alone with the baby. So he asked me to find out what I could and to look out for you while I did," Alex explained patiently.

Kari regarded him wordlessly, frowning as she tried, unsuccessfully, to assimilate what he was saying.

"Considering our past history, I didn't think you would take kindly to an offer of help, and I told him so. Since Devlin had to agree, he suggested I get you here by whatever means I could, then try to get you to talk to me."

Too stunned to speak, Kari stared at Alex, her mind racing. She should have known Devlin would realize something was wrong. After all, she'd hinted at her unhappiness with her job in general and Brandon in particular to both her brother and sister-in-law all weekend. But only because she'd hoped that in a roundabout way one of them might come up with a solution to her problem that wouldn't involve returning to the stable.

Now it seemed that all she'd succeeded in doing was worrying them so much that Devlin had gone to Alex and asked him to intercede.

"And you agreed to go along with his plan?" she asked, though his answer was obvious.

"Only because Devlin—and Laura—were so concerned," he stated simply.

His manner seemed much more distant than it had a few moments ago. More hurt than she would ever admit, Kari looked away.

Only because Devlin—and Laura—were so concerned.

What had she expected him to say? That *he* cared about her enough to come to her rescue? Not hardly, she thought with unwonted sadness.

She meant nothing to him. Nothing at all. Yet he was willing to saddle himself with her and her problems at Devlin's behest. But that didn't mean she had to sit by quietly and accept his charity.

No matter how much she feared going after Brandon on her own, she wasn't about to let Alex get involved. While he could provide her with the kind of protection she might very well need, she couldn't afford the emotional toll such dependence on him would inevitably take.

Already she'd caught herself hoping that maybe she meant something to him after all. There was no telling what kind of fantasies she'd start entertaining if she was forced to spend several days with him.

Unfortunately, she had a feeling she wasn't going to find it easy to convince him that her brother's imagination had been working overtime. Alexander Payton was no fool. No matter how much he felt he owned Devlin, he wouldn't have drugged her and abducted her unless he honestly believed her brother's concern was justified.

Well, she would just have to be equally persuasive, Kari decided, plucking nervously at the fabric of the robe she wore. Just make him believe Laura and Devlin had been mistaken and thus relieve him of any responsibility they'd conned him into feeling for her.

Pasting what she could only hope was a puzzled look on her face, Kari forced herself to meet Alex's gaze again.

"Why would they think I'm in trouble?" she murmured. "I did mention I was considering changing jobs, but only for a short time, and certainly not because of any problems I'm having with Brandon. I just thought it might be a good idea to vary my experience before settling down for good at Selby Stables."

"Oh, really?" Alex drawled with obvious skepticism.

"Yes, really," she snapped before she could stop herself.

Mentally cursing the hot flush spreading across her cheeks, Kari acknowledged that she wasn't any better at lying now than she had been in the past. Still, she couldn't afford to back off.

Drawing a deep breath, she counted to ten, willing herself to calm down as she added, "Actually, we're very close. And Brandon has promised that once we're married, we'll be equal partners. I want to have as much to offer *our* business as I can."

She really hated leading Alex to believe that she and Brandon were lovers. Lying to him about having an affair with a man she despised made her feel cheap and dirty. But what other choice did she have? Alex wouldn't let her go back to Selby Stables unless she convinced him that Brandon posed no threat to her. And getting away from Alex was absolutely essential to the maintenance of her already shaky emotional stability.

"Ah, I see."

Eyes narrowed, Alex nodded sagely, seeming to accept what she was saying as the truth. But he didn't look convinced. And though Kari would never admit that it made a bit of difference to her, he didn't appear the least bit jealous, either. Instead she caught the faintest hint of amusement edging his otherwise serious expression.

"So, you don't have to worry about me." Determined to ignore his irritating attitude and finish what she'd started, she offered him a bright smile. Then, glancing at the clock on the nightstand, she swung her legs over the side of the bed. "Now, I'd better get dressed and head back to San Antonio. Brandon is probably wondering what's happened to me."

"Laura called to tell him you were going to be delayed due to a touch of flu. He's not expecting you until the end of the week. Unless we need more time. Then Laura will call him again on your behalf," Alex stated, matter-of-factly.

"Well, we're not going to need any more time than we've already wasted on this nonsense," Kari retorted. "I've told you I'm not in any trouble. And I have a wonderful relationship with Brandon. Surely you must know that if I really needed help, I'd accept all you had to offer. But I don't. Believe me—"

"I'd like to, but I can't," he cut her off neatly.

"Why not?" she demanded, what little composure she had dwindling rapidly.

"Because you're lying through your teeth."

"I am *not*," she shrilled.

"Then tell me why you've been so scared you can't sleep?" he asked, his calm demeanor a maddening counterpoint to her own unwarranted outrage.

So scared she couldn't sleep? How could Alex possibly know...?

With a groan, Kari recalled the last words she had spoken to him before she'd passed out in his arms in the airport parking lot: *I want to sleep. But I haven't been able to. Been too scared.*

Unwittingly, she had sealed her fate with her own words. Words that proved Laura and Devlin had good reason to be concerned about her. Words that would have enabled Alex to know whether she was telling the truth, no matter how good a liar she was. And since she was a rank amateur at deception . . .

She really should have saved her breath.

Feeling utterly defeated, she drew her legs up under her and sat back against the pillows again.

"I've said all I'm going to say to you," she muttered, refusing to look at Alex as she crossed her arms over her chest defensively. "You can believe me or not. I don't really care. But I'm not subjecting myself to any more of your browbeating. I'm going to find my clothes, get dressed and go back to San Antonio."

"You're welcome to dress anytime you feel like it. I hung most of your clothes in the closet. The rest of your things are in the top drawer of the dresser. But you're not going anywhere until you give me some straight answers."

He stood, moved to the windows and closed them, shutting out the breeze that had warmed considerably with the growing heat of the day.

"You can't keep me here against my will," Kari said, her wavering voice belying her belief in the simple statement.

Pausing at the foot of the bed on his way back across the room, Alex met her gaze. "Oh, yes, I can. And I will. By whatever means I have to," he warned her. "Until I'm sure you're not in any danger."

"But I've tried to tell you—" she began all over again.

"And I've told you," he interrupted with seemingly inexhaustible patience, "I want the truth, the whole truth and nothing but the truth."

He stepped into the hallway and switched on the thermostat that activated the central-air-conditioning unit. A gust of cool air blew out of the vents in the ceiling, sending a shiver down Kari's spine.

Obviously not quite done with her yet, Alex loomed in the doorway again.

"Do you want to eat breakfast in here or would you rather come to the kitchen and eat at the table?" he asked equably.

"I'm not hungry," she replied, turning her back on him.

"You'll feel better if you eat something."

"I doubt it," she muttered.

Actually, she was ravenous. But she had no intention of giving Alex the satisfaction of knowing he was right. About anything.

"You can skip breakfast, then. But I'm not going to let you miss any other meals. You're much too thin already."

Too thin?

Stung by Alex's casually delivered criticism, Kari whirled around, ready to tell him exactly what he could do with his unkind assessment of her. But he was no longer standing in the doorway.

Thwarted yet again, she flopped against the pillows and stared at the ceiling. To her dismay, hot tears pooled in her eyes. Tears of anger and frustration and humiliation.

Much as she would like to tell herself otherwise, she wasn't going anywhere. At least not until she pulled herself together, physically and emotionally. Only then would she be ready to go another round with him.

She hadn't come close to convincing him that Brandon posed no threat to her. But she hadn't backed off when Alex accused her of lying, either. She had stuck to her story with a determination born of desperation. Just as she would continue to do.

Once she began to feel stronger, she would broach the subject again. If she repeated her lies often enough, maybe he'd finally begin to believe her. And then maybe he'd be willing to send her on her way.

Since he was only keeping her there at Devlin's request, he would probably be glad to see her go.

Granted, the likelihood that she'd be able to win Alex over on her own seemed rather slim. But there was no reason she had to. She could elicit a little help from her brother, as well.

All she had to do was persuade Devlin she wasn't in any danger. Then surely he'd call off Alex. He had gotten her into this mess, and she had no doubt he could get her out. But only if she could make him believe her.

Luckily, she'd always found lying long-distance to be much easier than lying face-to-face. Not that she'd ever made a habit of doing either one. But a little prevarication was better than allowing yourself to be put at the mercy of someone who had broken your heart once already.

With a renewed sense of determination, Kari glanced around the room, searching for a telephone. As she should have guessed, there wasn't one to be seen. However, she did spy a jack in the wall a couple of feet from the nightstand.

She'd bet every cent in her meager savings account that there had been a telephone in the room until quite recently. Apparently, Alex didn't want her making calls on her own. Well, fine. She'd get up, get dressed, then call Devlin under his watchful eye.

And then, she added ruefully as the aroma of freshly brewed coffee and frying bacon wafted into the bedroom, making her stomach growl, she would set aside her pride and eat breakfast.

No sense starving herself. Not when she would be heading back to San Antonio by afternoon. She would need the energy for the long drive home as well as for the inevitable encounter with Brandon that would ensue.

Although Laura had called on her behalf, he would also expect an explanation from her for her delay. She wanted to be able to give him one without tripping herself up. Otherwise she might arouse his suspicion, and that certainly wouldn't be smart.

Having settled on a course of action, Kari slid off the bed again slowly. She stood still for several seconds, afraid that she would feel light-headed anew, but the dizziness she had experienced earlier seemed to have passed.

The sedative Alex had given her must have finally begun to wear off. Still, she wasn't quite as steady as she'd like to be, she admitted as she made her way to the closet.

Inside she found the white cotton shirt and khaki pants she'd had on yesterday, along with her jeans, denim skirt, two brightly colored T-shirts, a lemon yellow blouse and the sleeveless pink silk dress she'd worn for Andrew's christening. Lined up neatly on the floor were her loafers, running shoes and the pink pumps that matched her dress.

Shoved to one side were some of Alex's clothes—shirts, jeans, sweaters and slacks—just a few of each, and all well-worn. Some old boots and a pair of deck shoes were also on the floor, and her bags had been stowed above, on the otherwise empty shelf.

Kari frowned and shook her head as she slipped her shirt and pants from their hangers. Alex certainly hadn't had any qualms about moving her into his house. But then, he'd thought he was going to be stuck with her awhile.

"Well, you were wrong," she muttered as she crossed to the dresser and opened the top drawer.

Her underwear, socks, long white nightgown, one pair of gym shorts and two pairs of tailored walking shorts had been carefully folded and placed inside. She added fresh underwear to the clothes she already held, then gave in to her curiosity and opened the other drawers, as well. One contained more of Alex's things—underwear, socks, shorts and T-shirts. The other two were empty.

He'd told her the house was his, but she doubted he spent much time here. Either that, or he'd moved his more personal belongings out before moving her in, she mused, her gaze drifting over the top of the dresser, bare except for one small lamp. One possibility saddened her as much as the other, though she had no idea why.

With a quiet sigh, she stepped into the bathroom and shut the door. She'd intended only to change into her clothes, but she was feeling so much stronger that she decided to take a quick shower first. The hot water revived her even more, and once she was dressed, she felt almost her old self again.

She toweled her hair dry as best she could, fluffed her fingers through the short strands, then walked back into the bedroom. The heady scents drifting in from the kitchen had intensified, making her mouth water. Maybe she would eat, *then* call Devlin. But first . . .

Wanting to familiarize herself with the lay of the land, she moved to one of the windows and raised the shade. Beyond the glass, she saw a neatly trimmed lawn slanting down to a thickly wooded area several hundred yards away.

Though she couldn't really judge by the view from one window, Kari sensed the house was fairly secluded. Which meant there probably weren't any neighbors nearby to whom she could go for help.

Not that she thought she'd have to seek outside assistance. But just in case Devlin refused to believe her, she ought to have an alternate plan of action. She was no match for Alex physically. However, she could be wily.

She would have to keep her temper under control, watch her mouth and act demure. Then maybe he'd let his guard down and she'd have a chance to slip away. But she didn't think she'd get very far on foot before he caught up with her.

And she seriously doubted he'd left the car keys lying around where she could find them.

Her thoughts whirling, Kari turned away from the window. A sense of panic seized her and her heart began to pound. She couldn't stay there with Alex. She just couldn't.

She had to get back to San Antonio. She had to deal with Brandon Selby as best she could, then salvage whatever was left of her riding career. Maybe find a job at a stable where she would have more of an opportunity to work with children than she did now.

And she would, one way or another, she vowed, taking a deep, steadying breath.

Her mental turmoil subsiding somewhat, she squared her shoulders and headed toward the doorway. One step at a time, she told herself. Eat, call Devlin and then take it from there.

The bedroom where she'd slept was at the end of a long hallway. Two additional rooms—one furnished with twin beds, a nightstand and dresser, the other set up as an office—opened off to the right and left respectively. There was also another bathroom just beyond the bedroom on the right.

The hallway itself opened into a large living room wide enough to accommodate two sitting areas. A huge blue-and-white-striped sofa sat in front of a cabinet holding a television and stereo components at one end, while a couple of matching armchairs and ottomans were angled on either side of a fireplace at the other. Antique oak tables, bookshelves filled with books, and several appropriately placed brass lamps completed the furnishings. Braided rugs in shades of blue and red added a touch of warmth to the polished hardwood floor.

Very nice, Kari thought, her gaze roving over the room, then lingering on the French doors, bordered by tall windows, that filled the far wall. Through them, she could see an expanse of tree-shaded lawn cut by a winding drive she assumed led to the main road.

Her way out. But not just yet.

Never one to rush her fences, Kari crossed the living room to the open doorway leading into the kitchen. She paused, then smiled slightly as she glanced around the cheery, sun-filled room, noting the plants on the windowsill as well as the basket of silk flowers and the placemats on the table. At least here the house looked lived in.

From where he stood by the stove, Alex eyed her warily, a pitcher of pancake batter in one hand. For just a moment, Kari wondered what he'd do if she decided to make a run for it. Throw down the pitcher and take off after her? Probably. And when he caught her—

The thought of his tackling her out on that luscious lawn sent a shiver of something closer to anticipation than anxiety creeping up her spine.

Good Lord! What was wrong with her? She must be crazy—imagining herself rolling around in the grass with Alexander Payton and enjoying it.

As a surge of heat spread across her cheeks, she lowered her gaze and moved to the table. "I realized I was hungry after all," she offered by way of explanation.

"I thought maybe you would," he replied as he turned back to the stove and poured four good-size puddles of batter on the hot griddle.

Obviously, she thought. He had set the table for two and was fixing her favorite breakfast—pancakes and bacon.

He knew her so well. But then, he always had. Why, there were even times she'd been sure he could read her mind.

Which meant she'd probably be wise to watch what she was thinking while he was around.

Again she imagined tumbling around on the lawn with him, and again she blushed.

"Help yourself to juice and coffee. There's milk in the refrigerator, too, if you want it."

"Thanks."

She risked a glance at him and saw him watching her, a glimmer of something like longing deep in his eyes. The same longing she'd experienced only a moment ago.

She stared at him wordlessly and he stared back. Her heartbeat quickening, she held on to one of the chairs, willing herself not to give in to the urge to go to him, to put her arms around him and—

With a blink of his eyes, Alex's expression grew cold and distant again. He picked up a platter and added the pancakes to the bacon already on it.

Feeling as if she'd been put in her place, Kari moved to the counter, filled a mug with coffee, then sat at the table.

When was she going to stop wishing he could love her as much as she loved him? He'd made it clear she meant nothing to him. Yet all she had to do was share a little space with him, and hope fluttered in her heart all over again.

Drawing on what little pride she seemed to have left, Kari took a sip of her coffee, then another and another. She'd already called herself a fool six times over. No sense wasting time repeating herself. Better to pull herself together and make the best of the situation.

She'd say as little as possible, eat what was offered, then call her brother. And no matter how much she wanted to put her head down and cry, she wouldn't. At least not until she was alone again.

Chapter 4

With a nonchalance he wasn't even close to feeling, Alex set the platter of food on the table. He wasn't sure if he wanted to shake Kari till her teeth rattled or kiss her senseless. Either way, the temptation to put his hands on her was almost more than he could resist.

He had been oddly off balance ever since he'd awakened to find her weaving like a drunken sailor beside his bed. He couldn't believe he hadn't heard her stirring sooner. He never slept like that. Never.

Luckily, he had managed to catch her before she landed flat on her face. But he'd had no time to distance himself emotionally from the impact physical contact with her still seemed to have on him. As he'd held her lithe body in his arms, his senses had reeled.

She had been just as irate as he'd anticipated, and with his defenses down, he hadn't been able to hide his amusement. Or his affection.

However, by the time she'd finished in the bathroom, he had collected himself. And a good thing, too, considering how she'd set about lying to him with such seeming aplomb.

Had he not had all his wits about him, he might have been fooled by her bright smile and brash tone. But with his emotions firmly under control again, he'd been able to study her with a certain amount of dispassion.

Though she'd appeared calm, Alex had realized almost at once just how flustered she really was. Granted, the explanations she'd offered had been reasonable enough. But her flushed face and averted eyes had contradicted almost every word she'd spoken. When he had also taken into account her earlier admission that she'd been too scared to sleep, he'd been sure she wasn't telling him the truth.

What he was still having a hard time understanding was why she'd chosen to lie to him. She herself had insisted that if she was in trouble, she'd welcome all the help she could get. Yet she seemed bound and determined not to let him run interference for her.

Not only had she vehemently denied that Brandon Selby posed a threat to her well-being. In her doggedness to throw him off, she'd gone so far as to imply the man was her fiancé. Thanks to Devlin, Alex knew better. But she'd been so adamant about it that he might have been fooled otherwise.

She must have a good reason for being so pigheaded. But for the life of him, he couldn't figure out what it was. Surely she had to realize he was much better equipped to deal with a man like Selby than she was. And she had to know he wouldn't allow her come to any harm in the process.

So what the hell was her problem? Did she really hate him so much she'd rather take her chances with a bastard like Brandon Selby?

With a sudden sinking feeling in the pit of his stomach, Alex answered his own question in the affirmative as he watched Kari fiddle nervously with her mug. After the way he'd betrayed her love and trust, he would have to be the last man on earth she'd willingly turn to for assistance.

Grimly, he poured a mug of coffee for himself, then sat down at the table. Without a glance in his direction, Kari forked two pancakes and several slices of bacon onto her plate, drizzled syrup over the pancakes and began to eat.

He had expected her to be hostile toward him. At least initially. But not so much so that she'd risk endangering herself instead of accepting his help. Which proved just how seriously he had underestimated the depth of her animosity toward him.

Looking back, he had to admit he'd given her good reason not to depend on him for anything. But that didn't mean the situation was entirely hopeless.

There was no way he could force her to cooperate with him. However, he could whittle away at her defenses until he won back her trust. Of course, he'd have to stop distancing himself from her. He'd have to be kinder, warmer and more gracious toward her or he'd never be able to convince her he was the lesser of two evils.

Considering how he felt about her, he wouldn't find that difficult to do. Once upon a time they'd shared a very special kind of camaraderie. And he still cared for her deeply. In fact, she meant more to him than any woman ever had.

Wooing her would be a pleasure. An honest pleasure. But therein also lay the problem.

Once he set about courting her favor, he could very well get caught up in the charade. And if Kari responded favorably, he might also begin to believe in happily ever after again. He might begin to hope and dream as he hadn't done in years.

And so might Kari. Only to realize he had misled her again—this time intentionally.

They had no more chance now of having any kind of future together than they had six years ago. His reasons for walking away from her then were still equally imperative. He would be staying around only long enough to get her out of whatever trouble she was in. Then he'd have no choice but to be on his way.

Of course, nowhere was it written that they had to be intimate. Merely establishing some kind of rapport with her ought to be enough to get her talking.

In fact, as angry and resentful as she appeared, that would probably be as much as he could hope to do. And, he assured himself, reestablishing a cordial relationship with her would certainly be justifiable if she then told him what he needed to know to keep her out of harm's way.

Aware he was having a much easier time talking himself into pursuing this new course of action than he should have, Alex helped himself to pancakes and bacon. He could tell himself he was going to be more congenial toward her only because she'd never confide in him otherwise. But somewhere deep in his soul, he knew better.

Having finally realized just how badly he'd hurt her, he wanted to make amends as best he could. He didn't expect her ever to have any honest affection for him again. But if at all possible, he'd like her to think of him in the future with something more akin to fondness than fury. That she now bore him such bitter enmity pained him greatly. Even though he most certainly deserved it.

His decision made, Alex supposed there was no time like the present to start winning her over. Crunching into a slice of bacon, he studied her silently for a few moments. She seemed just as intent on ignoring him as she had since he first sat down beside her. But he wasn't going to let her get away with that ploy any longer.

"Is the food all right?" he asked, allowing the very real warmth he felt for her to edge into his voice.

Obviously taken aback by his change in manner, Kari shot a startled look at him. She regarded him cautiously for several seconds, then lowered her gaze.

"Yes," she replied as she helped herself to another pancake and a few more strips of bacon. "The food is just fine."

"Would you like me to fix some more pancakes?" he offered.

"No, thanks."

Her overly polite tone grinding on his nerves, Alex schooled himself to be patient as he dug into his pancakes. After all, he reminded himself, he'd drugged her, abducted her and called her a liar. He couldn't expect her to respond to his overtures as if none of that mattered.

He ate in silence for a few minutes. Now finished, Kari sat across from him, head bent, hands in her lap, giving nothing away.

"Help yourself to another cup of coffee if you want," he said at last.

Without looking at him, she stood and retrieved the pot. She refilled her mug, hesitated a moment, then topped off his mug, too.

"Thanks." He glanced up at her, smiling, but she was already turning back to the counter.

"You're welcome," she murmured, then sat at the table again.

Her demeanor was all too impassive for his peace of mind. The way she was biding her time, she had to be up to something. She'd made it clear she'd said all she was going to say about Brandon Selby, and evidently she'd meant it.

Now he found himself wondering what she was planning to do instead.

With an inner sigh of frustration, he pushed his empty plate away and sat back in his chair. He knew better than to goad her. She'd clam up even more. But he wasn't about to let her brush him off, either.

"You look like you're feeling a little better," he began again, hoping to draw her out.

That she'd managed to shower, dress and come to the kitchen on her own meant the worst of the drug's effect had more than likely worn off. But her face was still pale and she still had dark circles under her eyes. Though she didn't appear quite as rough around the edges as she had earlier, he would have suggested she go back to bed if he hadn't been sure she'd snap his head off.

"Actually, I'm feeling a lot better." She glanced at him, her gray eyes stormy. "Even though you pumped me full of God only knows what last night."

"A relatively mild sedative," he reiterated in the blandest tone he could manage. "At your brother's request, and then only because you wouldn't have come here with me otherwise." He hesitated a long moment. Then, giving in to his curiosity, he asked, "Or would you?"

"Not hardly," she retorted, turning her face away.

"Look, Kari, I realize I haven't exactly endeared myself to you in the past. But right now I have only your best interests at heart. Regardless of what you say, I know you're in some kind of trouble. And I really do want to help you, if only you'll—"

"Help me?" she cut in, her anger getting the better of her despite her obvious attempt to stay calm. "You walked out on me without a word. Left me lying naked in my bed. And now, just because my brother *thinks* I'm in some kind of trouble, I'm supposed to forget what a jerk you are and welcome you back into my life? Well, guess again."

Without waiting for him to respond, she pushed away from the table, stood and crossed to the counter. Her back to him, she gripped the edge of the sink and stared out the window, her shoulders stiff and straight.

The pain in her voice cut through Alex like a knife. And though he knew he should stay as far away from her as possible, he couldn't seem to stop himself from going to her.

He had been so sure he'd done the right thing six years ago. That walking away from her then was better than subjecting her to the man he'd always been afraid he might become. He'd never thought that the wound he'd inflicted on her would still be so raw, so aching.

Pausing behind her, he put his hands on her shoulders.

"I'm sorry for leaving you the way I did. Believe me, I am. But I had my reasons."

He spoke without thinking, wanting only to ease her anguish. But as soon as the words left his mouth, he knew he'd strayed into forbidden territory, inadvertently opening a door he'd already vowed would forever remain shut.

"What reasons?" Kari murmured, glancing back at him. "Tell me, Alex. What reasons?"

"I can't."

"Can't or won't?" she shot back.

Refusing to be baited, he stared at her silently. She held his gaze, a pleading look in her eyes, for what seemed like a very long time. Finally, she broke away from him with an indignant toss of her head. And when she spoke again, her voice was cold as ice.

"I want to call my brother."

"Then call him," he replied, moving back to the table. "The telephone is on the wall by the refrigerator." He glanced at the clock on the wall, then added, "He's probably at the office. Do you know the number?"

"Yes."

Seeming surprised that he had given in to her request so easily, she crossed to the telephone, lifted the receiver and punched Devlin's number into the keypad.

More than happy to let her brother deal with her, Alex set about clearing the table and loading the dishwasher. He knew Devlin wouldn't be swayed by her story any more than he had been. But maybe he would have better luck convincing Kari to tell one or the other of them what was really going on with Brandon Selby.

Devlin answered almost immediately, and though Kari spoke softly and kept her back to him, Alex overheard most of what she said. In a teeth-grindingly cheerful tone, she told her brother, almost word for word, the same lies she'd told him earlier. Following her recitation, she paused, then seemed to be answering several questions.

As her responses grew terser and terser, Alex gathered she wasn't getting the reaction she had hoped she would. At last, after several minutes of silence—during which Alex assumed Devlin was lecturing her—she spun around and thrust the receiver at him.

He could only imagine what her brother had said to her, but from the wrathful look on her face, he figured it wasn't anywhere near what she'd expected.

"He wants to talk to you," she snapped.

As he took the receiver from her, she sidled past him, her chin tilted at a defiant angle, then stalked back to the table and flung herself into a chair, behaving just the way she had years ago whenever she failed to get her way.

Smiling to himself, Alex turned away from her just as she'd done to him.

"Yeah, what's up?" he asked, wasting no time on a more sociable greeting.

"She's lying, isn't she?" Devlin said matter-of-factly.

"I'd say so."

"And rather obdurately if I'm not mistaken."

"Rather obdurately, indeed."

"So, now what?"

"Actually, I was hoping you might have some suggestions," Alex admitted.

"Not having any luck charming her into talking to you?"

"I'm trying. But so far, it doesn't seem to be working."

"Any idea why she's being so stubborn?" Devlin asked, sounding as if he were truly perplexed.

"A real good idea," Alex muttered.

"Well, then, why don't you tell me?"

"I told you once already, but you wouldn't listen. I'm the wrong man for the job."

"Shall I start searching for a replacement?"

"Not yet." Alex had never been one to give up, and despite his better judgment, he wasn't about to start now.

"Give her a little more time to adjust to the situation," Devlin urged. "She'll come around."

"That's what I'm counting on," he replied.

However, as he glanced over his shoulder at her, Alex wasn't so sure he should. Sitting with her arms crossed over her chest, her mouth compressed in a narrow line, she looked more irate than ever.

"You think it's Selby who's scaring her?" Devlin asked.

"I'm almost positive," Alex replied. "It's *why* that's got me stumped. So far, she won't say. But I'm going to do a little digging on my own this afternoon."

"You've got your computer hooked up?"

"You bet. I'm ready to surf the 'Net. No telling what kind of interesting information I'll turn up out in cyberspace."

"Well, keep me posted."

"Will do," Alex agreed.

"You want me to talk to Kari again?"

"Only if you think it'll do any good."

"I doubt it."

"Yeah, so do I."

"Then I'll pass," Devlin said, his voice tinged with laughter.

"Coward."

Chuckling to himself, Alex hung up. Then, sobering once more, he turned to find Kari glaring at him.

"I wanted to talk to Devlin again."

"Then call him back."

"I will." Her chin tilted even higher, she regarded him challengingly. "From San Antonio."

He leaned against the counter, hands braced on his hips, and offered her a smile.

"Have a nice walk. A nice long walk."

"That's *my* car parked outside. I'm driving back."

"Not without your keys." His smile widening, he patted the side pocket of his shorts.

"All right, then. I'll walk."

Staring at him defiantly, she stood, then crossed to the opposite end of the counter, grabbed her purse, slung the strap over her shoulder and headed toward the door.

"Before you go, I should tell you there's six miles of gravel lane from here to the paved road. And it's at least ninety-five degrees outside. You might want to wait until dark, when it'll be a little cooler, but with only a flashlight to guide the way, the going will probably be even rougher then."

She whirled around, started to say something, then appeared to think better of it. After eyeing him a moment longer, she walked back to the table and, seeming utterly defeated, sat in her chair again.

The last thing he wanted to do was break her spirit. Yet he was greatly relieved she wasn't foolhardy enough to walk off just to spite him.

Not that he would have let her get far before hauling her back to the house. He'd meant it when he said he intended to keep her there by whatever means he found necessary. But he'd rather avoid having to use physical force on her. Even for her own good.

"You know, Kari, I'm not enjoying this any more than you are." He returned to the table and sat down, too. "But until you tell me exactly what's going on at Selby Stables, I won't let you go back there."

As if she were carved of stone, she sat still and silent, refusing to acknowledge him.

Reaching out, he touched her arm lightly as he added, "Whatever you've gotten yourself into, I'll help you get out, and I'll do my damnedest to see that you're not hurt in the process. I swear I will."

After what seemed like a very long time, but could have been no more than a minute or two, she turned her head slowly until she met his gaze. Her expression was so bleak it was all he could do to keep from going to her and gathering her into his arms. Only his firm belief that she would bitterly resent any offer of solace from him stayed the urge. But ever so gently, ever so encouragingly, he stroked her bare arm with his fingertips.

For one long moment, he sensed her wavering, and calling on what little patience he had left, he waited. Sadly, in vain. Instead of capitulating as he had anticipated she would, she drew her arm away and stood.

"As I told you once already, Alex, I don't want or need your help. I'm perfectly capable of taking care of myself.

I've done so in the past, and I have every intention of doing so in the future.''

Turning away from him, she moved toward the hallway, her demeanor haughty. And though he would have liked nothing better than to sit her down again and force her to see reason, Alex let her go.

She was angry enough already. Provoking her further, especially in her current state of mind, would only make her more obstinate. He'd do better to leave her alone for a while. Maybe then she'd come to her senses more readily.

While talking to her brother hadn't caused any significant change in her attitude, she hadn't seemed quite so resolute about keeping her own counsel. When he'd offered to help her just now, she *had* vacillated. As if, Alex thought, she'd been more than half-tempted to confide in him.

She was a smart woman. Surely, with Devlin's encouragement, she was already well on her way to realizing she had more to gain than lose by having him on her side. Perhaps given some time to herself, she'd finally be ready to act accordingly. Alex certainly hoped so. She needed him, despite her vehement denials, and he had every intention of being there for her. Whether she liked it or not.

The sound of the back bedroom door closing punctuated Alex's thoughts. Satisfied he'd done all he could for her for the time being, he crossed to the panel on the wall by the rear door and punched in the code that activated the outer perimeter alarm. Just in case she decided to slip out a window. Then he finished cleaning up the kitchen and headed for the room he'd set up as an office.

He'd meant to do his research on Selby last night. But then he'd gone into the bedroom to check on Kari one last time and made the mistake of sitting down in the chair. Only for a moment, he'd told himself as he gazed at her with a hunger that was almost unbearable. Instead of getting up again, he'd fallen sound asleep himself, and lost what chance he'd had of staying several steps ahead of her.

Now, with her in self-imposed exile, he had all afternoon to make up for lost time. He doubted she would seek him out again before early evening. And by then, with a little help from his friendly computer, he ought to know a whole hell of a lot more about Brandon Selby than he did at the moment.

That, in turn, would enable him to question Kari more adroitly the next go-around. Specific questions more often than not elicited specific answers. Especially when the questions were rapidly and relentlessly volleyed.

Alex worked steadily for several hours, tapping into one data bank after another, some accessible only via his security code. Slowly but surely, he began to see a disturbing pattern emerge.

Late in the afternoon he took a break. Having heard nothing from Kari since she'd taken refuge in the bedroom, he went to check on her. Much to his relief, he found her curled up on the bed, sound asleep. Glad she was getting some rest, he went back to the computer, leaving her undisturbed.

By the time he finally shut down for the day, he had a fairly good idea what was going on at Selby Stables. And if he was on the right track, and Kari was somehow involved, even inadvertently, he also understood why she was so scared she couldn't sleep.

Any man ruthless enough to kill show horses for a cut of the insurance money wouldn't think twice about eliminating someone who could incriminate him. He wouldn't want his reputation ruined. And with the expenses Selby had been incurring lately, neither could he afford to give up his little sideline.

What Alex hadn't been able to determine was why Kari seemed to be protecting the bastard. He hadn't come across any evidence that she'd benefited financially. Not that he believed she would willingly go along with such barbarity. But surely she had to have some inkling of what he was up to. Otherwise why would she be so afraid?

Yet she hadn't accused Selby of anything. And she wouldn't, Alex realized as he sat back in his chair. Not until she had absolute proof. She was too fair-minded to do anything else.

She was also too damned dauntless for her own good. Anyone else would have gotten out of there as fast as she could once she realized what was going on. But not Kari. Her conscience wouldn't let her do that. Instead she had decided to stick around long enough to gather whatever evidence she could in order to stop Selby on her own.

From the information Alex had managed to uncover, he had an idea she'd been playing a dangerous game of cat and mouse with the man for some time now. One that she must realize could get her killed. Yet she wasn't about to back off.

Alex shuddered to think what might have happened to her if Devlin hadn't sensed that something was wrong. But she was safe now, and he intended to make sure she stayed that way. She wasn't going anywhere near Brandon Selby again. Not as long as he had anything to say about it.

And he planned to have quite a lot to say about it.

Only not just yet, he reminded himself. He still had a little work to do before he was ready to confront her. Work that would have to wait until the following day.

First thing in the morning, however, he was going to make a few phone calls. Calls to find out if any law-enforcement agencies were involved yet. Insurance fraud was a major crime, and he didn't want to step on any toes. Once he'd gotten squared away with the proper authorities, he'd talk to Kari. And then . . . ?

Then maybe he'd take her away for a while. Far, far away. Maybe to a secluded island in the Caribbean where she'd be well out of reach until Selby was behind bars. Well out of reach of anyone but *him*.

With a rueful shake of his head, Alex stood and stretched. One of these days he was going to have to face the fact that he could never have that kind of relationship with her.

He gathered together the papers on his desk and shoved them in a drawer. Then, as his stomach growled, reminding him it was almost suppertime, he wandered down the hallway and tapped on the bedroom door.

"What?" Kari demanded, sounding supremely annoyed.

He opened the door and saw her standing by one of the windows, looking as if she'd just awakened.

"I thought I'd fix spaghetti for supper," he advised.

She shrugged indifferently as she gazed out the window. "Suit yourself."

"Want to give me a hand with the salad?"

"Not really."

"Then come sit at the table and keep me company."

"Are you asking me or telling me?"

"Asking," he replied, his temper finally starting to fray. She really could be a pain in the butt when she set her mind to it.

"I'd rather not." Shifting slightly so that he could no longer see her face, she leaned against the window frame.

"All right, then. I'll come and get you when the food is ready."

"I'm not really very hungry."

"Wait until you get a whiff of my special sauce. You won't be able to resist."

Without waiting for her to reply, Alex turned away, purposely leaving the door open.

He was half-tempted to send her back to Selby after all. But only for a moment. Much as he'd like to wring her neck, he didn't really relish the idea of anyone else doing it.

Pausing in the living room, he chose a CD from the stack on the shelf, slid the disc into the player and adjusted the volume. Then, letting the moody blues he loved soothe his weary soul, he set to work in the kitchen.

Kari could stay in the bedroom and sulk all she wanted. He was going to eat a good meal, maybe drink a glass of wine, then soak in the hot tub for a while. He was on vacation, after all. A well-deserved vacation. And he was going to make the most of it. Whether she cooperated or not.

Arms crossed over her chest, Kari stood by the bedroom window long after Alex left her, frowning as she weighed her options. To say they were limited would be an understatement. She could stay and tell Alex the truth, stay and continue to lie or try to get away.

As far as she was concerned, her alternatives were equally unappealing. But she had to make a decision soon. For her own emotional well-being.

She wished she hadn't slept away the afternoon. Maybe then she would have already come up with a plan of action. Instead she still seemed barely able to think straight.

But when Devlin had refused to believe her, and then Alex began badgering her again, she'd felt so damned defeated. Alone in the bedroom, she'd curled up on the bed and finally indulged in a few self-pitying tears. Eventually, she'd fallen sound asleep again. When she'd awakened less than an hour ago, rather than feeling rested and refreshed she'd been even more out of sorts than ever.

She couldn't understand why she'd let the two of them get her down. She ran several miles a day and rode for hours on end in the heat of summer. A six-mile walk wouldn't have done her in. She could have changed into shorts, a T-shirt and running shoes, slipped out the window and been long gone.

Actually, she admitted, she still could. Since Alex was busy in the kitchen, he probably wouldn't realize she was gone for at least thirty minutes or more. And if she kept to the woods rather than the gravel lane, he'd have a harder time finding her.

But was that what she really wanted to do? Was she that desperate to get away from him? So desperate she'd make her way back to Selby Stables any way she could, knowing she'd have to face Brandon on her own once she got there?

If Brandon had begun to suspect she was onto him, as she was afraid he had, Kari knew he would try to get rid of her permanently. And she'd have no one to watch her back. Was taking that kind of chance better than accepting whatever assistance Alex could offer her, as Devlin had urged repeatedly?

Granted, her brother had no idea just how hurtfully Alex had treated her six years ago. And, of course, he wouldn't know how susceptible she still was to his charms. He hadn't seen any problem with his best friend lending his little sister a helping hand. And he certainly wouldn't understand how devastating her resultant dependence on him could be.

In order for Alex to help her, they'd have to work together closely. And that kind of contact with him wouldn't do her any emotional good at all. She simply wasn't impervious enough to be with him on a daily basis and, at the same time, maintain the kind of distance necessary to keep from having her heart broken all over again.

The more time she spent with him, the more difficult it would be for her to remember he was only doing Devlin a favor. To remember that no matter how kindly he treated her, she meant nothing to him personally, and never would. To remember that when all was said and done, he'd leave her again just as blithely as he had before.

So why hadn't she changed her clothes yet? Why hadn't she crept out the window and run into the woods?

Because she wasn't about to allow Brandon to get away with what he'd done, and taking him on alone was just too dangerous. She didn't really want to end up dead.

Like it or not, she had a better chance of stopping Brandon with Alex's help than she had on her own. And as long as she attained her ultimate goal, surely she would be able to survive whatever anguish ensued.

She had another, more personal, reason for staying put, too, she admitted, watching the shadows of early evening play across the lawn. While they were together, she was going to find a way to make him tell her why he walked out on her the way he did.

He'd already acknowledged that he'd hurt her. He'd even gone so far as to apologize. But he hadn't wanted to explain his actions. When she had pushed him, he had withdrawn from her so completely he could have been on another planet.

That didn't mean she couldn't keep asking and asking, though. Just as she was going to be stuck with him, he was going to be stuck with her. So why not make the most of it?

Sooner or later, out of sheer exasperation, he'd give her an answer. And then maybe she'd find it easier to live with what he'd done to her.

Even if the truth was that he had never really loved her, knowing would be better than wondering for the rest of her life. She'd much rather have her hopes dashed once and for

all than go on longing for the improbable, as she so foolishly continued to do.

Her course set, Kari finally turned away from the window and headed for the bathroom. To her surprise, she felt
almost lighthearted as she washed her face and brushed her
hair. At long last, she seemed to have come to her senses.
And now that she had put things into perspective, she was
ready to move ahead.

Yes, Alexander Payton had hurt her badly. And yes, he
would more than likely hurt her again, no matter how careful she was. But with luck, when all was said and done, she
would be free. In more ways than one.

In all probability, she wasn't going to like Alex's reasons
for leaving her. But at least she would know where she stood
with him. Then maybe she'd be able to get on with her life
at last.

Breathing in the spicy aroma of sautéing garlic, onions,
green peppers and Italian sausage, Kari made her way to the
kitchen. So far, she had behaved rather badly. However,
that was going to have to change. She knew as well as anyone that you caught more flies with honey.

Still, just outside the kitchen doorway, she stopped short
and wiped the slight smile from her face. No sense going
overboard just yet. She'd only end up tipping her hand. If
she turned cheerful all of a sudden, Alex would wonder
what she was up to, and she'd never get him to lower his
guard.

She'd be wiser to take it slow and easy. She could soften
toward him a little now, then a little more in the morning.
Then tomorrow afternoon, when she told him everything,
he'd assume she had finally come to her senses. And once
they were working together against Brandon, she would
make the most of their newfound affinity for each other.

Braced for the worst, she would use whatever means necessary and find out, once and for all, exactly why he had run out on her at the very moment she'd begun to believe he truly loved her.

Chapter 5

As Kari entered the kitchen, Alex glanced over his shoulder at her. He seemed surprised to see her, but he didn't say anything to confirm her suspicion. Turning back to the skillet on the stove, he stirred the contents without speaking at all. And for several uncomfortable moments, neither did she.

She didn't know about him, but she didn't want to get off on the wrong foot again. Still, after what he'd done to her, she wasn't about to offer him explanations or apologies, either. He already knew he had the upper hand. No sense reinforcing that fact by admitting she'd said or done anything that required his understanding or forgiveness.

So, what *could* she say to break the silence stretching between them without offending or empowering him?

"Still want some help with the salad?" she asked at last, then cringed inwardly at the inanity of her question.

"It's already done," Alex answered matter-of-factly.

"Oh."

She paused by the table uncertainly and ran her hand over the back of a chair, watching as Alex transferred the sausage and vegetables from the skillet onto a plate covered with a paper towel. She had no idea what to say or do next, and he didn't appear inclined to offer her any hints.

After what seemed like an eternity, he gestured toward a loaf of French bread in a red-white-and-blue wrapper and said, "You can fix the garlic bread if you want."

"Okay."

Thoroughly discomfited, she crossed to the counter. Somehow she had thought he would be more welcoming. But after the way she'd been acting, how could she expect him to be glad she was gracing him with her presence?

She'd all but snapped his head off when he'd come to the bedroom to make amends. And there had been an edge of resentment in her voice when she'd asked about the salad. If she had heard it, then of course he must have, too.

Alex had never been a glutton for punishment. And with the way her anger and frustration kept soaring out of control, she had yet to be what anyone would call good company. So why would he be anything but wary of her now?

Damn, damn, *damn...*

He would never lighten up unless *she* did. And in a genuine way. He had already proved he knew her too well to be taken in by any prevarication on her part.

Racking her brain for an opening gambit that might get him to lower his guard, Kari slid the bread out of the wrapper and set it on the cutting board. As she reached for the knife, she spied two empty glass jars sitting on the counter near the stove. Identical to ones she kept on hand in her own pantry, they not only revealed the source of Alex's so-called special sauce, but also provided her with something relatively innocuous to tease him about.

"*Your* special sauce, huh?" she asked, allowing the merest hint of laughter to edge her voice as she picked up one of the jars and pretended to study the distinctive green label. "Looks just like *my* special sauce."

"Okay, I admit I start with that stuff." He glanced at her, a sheepish smile curving the corners of his mouth. "But by the time I get finished with it, I guarantee you'll be impressed."

Turning away again, he dumped the sausage and vegetables into the pot already bubbling on a back burner, added half a cup of Parmesan cheese and a generous measure of red wine from the open bottle on the counter. He gave the sauce a good stir, then lowered the heat so it could simmer.

"How creative of you," Kari murmured approvingly as she finished slicing the bread and began to butter it.

"That's nothing. Wait till you see what I can do with a box of brownie mix."

Taking the said item from the pantry, Alex ripped off the top, opened the plastic bag, poured the contents into a mixing bowl and added one cup each of chocolate chips and chopped walnuts.

"Oh, please, I do that all the time," she countered, unimpressed.

"Yeah, but have you ever used a combination of amaretto and cream instead of the water called for in the recipe?" he inquired with a superior arch of one eyebrow.

"Never," Kari admitted, sprinkling garlic powder on the bread.

"Well, get ready for a real treat."

"Dessert and an after-dinner drink all in one, huh?"

"You got it," he agreed.

Finished with the bread, Kari wrapped it in a piece of tin foil. Then, with a strange sense of déjà vu, she leaned against the counter as Alex opened the amaretto he'd taken from the pantry.

Their bantering had a familiarity about it that tugged at her heart. But then, they had prepared more than one meal together when he'd come to stay with her after her parents died. So, naturally, working side by side the way they had been would seem just like old times.

But she wasn't about to admit as much to Alex. She'd only stir up her anger and frustration again by talking about the past. Just as she would if she made any kind of comment about the future. And, unfortunately, she had a feeling they'd said almost all there was to say about his culinary expertise.

"Do you want me to put the bread in the oven?" she asked.

"Yeah, sure. I'm just about ready to start the spaghetti."

"What about the brownies?"

"They can bake while we eat."

As Alex poured the brownie mix into a pan, then lit the burner under the large pot of water already atop the stove, Kari searched desperately for something else to say or do. She couldn't afford to stand by silently too long. He might start in about Selby Stables again.

He had restrained himself so far. And she had already decided to tell him everything anyway. But she wasn't in the mood to be interrogated tonight. She'd much prefer to share a quiet dinner with him as if they really were friends again.

Her gaze drifting to the table, empty except for the pretty little basket of blue and rose and white silk flowers she'd seen there that morning, she asked, "Do you want me to set out the plates?"

"I thought we'd eat on the deck. Unless you'd rather stay in here."

"Oh, no, I'd *love* to have dinner on the deck," Kari hastened to assure him, then winced as she realized she'd gone a bit overboard in her enthusiasm.

After spending the day cooped up in the house, she was eager to get out for a while, though. The long hours indoors, doing nothing but staring into space, had left her feeling much too restive.

"Good." Nodding agreeably, Alex pulled a tray from one of the lower cabinets. "The deck is shaded this time of evening, so it should be fairly comfortable." He added place mats, napkins, plates and silverware, then asked, "What would you like to drink? Iced tea, a soft drink, a glass of red wine?" He gestured toward the bottle on the counter.

For one long moment, Kari was tempted to ask for a glass of wine. She loved red wine and she knew by the label that the cabernet sauvignon Alex had offered her was an especially good one. But she didn't dare. One glass of wine could, and probably would, lead all too easily to two. And two glasses of wine would leave her much too relaxed for her own good.

With her emotions still so near the surface, there was no telling what she might say or do. And she didn't want Alex to know just how vulnerable she was feeling.

"Iced tea, please," she answered stoically.

"Are you sure? You used to like red wine, and this one is better than average."

"I'm sure."

"Iced tea it is, then," he muttered, sounding vaguely disappointed.

He filled two tall glasses with ice, set them on the tray, then added a glass pitcher of tea he took from the refrigerator.

"You don't have to abstain on my account," she said.

As she recalled, Alex rarely drank, and then only in strict moderation. But a little wine might loosen him up, and that would definitely be to her advantage. Of course, that was probably what he'd been hoping would happen with *her*....

"I'm not," he replied. Then, as he lifted the tray and held it out to her, he added, "Sure you can manage all this?"

"Yes." Giving him a smug smile, she took the tray from him easily and turned away.

He might consider her too thin, but she certainly wasn't any weakling. She couldn't afford to be. Not when she rode high-strung young horses on a daily basis.

"Well, then, let me get the door for you."

Moving past her, he fiddled with a keypad on the wall by the back door.

"What's that?" she asked, eyeing him questioningly.

"One of the control units for the security system."

"Security system?" Puzzled, Kari shook her head. "Don't tell me you're afraid someone is going to sneak out here and try to break into your house. You said yourself this place is out in the middle of nowhere."

"Actually, I am. There's been a lot of vandalism around here lately. I'm gone most of the time, and I don't want my house trashed in my absence," he replied. Then, the barest hint of amusement in his bright-blue eyes, he added with unexpected candor, "However, this afternoon I was more concerned about somebody slipping out a window and trying to make a run for it."

Though taken aback by his honest admission, Kari forced herself to meet his gaze, widening her eyes innocently as she asked, "You thought I'd do that?"

He knew her too well. Much, much too well. But she had no intention of acknowledging how disturbed she was by that fact.

"Well, you seemed awfully anxious to get away earlier."

"Not anxious enough to walk six miles of gravel lane in the heat of the day with no real idea of where I'd end up," she stated pragmatically.

"What about now?" he asked, opening the door.

"Now I'm too hungry to do anything but wait for dinner to be served," she assured him quite truthfully.

"And after dinner?" He held her gaze, a searching look in his eyes.

"I'm not sure." She tipped her chin up and smiled slightly. "Guess you'll just have to wait and see."

"Yeah, I guess I will." He moved away from the doorway so she could pass. "I'll have the food out just as soon as it's ready. Shouldn't be more than ten or fifteen minutes max."

Relieved that Alex had chosen not to pursue the track their conversation had been taking, Kari walked out to the deck. She wasn't quite ready to tell him she'd decided to stay put. He'd want to know why, and she'd have to admit she needed his help. Then she'd be beholden to him. And tomorrow would be soon enough for *that*.

As he closed the door behind her, Kari crossed to the round redwood table and matching chairs. Breathing in the summer-scented evening air, she set the table, then poured a glass of tea for herself. As she sipped her drink, she wandered the length of the narrow deck, one hand trailing along the wood railing until she came to the hot tub at the far end.

Nice, she thought rather wistfully, gazing down at the crystal-clear water that rippled gently under the faint breeze drifting across the lawn. Had she been alone, she would have found the switch and started the water churning, then stripped out of her clothes and slid in.

But, of course, she wasn't alone. And she wasn't getting naked anywhere near Alexander Payton. Not that he'd be interested, she reminded herself sternly.

Trying not to think about how enjoyable it would be to loll in the hot tub—even alone—Kari paced back to the table. As she surveyed the rest of Alex's domain, her surprise grew as the potential of the property he owned dawned on her.

Beyond the neatly manicured lawn that surrounded the house she saw what appeared to be a large horse barn set in the middle of several small paddocks, one of which contained a mechanical walker. All were enclosed by sturdy wood rail fences, as was the far pasture. And though deserted, the barn, the paddocks, the fences, even the far pasture, all appeared to be well maintained.

As she gazed out across the lawn, she couldn't help but imagine what the place would be like if it were truly lived in. There would be horses grazing in the paddocks and the far pasture. There would be dogs and cats and kids running loose in the house and the yard. And there would be a man and a woman—husband and wife—working together to build up their stable. Just as she and Alex had once talked of doing.

This place could be everything she had ever wanted, she mused. Could be, but wouldn't.

Sadly, she turned away from the beguiling vista as Alex walked out carrying a second tray loaded with food.

"Want to get the door?" he asked.

"Sure."

Blinking back the prickle of tears in her eyes, Kari did as he asked. Then, fighting to bring her emotions under control again, she joined him at the table. As he set out two small plates of salad, a large bowl of spaghetti, the bread basket and various other odds and ends, she filled his glass with tea and topped off her own.

"I hope you're as hungry as you said you were."

"I am," she assured him as they sat down across from each other.

"Salads first?"

"Okay."

She selected one of the bottled dressings Alex offered her and added a generous dollop to her salad. Picking up her fork, she toyed with a slice of tomato, then ventured, "You have a really nice place here."

"Just a house and some land."

Digging into his own salad, Alex shrugged dismissively, but Kari sensed it was more to him than that.

"When did you buy it?"

"About four years ago." He gestured toward her yet-to-be-touched salad. "I thought you were hungry."

"I am." She ate a few bites, but couldn't seem to quell her curiosity. "Why?" she asked at last, unable to let the subject drop despite his uncommunicativeness.

"Why what?"

"Why did you buy this place? Whoever owned it before raised horses, didn't he? But obviously, you're not doing that. So why?" she prodded, determined not to be dissuaded.

"I thought it would be a good investment," he said, shrugging again. "Ready for some spaghetti?"

"Yes, please."

Sensing his increasing annoyance, Kari said nothing as she held up her dinner plate so he could serve her. Then she helped herself to a slice of garlic bread and ate quietly for a few minutes.

She was sure there was some truth to what he'd told her. The property he owned *was* valuable. But from the care he seemed to have lavished on the house and the land around it, this place meant more to him than the money it was worth.

Whether he wanted to admit it or not, Alex had made a home for himself here—a home he rarely visited, but a real home nonetheless.

But why here?

Although he had never talked much about his past, Kari knew he had been born in Philadelphia and had lived there until his parents were killed in an automobile accident when he was eight years old. According to Devlin, they had been very wealthy, but they'd had no close relatives. Eventually, an elderly cousin had been located in Chicago. A childless widow, she had taken Alex in, not only giving him a good home, but seeing to it that he got an excellent education, as well.

She died just after Alex had graduated from West Point, and since then, as far as Kari knew, he hadn't had any one place that he'd called home. Whenever he'd had leave, he had come to San Antonio with Devlin. And now he owned his own place in the Texas Hill Country.

Did that mean he felt some special affinity for the state? Or was there more to his making a home for himself—the kind of home she had once told him she wanted—so close to where *she* lived?

Frowning, she glanced at Alex and saw him watching her.

"Something wrong with the spaghetti?" he asked with apparent concern.

Looking down at her plate, Kari realized she'd eaten no more than a bite or two. For the past few minutes, she'd been idly twirling several strands of pasta around the tines of her fork.

"It's fine, really. Just fine."

As she lowered her gaze and lifted her fork to her mouth, she chided herself for indulging, yet again, in what could only be wishful thinking.

Why on earth would Alex buy a piece of property with her in mind? He'd walked away from her without a backward glance six years ago. Since then she hadn't seen hide nor hair of him. Not until a few days ago. And then, only because Devlin and Laura had brought them together for Andrew's christening.

And she certainly wasn't here now because that's what he wanted. He hadn't brought her to his home of his own free will, but rather as favor to her beloved brother. And once he'd done what he seemed to consider his duty, he would no doubt be glad to get rid of her again.

With a sigh of regret, Kari finished her spaghetti, then pushed her empty plate away and sat back in her chair. For her own good, she was going to have to stop grasping at straws. And yet...

As her gaze wandered back to the horse barn, she found herself wondering—again—why Alex had chosen to make his home in a place that epitomized her dream. Given his reluctance to talk about it, she wondered, too, if she would ever know.

Of course, she hadn't begun to bedevil him with questions yet. She had backed off a few minutes ago, but only to give herself time to think before ruffling his feathers any further. Earlier she'd vowed she was going to get some answers out of him before they went their separate ways. Now she was more determined than ever to follow through with that plan.

Beside her, Alex stood and stacked her empty plate atop his.

"The brownies should be just about ready to come out of the oven." He set their plates and silverware on one of the trays, then added the bread basket and the bowl of leftover spaghetti. "I'd better check on them."

"Want some help cleaning up the kitchen?" Kari offered, standing, as well.

"Thanks for asking, but there's not much to do." He lifted the laden tray and turned away.

Willing herself not to be bothered by his standoffishness, she hurried ahead of him and opened the door. Obviously there were some things—like his property—that he didn't want to talk about. But if he thought distancing himself from her would deter her, he was in for a big surprise.

"Will you drink some coffee if I make a fresh pot?" he asked as he moved past her.

"Sure."

After sleeping away most of the day, the last thing she needed was another dose of caffeine. She'd have enough trouble sleeping tonight. But she couldn't imagine eating a brownie without also indulging in a cup of coffee. She loved the way the dark, bitter brew enhanced the sweet, rich taste of chocolate too much to forgo it. And she'd already denied herself the pleasure of having a glass of wine as well as lolling naked in the hot tub.

Too restive to sit again while Alex was in the house, Kari walked along the deck as she had earlier. The sun had begun to dip behind the treetops, lengthening the shadows spreading across the lawn while at the same time bathing the barn in a golden glow. Pausing, she flattened her palms against the railing and leaned forward, unaccountably drawn by the white, wood-frame building.

It wasn't all that large. Nor was it all that new. But to her it seemed just right. At least from what she could see of the outside.

"We can take a walk out there if you want," Alex said as he came to stand beside her.

Disconcerted, she glanced up at him, then looked away again. She hadn't meant to let him catch her daydreaming, but he'd crossed the deck so quietly he'd caught her by surprise.

She certainly didn't want to give her thoughts away. Not when they were so ludicrous. Yet she couldn't seem to make herself refuse his offer, either. Pretending that kind of nonchalance was simply beyond her.

"All right," she agreed, hoping she didn't sound quite as eager as she was.

Alex led the way down the short flight of steps off to one side of the hot tub. Then they walked across the lawn side by side, neither of them speaking as the evening breeze ruffled their hair. When they reached the barn, Alex punched in a code on the keypad beside the door, ushered her into the surprisingly cool, dark interior and flipped a switch.

Blinking in the sudden bright light, Kari moved away from him, walking slowly, wonderingly, between the rows of tidy box stalls. She counted ten on each side, all empty except for a scattering of fresh straw on the floor. At the far end, one doorway opened into a tack room, also empty, while another led into an office.

Stepping across the threshold, she saw that the previous owners had left behind a small wooden desk and chair, a four-drawer metal filing cabinet and an old refrigerator. All ready for someone to move in. Someone other than her.

"So, what do you think?" Alex asked as he joined her in the office.

"It's very nice," she replied, cursing the slight quaver she heard in her voice. "You've invested wisely."

Why was she tormenting herself this way? Anyone with any sense would have given the damn barn a wide berth. But not her. Oh, no. She had to go and tease herself with what-ifs that would never be.

Granted, where Alexander Payton was concerned she'd never been able to think straight. But she wasn't an innocent young girl anymore. She was a grown woman, and as such, the time had come for her to face reality.

She could fantasize all she wanted about their living happily ever after as husband and wife, raising kids and horses here. But Alex didn't love her as she still foolishly loved him. And without that essential element, they had no future together. None whatsoever.

Turning, she brushed past him, afraid that if she stayed there any longer she'd end up crumpling into a little heap and sobbing her heart out like a disenchanted child.

"Kari, wait," Alex called after her.

Ignoring him, she hastened past the empty stalls. She had almost made it to the open doorway, when he caught up with her, halting her with a hand on her shoulder.

"Hey, what's wrong?" he asked, turning her to face him.

As she met his gaze, she saw the confusion in his eyes, the same confusion she'd heard in his voice, and realized he didn't have a clue why she'd left him standing alone in the office. And she wasn't about to enlighten him. Not when all she'd get in return was his pity.

"Nothing." Forcing herself to smile, she shook her head. "Nothing at all."

"You seemed upset a moment ago." Not quite convinced, he eyed her steadily as he gently kneaded her shoulder.

"Why would I be upset?" she countered, shrugging away from his all-too-comforting touch.

"I don't know." Obviously still uncertain, Alex frowned down at her. "But are you?"

"Of course not," she replied, turning toward the doorway again. "I really enjoyed seeing your barn." Airily, she waved a hand at the stalls. "Like I said, it's very nice."

As she walked outside, Kari was tempted to head for the long, curving drive that would take her to the six miles of gravel lane and, eventually, the main road to...wherever. Getting as far away from Alex as quickly as possible suddenly seemed like the smartest thing she could do. The longer she stayed with him, the more heartache she was going to bring upon herself.

What difference did it make why he'd left her? Or why, for that matter, he'd bought this place? He had made sure she understood that he didn't want her to be a part of his life. So why not just accept it and be gone?

Of course, she'd still have to deal with Brandon, she thought, gazing longingly into the distance. And stumbling around alone in the dark, more than likely lost—as she'd no doubt end up doing at this time of night—wasn't exactly her idea of fun.

Cursing her predicament for the umpteenth time, Kari reluctantly turned toward the house. For now, she was stuck here with Alex. Which meant she was going to have to toughen up emotionally. Either that, or leave well enough alone where he was concerned.

She'd been so sure that knowing why he'd left her would loosen the hold he still seemed to have on her heart. But maybe ignorance *was* bliss after all. Going on as she had for the past six years just might be easier on her in the long run.

Her shoulders slumping, she climbed the steps to the deck, then glanced back to see where Alex was. Not far behind her, she noted glumly, though she hadn't heard him crossing the lawn. And in the growing darkness his expression was unreadable.

She thought about retreating to the back bedroom again. But hiding out now would only make it that much more difficult for her to face him in the morning, admit that she'd lied, then ask for his help.

Talk about being caught between a rock and a hard place.

Her hands clenched into fists, Kari strode across the deck to the table and sat in her chair. She wasn't sure if she wanted to laugh or cry. But she knew that if she dared do either, there was good chance she wouldn't be able to stop.

"Ready for dessert?"

As Alex paused by her side, he eyed her warily just as he had when she'd joined him in the kitchen earlier. Despite the light pouring through the windows, he couldn't see her face. But he knew she was upset. Whether she wanted to admit it or not. And for the life of him, he didn't know why.

"If you are," she replied, her tone much too cheery considering how rattled she'd been out in the barn.

"I've got a carton of vanilla ice cream in the freezer. Want a scoop on your brownie?"

"Sure."

Reluctantly, he turned away. He hated leaving her alone. Not because he thought she'd take off. He figured she had more sense than that. But he was concerned about her sudden mood swings.

After their exchange in the bedroom, he'd thought she would skip dinner just to be obstinate. So of course he'd wondered what she was up to when she wandered into the kitchen and offered her assistance. She had seemed to want nothing more than to make peace. And he had gladly gone along with her, following her lead.

He had thought she might be ready to tell him what was really going on at Selby Stables. But so far she hadn't mentioned it.

None too eager to stir her up again, Alex hadn't broached the subject, either. He'd wanted to enjoy her company, at least for a little while. And he most certainly had. Until she'd started questioning him about his property.

As he sliced the brownies, scooped ice cream and poured coffee, he admitted that her persistence had made him extremely uncomfortable. She had poked and prodded, seemingly intent on finding out exactly why he'd bought what she'd been correct in assuming had once been a horse farm.

There had been no way he could tell her the truth. Not without revealing the depth of his feelings for her. Feelings he had no right to act upon except in the most circumspect of ways.

Here he had been able to hold her close in mind if not in body. Here he had been able to imagine her riding like the wind across the far pasture or working patiently to teach a small child—their small child—the finer points of horsemanship.

But he could never allow her to know that. Not when he couldn't allow himself to turn such fantasies into reality. He'd led her on once and hurt her deeply. He couldn't, *wouldn't,* do that to her again.

She'd seemed satisfied with the answer he'd finally given her. At least enough to stop questioning him. But unfortunately, he hadn't had sense enough to let it go at that.

When he'd caught her standing on the deck, gazing at the barn, her longing obvious, he'd wanted her to see it up close. He wasn't sure why. Perhaps so she'd give it her seal of approval.

And she had. With a kind of sadness that had torn at his heart. As though she, too, had been imagining all that might have been if only he could have trusted himself.

But no. She couldn't possibly have been entertaining that particular flight of fancy—not hating him the way she surely must after all he'd done to hurt her. Such wishful thinking was his, and his alone. And he'd do well to remember it.

He added a couple of citronella candles and a book of matches to the tray holding their coffee and dessert. Then, juggling it in one hand, he managed to open the door on his own.

From her place at the table, Kari glanced up at him and started to stand.

"I've got it," he said, pulling the door closed.

"I'm sorry," she apologized, sounding sincere. "I should have given you a hand instead of sitting here waiting to be waited on."

"Hey, I don't mind. After all, you're my guest."

"Well, I guess *you* could say that," she retorted, her quiet voice heavily laced with sarcasm.

"Don't tell me you're still mad at me for kidnapping you," he teased, admiring her spirit in spite of himself.

Had she been the docile type, he would have had an easier time of it. But no matter how aggravating she could be, he liked her just the way she was.

"All right, I won't."

She helped herself to a brownie topped with vanilla ice cream, and a mug of coffee, while he set the candles on the railing and lit them. In the flickering light, she regarded him steadily for several seconds, then dug into her dessert.

Luckily, looks couldn't kill, Alex thought, smiling to himself. Otherwise he'd be dead and gone. Still, he was definitely skating on thin ice with her.

For whatever reason, she'd stopped fighting him. But she wasn't quite ready to confide in him yet. Until he could win her over completely, he'd have to at least try to mind his manners.

But she was so damn teasable. She always had been. Which was only one of the many reasons he'd fallen in love with her in the first place. She'd brought out the boy in him.

The boy his sadistic parents had come all too close to destroying—

"If you're not going to eat that, I'll be glad to take it off your hands and dispose of it properly."

Drawn from his reverie, he eyed her with amusement.

"Oh, really?"

"Well, I can't see letting a perfectly good brownie go to waste," she replied.

"Perfectly *good?*"

"All right, absolutely fabulous," she amended, albeit grudgingly.

With an audible sigh, she popped the last bite of her brownie into her mouth and sat back in her chair.

"I'm going to eat mine, but if you want another, help yourself."

"Much as I'd love to, I'd better not." She shifted in her chair, tucking one leg up under her, and stared out into the darkness. "It's really pleasant out here. Living so close to San Antonio, I forget how cool it gets at night in the Hill Country. And it's so peaceful. Considering the kind of work you do, I'm not surprised you come here when you have time off."

"It's a nice change," Alex conceded, surprised she was making an effort at polite conversation. Surprised and slightly suspicious.

He had assumed she would beat a hasty retreat to her room once they'd finished dinner. But she seemed to want to talk. About *him*.

"Of course, from what Devlin said, your stay in Mexico must have been kind of dull compared with some of the other places you've been."

"Collecting and analyzing information isn't exactly my specialty. But McConnell needed someone down there when your brother left, and I was at loose ends." He pushed his empty plate away and reached for his mug of coffee. "I agreed to take over until a permanent replacement could be found."

Alex didn't mind discussing his work with Kari. She was aware of what he and Devlin did for a living. And in the past, she had always been fascinated by their adventures—what they'd been able to tell her about them.

"And you're on leave now?"

"For four weeks."

"Then what?" she asked, turning to look at him.

"Then I'll head back to Virginia, prove to McConnell that I'm fit enough to go out in the field again, and take whatever he's got to offer in the way of covert operations in the Middle East."

"I thought maybe you'd be ready to give that up. After last year..."

She regarded him steadily, an odd expression on her face. As if what he'd just said had filled her with regret. But that would mean she still cared for him, and he knew better than to think that was possible.

"Not me. Sifting data in Mexico was boring as hell. And I'd go crazy sitting behind a desk the way your brother does now. I like working covert operations. I'm good at it, and I don't have anyone to worry about except myself," he stated pragmatically.

"No, I guess you don't, do you?"

Though she'd agreed with him easily enough, Alex could have sworn he'd heard a slight catch in her voice. And for just an instant, before she turned her face away, he thought he saw what he could only describe as anguish in her eyes.

Again he told himself he must be mistaken. After the way he'd hurt her, what difference could it make to her whether he lived or died?

"Hey, you used to think spy work was exciting," he said, hoping to lighten her mood by using the description she'd once applied to his job.

"I used to think riding bareback without a helmet at a full gallop across an open field was exciting, too." She shifted in her chair again and stood, then added a little too brightly, "But I guess I've gotten more cautious in my old age. Maybe too cautious."

Utterly dismayed by her casual comment, Alex stared at her.

"Tell me you didn't do that," he demanded.

"Oh, yes, I did. Many times. And now that I think about it, maybe I'll try it again. Especially since I don't have anyone to worry about except myself, either."

"Are you crazy?" Alex stood, too, and glared across the table at her. "You could break your neck."

"No crazier than you. You could be blown to bits," she shot back.

"That's the risk I take to do my job."

"Not because you have to. Because you want to. And if I want to ride bareback at a gallop across an open field, I will." Angrily, she moved past him and headed toward the door.

"Kari, wait."

Reaching out, Alex caught her arm, halting her in mid-flight. She whirled around, her eyes shooting sparks, and tipped her chin up challengingly.

"What?" she demanded.

He wasn't sure whether he wanted to turn her over his knee or grab her and kiss her until the last of her defiance disappeared. Either way, he'd no doubt cancel out any headway he'd made toward convincing her he only had her best interests at heart.

She'd resent the hell out of being bullied physically. And more than likely, kissing her would only stun her into momentary silence. He wouldn't mind *that,* but there would be hell to pay later. Which left him little choice but to pacify her verbally.

Taking a deep, calming breath, he met her gaze and smiled ruefully.

"Of course, you're free to do whatever you want. But I wish you wouldn't take any unnecessary chances. I'd really hate for you to get hurt."

"And I'd really hate for you to get hurt again," she replied, that faint quaver in her voice once more. "Last time, when Devlin told me you might die, I—"

She stopped, obviously alarmed by what she'd almost admitted, and looked away.

"What?" he asked, almost afraid to hear her answer.

Was it possible that she still harbored some fond feelings for him? He desperately needed to know. And yet—

"It doesn't matter." Not quite meeting his gaze, she eased her arm from his grip and stepped back. "I'd better go in. I'm kind of tired."

In the candlelight, she looked weary beyond words. Still, Alex hated to let her go. Their conversation had taken an odd, totally unexpected turn, leaving him with questions he wanted answered.

But he was afraid that if he blocked her way, she'd start to unravel. Although he'd gone out of his way to treat her with beneficence, he knew she'd been deeply dismayed to find herself at his mercy.

Pushing her too hard now could be disastrous. Especially if he pushed her in a direction she suddenly seemed determined not to go. Better to give her a chance to regroup, and do the same himself. Otherwise they both might say things they'd regret.

Much as he'd like to know that she still cared for him, what good would it do? He couldn't admit that he still cared for her, as well. Not when he couldn't allow himself to do anything about it.

"I usually turn the air-conditioning off at night and open the windows, but if you'd rather—"

"I like sleeping with the windows open," she assured him as she edged toward the door. Then, eyeing him thoughtfully, she paused and asked, "But won't that cause a problem with your security system?"

"I've got it rigged so the windows can be opened up to six inches without tripping the alarm," he replied with a slight smile.

"Oh." She lowered her gaze and shrugged with seeming indifference. "I was just curious."

"Don't worry," he said. "The bogeyman won't get you while you're here."

"As far as I'm concerned, he's already got me."

"Hey, I haven't treated you that badly, have I?"

"Not today," she said as she stepped into the house and pulled the door closed.

Not today, he thought, but six years ago...

Her simple statement a subtle reminder of what he'd done to her once, Alex tilted his head back, stared at the stars sparkling in the night sky and cursed himself for being such a fool.

Chapter 6

Gradually becoming aware of the birds twittering in the trees just outside the windows, Kari opened her eyes. From the pale sunlight playing across the bedroom floor, she surmised, with surprise, that it must be just past dawn. A glance at the clock on the nightstand confirmed her suspicion. Six-fifteen. The time she normally awoke.

Despite all her tossing and turning after she'd crawled under the covers and switched off the light last night, she was back on schedule. And, miracle of miracles, she actually felt rested, even though she had still been awake around midnight.

She hadn't really expected to sleep at all. Not after the lazy way she'd spent the day. And especially not after that last little exchange she'd had with Alex.

She'd started out asking about his plans for the future, not only to make conversation but to satisfy her curiosity. Then, all of a sudden, she'd found herself baiting him purposely.

She had wanted him to admit she still meant something to him. She had given in to a contrariness she couldn't seem to control, tossing off that comment about riding like a wild woman—something she had done years ago when she had thought she was invincible.

But Alex hadn't reacted as she'd hoped he would. He'd been more angry than anything. And, her own temper flaring, she had almost gotten caught in her own trap.

She had come close, much too close, to revealing just how devastated she'd been eighteen months ago when Devlin told her Alex might die. She'd managed to stop herself just in time. But she had a feeling Alex had gotten her drift anyway.

Not that he had seemed to care. He'd been more than willing to let the subject drop, easily allowing her to use her weariness as an excuse to put some distance between them.

Actually, more than anything she'd been suffering from a sense of defeat, and taking refuge in the back bedroom had seemed the wisest thing she could do.

Trying to lure Alex into admitting he cared for her had been an exercise in futility. And now, more than ever, Kari knew that the time had come for her to accept that fact and move on emotionally.

Were she also able to move on *physically,* she'd have an easier time of it. Up until the past few days, she'd actually been able to go an entire day, sometimes two, without thinking about him . . . much. But that wasn't possible now. And wouldn't be until they'd dealt with Brandon Selby.

She could only hope Alex would have some idea how to stop him quickly and efficiently. Then she would be free of both of them. After last night, that was all she really wanted.

Wishing she could think of something—anything—else, Kari threw back the light cotton blanket and sat up. Unlike yesterday, she wasn't woozy at all. She was wide-awake and raring to go. Had she been at home, she would have thrown on shorts and a T-shirt and gone for a run. Come to think of it, she might just do that anyway, she thought, as she stood and stretched.

Though she had closed the bedroom door last night, she noted it was now half-open. Alex, of course. He'd probably come in to check on her during the night. Come and gone again, evidently not the least bit tempted to—

"Stop it," she muttered, taking a T-shirt and her running shoes from the closet, then moving to the dresser for a pair of shorts, underwear and socks.

In the bathroom she dressed quickly, washed her face, brushed her teeth and ran a comb through her hair, her determination to get some exercise building steadily.

If Alex could run with Devlin, he could just as well run with her, or trust her to return to the house after running on her own. She'd lazed around for the past four days, which probably had a lot to do with the maudlin turn her thoughts kept taking.

She'd definitely had way too much time on her hands lately. More than she was used to having, anyway. And she was beginning to feel it in her bones, she thought, acknowledging again the restlessness that had been stirring in her since she'd first awakened.

Pounding cross-country at a good clip ought to use up some of her excess energy and help clear her head. Telling Alex the truth about Brandon would be easier if she felt a little more in control. As with riding, running always gave her a sense of freedom as well as a sense of power over herself and her destiny. And now, more than ever, she needed that.

Breathing in the aroma of freshly brewed coffee wafting down the hallway, Kari glanced into the other rooms on her way to the kitchen. Alex's office and the spare bedroom were both neat and tidy—the desk in one cleared of papers, the twin beds in the other made up just as they had been yesterday.

What had Alex done last night after she'd left him standing on the deck? Come to her room sometime after she'd fallen asleep. She knew that. But had he slept in the chair by her bed again or alone in the spare bedroom?

Since he would have spent the night in her room only to keep tabs on her, she tried to tell herself it made no difference. Yet a part of her wished she knew for sure. The part of her that couldn't quite let go of her youthful dreams no matter what he said or did to dispel them.

She expected to find him in the kitchen, but he wasn't there. Moving to the window over the sink, she glanced outside and saw him sitting at the table, his back partially turned to her, his bare feet propped up on the railing.

She wondered how long he'd been out there. Most of the night? Knowing how little and how lightly he slept, she wouldn't have been surprised.

He'd changed clothes, though. He now wore gray knit shorts and a white T-shirt. And he seemed relaxed. As she watched from her place by the window, he lifted his face to the morning sun and smiled slightly as the breeze ruffled his hair.

For a moment, he looked so boyish, so carefree, that her heart ached with longing all over again. She remembered seeing him like that years ago when he'd come to visit with her brother. Not at first. But after a while, when he'd finally begun to feel comfortable enough to set aside his natural reserve.

She also remembered believing she had somehow had a hand in his transformation, not only as Devlin's often capricious little sister, but in her own right, as well. Especially as she'd grown into a young woman.

But if that had been the case, then why had he walked out on her? What man in his right mind would intentionally avoid a woman who brought him happiness?

Looking back, she could only assume she'd given herself more credit than she deserved. Perhaps she had wanted to be the light of his life so much that she'd found ways to convince herself she was.

But not anymore. As she'd reminded herself more than once already, she was older and wiser now. And by no stretch of the imagination could she think that Alex's current contentment had anything to do with her. He was simply enjoying the early morning alone, as he obviously believed himself to be, while she spied on him shamelessly.

Forcing herself to turn away from the window, Kari bypassed the coffeepot, deciding to wait till after her run to indulge, and headed for the kitchen door. As she stepped onto the deck, Alex glanced over his shoulder, his expression guarded. Then, moving his feet from the railing, he straightened in his chair.

"Don't let me disturb you," she said, halting a few feet from the table as he stood and faced her.

"You're up early." He continued to eye her warily, as if expecting her to bolt.

"Not really. I'm usually getting ready to start work by now."

"There's fresh coffee in the pot on the counter."

"I saw it." She hesitated uncertainly. Then, determined not to let him intimidate her, she added, "I thought I'd go for a run first."

To let him know she was serious, she crossed to the railing and began her warm-up routine of bends and stretches.

"Sounds like a good idea to me. I've been kind of a slug the past few days. Give me a couple of minutes to put on my shoes and I'll go with you."

"Sure," she agreed, as if she really had a choice.

Granted, he had offered to accompany her. However, she knew better than to think he'd allow her to go off on her own. But then, she didn't mind having him along. Not at all.

Ten minutes later, they moved down the drive, side by side, at a moderate pace.

"How far do you usually run?" Alex asked.

"About five miles."

"Every day?"

"Usually only three or four times a week," she replied, smiling slightly at the hint of awe she'd heard in his voice. "When I'm scheduled to ride most of the day, I shorten my run or skip it altogether."

"From the way Devlin talked, you've been winning a lot lately for your owners."

"Yeah, I've had some good days," she admitted, her smile widening. "And I still enjoy riding in competition. But what I really love is working with the kids who come to us for lessons. Watching them gain poise and confidence in the saddle is such a pleasure. And when they start winning at shows it's a real thrill. Some of them have so much potential—more than I ever did."

"What about Selby? Does he give lessons, too?"

Despite the direction their conversation had been taking, Kari was momentarily taken aback by Alex's question. She wasn't quite ready to talk about Brandon yet. But obviously Alex was.

"Hardly at all anymore," she answered at last. "And it's just as well. He's not what you'd call patient or understanding. After he drove off three of our most promising students, I finally convinced him to let me do most of the teaching. Now he only works with a couple of boys in their late teens. Ones he considers to have the potential to become Olympic contenders. He's also taken over most of the training of our various owners' younger horses."

"How many other people does he having working for him?"

"Half a dozen stable hands on average. They come and go. Mostly go, considering his penchant for temper tantrums. And about the same number of college students who help out with riding classes or stable work on a part-time basis in exchange for boarding their horses. He's been talking about hiring another trainer and expanding, but as far as I know, he hasn't interviewed anyone for the job yet."

"Shouldn't you have a say in that? Since you're going to be partners and all?" Alex asked, reminding her, with seeming innocence, of what she'd told him yesterday.

Refusing to look at him, Kari ran on in silence for several seconds. At his instruction, they turned back toward the house. Still she didn't speak, though she knew the time had come to tell him the truth. And neither did he, evidently willing to wait as long as necessary for her to respond.

Admit that you lied to him, she told herself. *Admit it and get it over with.*

"Brandon and I aren't going to be partners."

"But I thought you said—"

"I lied," she cut in before she lost her nerve. Then, with a surge of speed she hadn't known she could muster, she sprinted ahead of him, her gaze locked on the house.

She had no choice now but to tell Alex what she suspected Brandon was up to. And in all honestly, the prospect of finally coming clean with him left her feeling more relieved than anything.

Lying, even out of a false sense of self-preservation, had never sat well with her. She'd always tried to be honest in her dealings with other people, whether they were friends or foes. And from now on, she intended to be honest with Alex, as well. About everything. Even her feelings for him . . . if the occasion warranted.

Whether by design or due to the damage that had been done to his leg, Alex allowed her to go on ahead of him. He didn't bother to catch up with her when she slowed to a walk so she could cool down, and he was still several hundred yards away as she climbed the steps to the deck.

Pausing, she glanced back at him. He met her gaze, his expression unreadable as he continued toward her, limping slightly. She eyed him uncertainly, trying to decide whether to stay outside or go into the house.

"Why don't you shower and change clothes," he suggested. "Then I think we'd better talk."

She nodded, then headed for the door, grateful for the momentary reprieve he'd offered her. Thinking about telling him the truth was a lot easier than actually doing so was going to be. Not because she had any qualms about sharing her suspicions with Alex. But because she had a feeling Alex was going to want to know why she'd lied in the first place. And answering him truthfully, as she intended to do, could prove to be distressing. For her, and perhaps for him, too.

Twenty minutes later, dressed in fresh shorts and the last of her clean T-shirts, Kari returned to the kitchen to find Alex at the counter, sliding a huge brownie onto a plate.

"Ah . . . amaretto-laced chocolate decadence," she said as she filled a mug with coffee. "The breakfast of champions."

Looking not the least bit abashed, Alex glanced at her. "Want one?" he asked. Then he gestured toward a box of muesli Kari knew for a fact was actually quite tasty as he added, "Or would you rather indulge in a bowl of that nuts-and-twigs stuff?"

"I should eat the cereal, but..." Kari shrugged and smiled. "If you're going to throw caution to the wind and start the day on a sugar high, I might as well, too."

"I had a feeling you would." He sliced an equally large brownie for her and put it on a plate, then nodded toward the door. "Why don't we go back outside while it's still cool enough to be comfortable?"

Kari followed him out to the deck and took the same chair she'd sat in the night before. Suffering only a moment or two of regret for her intemperance, she dug into her "breakfast" with undisguised relish. She could easily afford to gain a few pounds, though doing so by eating sensibly would be wiser. However, considering all the explaining she had ahead of her, having a little treat first didn't seem like that bad an idea.

To Alex's credit, he let her eat in peace. But when he took their empty plates inside and returned with the coffeepot, Kari knew her grace period was about to end. As Alex refilled her mug, he verified her suspicions.

"So, you and Selby aren't making wedding plans, after all," he said.

"No, we're not." She turned toward him and saw that he was watching her intently.

"Want to tell me what's really going on between the two of you, then?"

"Nothing personal," she replied. "He did ask me to marry him before I left for Virginia, and I told him I'd think about it. But I never had any intention of accepting his proposal."

"Why not?" Alex prodded.

"Because I'm not in love with him." Her face warming, she lowered her gaze.

"From the way Devlin talked, you really admired the guy when you first went to work for him. And the two of you do have a lot in common."

"You know that old saying about familiarity breeding contempt? Well, it took me a while, but eventually I realized Brandon Selby was a real bastard."

"How so?"

"One minute he can be intentionally cruel without the slightest provocation, and the next minute he can be so...solicitous you're tempted to believe you only imagined having a strip torn off you for some minor failing. And, of course, any abuse he metes out is always for your own good. Or so he always insists. After a while—a longer while than I like to admit—I began to see a pattern to his behavior. A pattern designed to undermine my confidence while keeping me in a continual state of uncertainty."

"Has he ever hurt you physically?" Alex asked, his voice low, yet so cold, so hard, that Kari regarded him with sudden consternation.

"Oh, no." She shook her head vehemently. "He's much too good at verbal chastisement to have to lay a hand on anyone. Even now, knowing how he operates, I still end up in tears whenever he's displeased with me."

"Yet you still continue to work for him." As if needing to put some distance between them, Alex stood and moved to the railing, then turned to face her. "With your background and reputation, surely you could find a job at another stable. So why stay with Selby?"

"Because I'm fairly sure he's been getting away with murder, and I intend to find a way to stop him," she stated simply.

Alex met her gaze, seemingly unfazed by what she'd revealed, though his eyes narrowed almost imperceptibly. Kari wasn't sure how she'd expected him to react. But his lack of surprise disconcerted her. Until it dawned on her that he might already know what was going on at Selby Stables.

She knew how clever Devlin was at tracking down bits of information, then piecing them together. And Alex was her brother's protégé. Which would make him equally adept at ferreting out—

"That's what I suspected," he said, as if reading her mind.

"Well, if you already knew, then why give me the third degree?" she demanded, her voice rising angrily. She really, truly, hated being manipulated.

"I don't *know* much," he replied, his tone placating. He sat back against the railing and crossed his arms over his chest. "I went hunting on the computer yesterday and came up with some interesting bits of information about your boss and his business dealings over the past five years or so."

"Ever since I went to work for him."

"Yes, ever since you went to work for him," Alex acknowledged. "And from what I discovered, I've come to the conclusion that Brandon Selby has profited from the death of other people's horses on at least two occasions, and more recently, from the death of one of his own animals. There's also a fourth instance I'm not sure about." He paused, eyeing her thoughtfully. When she could do nothing but stare at him in astonishment, he added, "Am I on target, or what?"

"Oh, yes. You're right on target." She shook her head, still somewhat bewildered. "You put all that together after working on the computer one afternoon?"

"I got enough information from newspaper and magazine articles, insurance-company records, financial transactions and bank statements to put two and two together and come up with a plausible four. I assumed he was up to no good, and that whatever he was doing had to be benefiting him monetarily."

"And there I was, right in the middle of it, yet totally oblivious until a couple of months ago," Kari muttered disgustedly. "I can't believe I was so blind. So blind and so stupid."

"What happened to raise your suspicions?" Alex asked.

"A young gelding Brandon had pinned high hopes on wasn't coming along nearly as fast as he'd anticipated. He'd paid top dollar for the horse about two years ago and had been working with him personally, bragging to everyone on the grand prix circuit that Moonwalker was going to win big.

"But Moonwalker just wouldn't perform for him, at least not the way Brandon had led people to believe he would. After the horse placed low in several shows during the fall and winter, Brandon was beginning to worry about his reputation. He decided to put Moonwalker up for sale, but a rumor had started that Brandon had ruined him. As a result, nobody was willing to pay anywhere near Brandon's asking price."

"Was there any truth to the rumor?"

"No truth at all. Moonwalker had a lot of potential, but not as much as Brandon insisted he did. As a result, all his bragging backfired on him."

"So he got rid of the horse the only way he could without losing most of what he'd invested," Alex said.

"Yes," Kari agreed. "I believe that's exactly what he did."

"How?"

"He arranged for Moonwalker to have an accident. Or at least that's what I think he did. No matter how hard I've tried, I can't think of any way Moonwalker could have gotten out of the barn the night he broke his leg and had to be put down, unless someone unlatched his stall door intentionally.

"We had a bad storm brewing all evening and the horses were nervous. Just to be on the safe side, I checked on them myself one last time before turning in for the night. All the stall doors were secured just the way they should have been. Yet sometime after midnight when the storm finally broke, Brandon claims he came upon Moonwalker sliding around out on the paved driveway, crazed with fear, his left foreleg shattered, supposedly from a fall."

"Did Selby have any idea how the horse got out?"

"He claimed Moonwalker must have kicked open his improperly latched stall door, and the insurance company accepted his story. The horse *was* extremely high-strung, he *did* have an aversion to lightning and thunder and he *had* kicked his stall door open in the past when it *was* unlatched. But I'd been out there myself less than two hours earlier, and I'd checked—"

Angrily, Kari got up and paced to the railing much as Alex had done a few minutes earlier. Standing beside him, she recalled all that had occurred that awful night and shuddered inwardly. Poor Moonwalker hadn't deserved to die that way.

"Did you confront Selby about the discrepancies in his story?" Alex asked.

"I tried, but he put me off. Said I'd probably been in such a hurry that I hadn't really noticed. And when I started to argue with him, he was furious. He asked me if I was calling him a liar, then hinted that perhaps I ought to be more grateful he was willing to cover up *my* carelessness by blaming the open stall door on the stable hand who'd been on duty that night.

"Until then, I didn't really suspect Brandon. I thought maybe someone else had sabotaged the stable. Vandals or a disenchanted former employee. But he was so determined to pin the blame on Marco while at the same time insisting I'd be wise to leave well enough alone or risk being blamed myself. That's when I began to realize that Brandon must have something to hide.''

"What about the stable hand? Surely he must have had something to say in his defense."

"He didn't have a chance. Brandon fired him early the next morning. I've tried to find him in the hope that he could corroborate my story, but so far, I haven't been able to track him down. He's not working for any of the larger stables in Texas or Louisiana."

"So it's your word against Selby's."

"Yes."

"What about the other horses you've lost over the past few years?"

"After Moonwalker, I began to wonder about them, too. But again, I have no real proof of any wrongdoing on Brandon's part. All three horses were causing problems for either the owners or for Brandon. But all three died of colic. That's not unusual, although three horses in the same stable dying of colic within a three-year period is somewhat out of the ordinary.

"However, when I thought back, I realized that shortly after two of the horses died, Brandon suddenly seemed to have a lot of money to spend. He bought an expensive foreign car, ordered improvements done on the house and barn and started work on a new riding arena. I didn't think much of it at the time. Business had been good and our horses had been winning regularly. But now..." Kari shrugged and shook her head despondently as she gazed into the distance.

"What about the third horse?" Alex prodded.

"I thought maybe losing Wylde One was just a fluke. But though I don't think money was involved, her death worked in Brandon's favor, as well. Like Moonwalker, the mare wasn't doing as well as expected, and the owner had begun hinting about trying another trainer. After she died, Mr. Chambers bought another mare and Brandon talked him into letting him work with her. Within months, she was placing in the money, making Brandon look good again."

"According to the records I checked, Selby deposited large sums of money into his account in October 1992, and again in June 1994. Do those dates coincide with the deaths of two of the horses?"

"Yes." She glanced at Alex hopefully. "Is that proof of any kind?"

"No," he admitted. "He included the sums in his tax returns as income. That means he probably issued invoices for services of some sort as backup."

"Probably." Kari slumped against the railing, turning her back on the lovely view. "Damn it, he's going to get away with what he's done, isn't he? Unless I can find some concrete proof or catch him in the act."

"That's why you haven't left, isn't it?"

Kari nodded.

"Do you think he's realized you're onto him?"

"I'm not sure."

"Why do you think he asked you to marry him?" Changing tack without warning, Alex caught her by surprise.

Highly miffed, Kari straightened her shoulders as she turned to face him. "What? You don't think he's madly, passionately, in love with me?"

She *knew* Brandon wasn't in love with her, but she was offended that Alex obviously hadn't considered it a possibility. Just because *he* didn't care about her was no reason to assume another man wouldn't.

"I didn't say that," Alex replied, his tone conciliatory. "I was just wondering if you thought he had some ulterior motive..." His voice trailing off, he winced, as if realizing he was only making bad matters worse. "I'm sorry. I didn't mean to imply—"

"That I'm not a desirable woman in my own right?"

Pleased to see him so discomfited, she eyed him with a slight smile.

He met her gaze steadily, an odd light in his bright-blue eyes. "You're the most desirable woman I've ever known," he stated simply.

Her smile fading, Kari looked away, her thoughts confused. How could he feel that way, yet abandon her?

Aware that now was not the time to travel down that particular road, she chose, instead, to answer his original question.

"I think Brandon asked me to marry him because he figured a proposal would throw me off, at least temporarily. I made no secret of how infatuated I was with him when I first went to work for him. But he never showed any romantic interest in me. Not until after I questioned him about Moonwalker.

"First he made those veiled threats about my being to blame for the horse getting loose. Then a few days later he came on to me as if he'd suddenly realized I was the love of his life. He started talking about marriage and a partnership in the stable as though it were almost a done deal."

Staring out across the lawn, she recalled, with utter distaste, the way he'd backed her into an empty stall and kissed her and fondled her. She'd wanted to fight him off, but she'd been too afraid. And there had been no one around to help her.

Luckily, he hadn't expected anything more of her or the jig would have been up. No matter how much she wanted to bring him to justice, she wasn't about to have sex with him. And he'd seemed willing to comply with her wishes on that score.

Or lack of score, she thought, barely suppressing a wholly inappropriate giggle.

"What's so funny about that?" Alex demanded.

Understandably, he failed to see the humor in the situation she'd described.

"Nothing," she assured him soberly. "Nothing at all."

"I take it you've been stringing him along since then."

"To a certain extent, yes," she admitted. "But only to give me time to gather some evidence against him."

"By granting sexual favors?" he asked, his voice cold, his words clipped.

"Not that it's any of your business, but no, I haven't granted him any sexual *favor*." Angry all over again, she returned to her chair and sat down, refusing to look at him. "I told him I needed a few weeks to consider his proposal and he agreed. But he's not going to wait much longer for my answer. That means I don't have much time left to find a way to stop him. Which is why I decided to accept your offer of help."

"I was wondering what changed your mind."

"Sheer desperation," she muttered. "I honestly don't know what to do next. And the longer I'm away, the more likely it is that he's going to get suspicious. So, Alex, got any ideas?"

"Yeah, I think you'd be wise to give Selby as wide a berth as possible," he snapped, his expression grim.

"I wish I could. But until he's been stopped, that's not an option. As far as I know, I'm the only one who's aware of what he's doing. Except for the owners who appear to have been in league with him. And I doubt they'll rat on him when they're just as culpable.''

"Maybe you're not the only one whose suspicions have been aroused."

"I'd like to believe that, but I've been right in the middle of it for almost five years and I began to catch on only a couple of months ago. I may not be the brightest person alive, but I'm no dummy, either."

"No one has so much as hinted to you he might have some qualms about Selby losing four horses in just over three years?"

"No one at all."

"What about you? Have you said anything to anybody about what you suspect?"

"Only to you," she replied. "My suppositions wouldn't carry the same weight as proof. And who would take the word of a disgruntled employee—as I'm sure I'd be portrayed—over that of someone of Brandon's stature?"

"So there's a good chance no one else is aware of what's going on."

"I'd say that."

"Before we go any further, I'd like to find out for sure."

"But how?"

"I'm going to contact a few friends of mine. Friends who would know if Selby is being investigated. There's a chance one or another of the insurance companies involved may have become suspicious and gone to the authorities without your knowledge."

"Then what?" she asked.

"Then we'll see," he answered cryptically.

"How long do you think it'll take you to get in touch with your friends?"

"Not long." He checked his watch, then added, "I should have some idea who knows what by late this afternoon."

"I guess that means I won't be able to go back there today."

"If I have anything to do about it, you're never going back there," Alex growled.

"But how else will I be able to prove—"

"I'll think of something." He moved away from the railing, picking up his empty mug and the coffeepot. "But first, I have some calls to make. Are you coming in?"

"Yes." Reaching for her empty mug, Kari stood and followed him into the house. "If I'm going to be here a while longer, I'll have to do some laundry."

After that, she'd have to find something else to occupy her time. Maybe bake bread. She hadn't done that in ages. And kneading dough would be as good a way as any to work out some of her frustration.

"The washer and dryer are in here." He opened a set of louvered doors just inside the kitchen entryway to reveal a cubbyhole where the machines sat side by side.

"Do you want me to toss in any of your things?"

"No, thanks."

"I thought I might bake some bread, too."

Halfway across the kitchen, Alex paused and shot her a quizzical look.

"Unless you'd rather I didn't," she amended hastily.

"Oh, no. Be my guest." He gestured toward one of the upper cabinets. "Estella, my caretaker's wife, keeps several cookbooks in there." He opened the pantry door and glanced inside. "And it looks like she's stocked everything you'll need in here, including yeast."

"Well, then, as long as you're sure you don't mind..."

"I'd have to be nuts," he said, offering her a wide smile. "The bread you used to bake was the best I've ever tasted, and your cinnamon rolls weren't bad, either."

Inordinately pleased, Kari smiled, too.

"If you want cinnamon rolls, as well, I'd better get to work."

He could irritate the hell out of her, yet all he had to do was flash that boyish grin her way and she was putty in his hands.

"Let me know if you need anything else," he advised.

Having decided to start the bread dough before loading the washer, Kari stayed in the kitchen as Alex headed toward the hallway.

"I will," she murmured, watching him go, remembering a time when he wouldn't have left her without a hug and a kiss first.

But those days were gone for good. And that *need* was one she could never again ask him to meet.

Chapter 7

Under almost any other circumstances, the enticing aroma of homemade bread and cinnamon rolls drifting into his office would have filled Alex with a sense of contentment. Especially since Kari was the one busily doing the baking in his kitchen. But as he cradled the telephone receiver and sat back in his desk chair, he was feeling far from gratified.

Given a choice, he would have preferred she was anywhere but there. Well, almost anywhere. He wouldn't have wanted her back at Selby Stables. He wanted her somewhere safe. Unfortunately, after his conversation with FBI agent Kevin Wyatt, Alex was afraid such a place no longer existed.

Unwittingly, in his attempt to find out who suspected what about Brandon Selby, Alex had come upon Wyatt, and inadvertently, he'd handed the agent the potential ally he needed inside Selby's operation. Alex had wanted only to protect Kari. Instead he was about to deliver her into the hands of a man determined to bring Selby down. Not only

for the killing of show horses for a cut of the insurance
money, but for the suspected murder of a former assistant
who, much like Kari, had apparently stumbled onto the
trainer's little sideline.

Alex wasn't sure why he hadn't considered that Selby's
nefarious scheming had begun long before Kari went to
work for him. But now, thanks to Kevin Wyatt, he knew the
trainer had been connected to the deaths of at least two or
three horses prior to Kari's employment. And shortly before Kari had been hired, her predecessor, a young woman
by the name of Amanda Holcomb, had died unexpectedly
of a drug overdose. Though it had been ruled a suicide, due
in part to Selby's insistence that she'd been unstable, the
woman's family had believed that she'd been murdered, and
that Selby had had something to do with it.

Agent Wyatt had agreed, having traced Selby's financial
gains to the deaths of an unusually large number of horses
housed in his stable. But he'd had no proof, nor any way of
obtaining it. Until now.

Alex had to admire Wyatt. The man had led him along
expertly, asking all the right questions in such a nonthreat-
ening way that he'd answered readily, sure he was getting as
much information as he was giving. Only too late did he realize he'd put Kari in a dangerous position.

Wyatt needed someone to help him catch Selby in the act,
and he had every intention of using Kari as that someone.
And there wasn't much Alex could do about it. Not without obstructing justice, and thus possibly endangering Kari
even more.

Of course, she would be given a choice whether or not to
come to Wyatt's assistance. But were she to refuse, she could
be charged with complicity. Or so Wyatt had made a point
of informing Alex.

Not that Alex thought for a moment she would refuse. Knowing Kari, he doubted she'd need any coaxing at all. She was out to get Selby herself. And more than likely, brave little fool that she was, she'd be eager to help Wyatt any way she could.

God help him, Devlin was going to nail his hide to the wall. He was supposed to be keeping her out of trouble, not delivering her into the hands of a ruthless FBI agent out for blood.

For one long moment, Alex considered contacting his friend in the hope that *he* could call off Wyatt. But Devlin had no more authority over an FBI agent than Alex himself did. And Wyatt had given every indication that he wasn't going to back off for any reason where Selby was concerned.

Alex also thought about hustling Kari out to the car and heading for the Mexican border. With the kind of training he'd had, he could make sure they stayed lost for years if necessary. But she would never cooperate. And he certainly couldn't keep her bound and gagged indefinitely.

A glance at the clock on his desk warned he had just over an hour until Wyatt was due to arrive from San Antonio. Before then, he had to talk to Kari and prepare her for what the agent was going to ask of her. He was also going to have to think of a way to stay close to her without arousing Selby's suspicions when she went back to the stable. Because she wasn't returning alone. No matter what Wyatt had in mind. That much Alex could guarantee.

He found her in the kitchen as he'd expected. She was sitting at the table, spreading creamy vanilla icing over a plateful of cinnamon rolls as the dryer hummed busily in the background.

He halted in the doorway, eyeing her with a hunger that only seemed to intensify with the passage of time. He'd never gotten her out of his system, and he probably never would. The mere sight of her made him ache with desire. A desire he was having more and more trouble keeping under control.

Even now, he ought to be considering how best to tell her about Kevin Wyatt. Yet all he could think about was how much he'd like to come up behind her, cup her breasts in his hands and press his mouth against the back of her neck.

Banishing his lascivious thoughts with a muttered curse, he headed toward her.

From her place at the table, Kari turned to greet him. Her smile faded as she met his gaze.

"Someone knew something," she said as he took a seat across from her, just out of touching distance. When he didn't answer immediately, she added, "Something disturbing."

"Yeah, you're right. Something damned disturbing," he acknowledged.

"What?" she asked, setting aside the bowl and spatula, then folding her hands on the table.

Though her voice was steady and she regarded him in a calm manner, Alex couldn't help but see the glimmer of fear in her pale-gray eyes. Chastising himself yet again for putting her in such an untenable position, he locked his hands together on the table, too. Then, matter-of-factly, he told her about his little talk with FBI agent Kevin Wyatt.

To her credit, she listened quietly, betraying little of the turmoil she had to be experiencing. Only the whitening of her knuckles as she clenched her hands tighter, then tighter still, gave her away.

"So, Brandon has been carrying on his sideline much longer than I thought," she said when he'd finished relating the information Wyatt had given him.

"There's also a good chance his last assistant began to suspect him just as you have. Only she ended up dead before she could do anything about it."

"But from what I recall, Amanda Holcomb committed suicide. She had taken a bad fall and was having trouble getting her nerve back. Rumor had it she was severely depressed . . ." Her words trailing away, Kari hesitated.

She didn't seem to want to believe Selby was capable of murdering a young woman. But from the look on her face, she'd already begun to accept the possibility that he had.

"She took the fall at the stable, didn't she?'

"Yes," Kari replied. "And now that I think about it, I remember overhearing Brandon telling another trainer he had to let her go because she couldn't cut it anymore. There was also talk about her using both tranquilizers and painkillers. Then her parents found her dead of a drug overdose."

"Wyatt told me they never believed she killed herself. But they had no proof to the contrary. All they knew for sure was that she both feared and hated Brandon Selby in the weeks after she was injured."

"How did Kevin Wyatt get involved?"

"I gather he's a friend of the family. Up until recently, he'd been investigating on his own. Then about six months ago he was contacted by one of the insurance companies. An adjuster had become suspicious after paying yet another claim made by an owner whose horse had died while at Selby Stables."

"And he's coming here to talk to me." Kari frowned as she stared at her hands, now twisted together in her lap. "Does he think I'm involved?"

"No, he doesn't," Alex assured her.

"Then what could he possibly want?"

"He didn't elaborate over the telephone, but I suspect he's going to ask you to help him catch Selby in the act."

To Alex's dismay, Kari eyed him eagerly, as if she were actually pleased by the prospect.

"Do you think he has some sort of plan?"

"Oh, I'm sure he does. But there's a good chance you're not going to like it," Alex replied, hoping to nip her enthusiasm in the bud.

"Well, we'll find out soon enough, won't we?" Pushing her chair back, she stood and picked up the empty bowl and the spatula she'd used to frost the cinnamon rolls. "What time did you say he'd be here?"

As she started past him on her way to the sink, Alex reached out and caught her by the arm. She seemed to have no idea what she could be getting herself into. Or maybe she was simply choosing to ignore the risks involved.

"You don't have to go along with Wyatt, you know. He can't force you to put yourself in a potentially dangerous situation. And any plan that involves your going back to Selby Stables will be just that. If Selby did kill Amanda Holcomb, he's not going to think twice about getting rid of you, too. Not if he considers you a threat."

"I realize that," she replied, her voice low. "But I also know I wouldn't be able to live with myself if I didn't do everything I could to put him behind bars."

Alex wanted to argue with her, but he understood all too well where she was coming from. Walking away while she still had the chance was something she simply would not consider doing. That she would equate with cowardice. And Alex knew for a fact that she didn't have a craven bone in her beautiful body.

"Well, if Wyatt wants you to go back there, don't think I'm letting you go alone," he muttered, releasing her.

"I don't see how you could do otherwise," she retorted as she stepped away from him.

"Oh, really?"

"The man asked me to marry him a couple of weeks ago."

"So?"

"So..." She gazed at him as if he were dumber than a doornail. "How long do you think he'd keep me around if I came back with a strange man in tow?"

"I hadn't planned to be that obvious," he replied, smiling slightly as he thought of the wig, the beard and the glasses.

He'd have to stain his skin a darker shade of tan, use the tinted contact lenses that turned his blue eyes brown and remember to speak mostly Spanish. But he shouldn't have any trouble at all posing as a stable hand of Hispanic descent.

"What did you have in mind instead?" she prodded.

"Something guaranteed to get me in the door. At least the stable door," he answered enigmatically.

She glared at him a moment longer. Then, knowing when to quit, she turned back to the sink and changed the subject.

"I found a chicken casserole in the freezer. I thought we could have it for dinner along with a salad. There should be enough for Mr. Wyatt, too."

"Wyatt won't be staying for dinner," Alex stated as the sound of a car coming up the driveway reached his ears.

"But surely the polite thing to do—"

"Right now, I'm not feeling particularly polite," he shot back. He stood and headed toward the kitchen door. "He can say his piece and go back to San Antonio."

He couldn't keep Wyatt away from Kari. But nowhere was it written that he had to make the agent's job easy. Not when the man was more than likely going to ask Kari to put her life on the line to catch a dirtbag like Selby.

"Well, it's your house." Her disapproval evident, she slid the casserole in the oven, then set about washing the pans she'd used to bake the bread and rolls.

Having nothing to say to that, Alex walked out to the deck and waited there as a dark-blue sedan rolled to a stop alongside Kari's car. A tall, trim man emerged, dressed in a gray suit, white shirt and paisley tie, his dark hair stylishly cut. He strode purposefully toward the house, his attitude all business.

"Mr. Payton?" the man inquired as he started up the steps.

"Alex," he replied, grudgingly extending his hand in greeting as he moved to meet the agent.

"Kevin Wyatt." His handshake firm, he assessed Alex with the same undisguised interest Alex directed toward him. "Thanks for agreeing to let me talk to Ms. Gray."

"I wasn't aware I had a choice," Alex drawled, turning back to the house.

"Look, Payton, I don't want to see her come to any harm, either," Wyatt advised.

"But if you think she can help you put Selby out of commission, you'll use her any way she'll let you." He paused and glanced at the other man, making no effort to hide his animosity. Then, in a deceptively mild tone, he added, "Just remember that if anything happens to her, anything at all, I guarantee your life won't be worth living anymore."

"Are you threatening me?"

"No, Wyatt, I'm making you a promise—government agent to government agent."

His point made in a way that left the other man no room for doubt, Alex led him into the kitchen, where Kari stood by the counter, drying her hands on a towel. As he did the introductions, she offered Wyatt a gracious smile and extended her hand.

That she seemed glad to see the FBI agent only intensified Alex's concern for her. She'd made it clear she was fully prepared to cooperate with Wyatt, and meeting the man in person hadn't put her off in the least. Of course, Wyatt was doing his damnedest to be personable, returning her smile in a way designed to hide the fact that he was actually appraising her with well-trained eyes.

"We can sit at the table while we talk," Alex directed.

"Yes, please have a seat," Kari said, frowning at Alex's lack of cordiality. "Can I offer you something to drink? Coffee, iced tea or a soft drink?"

"I'd love a cup of coffee," Wyatt replied, gazing at her with appreciation.

"I'll get it," Alex growled, refusing to let her wait on the man. "You sit down and listen to what he has to say."

"Alex," she said, bristling, her voice low. Then, a little louder, she added, "I'll have coffee, too. And bring some plates and forks so we can sample my cinnamon rolls."

Why she was so determined to turn what was damned serious business into a social occasion, Alex didn't know. Until she looked up at him pleadingly. Then he realized she wasn't finding it easy to be as brave as she thought she should be.

Mentally cursing himself, he reached out and gave her shoulder a reassuring squeeze.

"Sounds like a good idea to me. Now, go and sit down."

Her gratitude almost palpable, she nodded, then turned back to the table.

Wyatt wasted no time apprising them of the situation. After ascertaining that Alex had already relayed the details of their telephone conversation, and assuring himself that they had no questions concerning the results of his investigation to date, he launched into the plan he'd devised to catch Selby in the act of destroying a horse for the insurance money. A plan that involved Kari, just as Alex had feared.

Simply put, she and Wyatt would approach an owner she believed they could trust. They would explain the situation, then ask the owner to talk to Selby—while wearing a wire—about destroying a horse. Then, with Kari and Wyatt keeping watch on the barn after hours, they'd wait to catch him in the act, and with luck, stop him before the deed was actually done.

Alex had to concede that the plan had some merit. While there would be some risk to the horse, with careful monitoring the animal shouldn't come to any harm. But he had no intention of allowing Wyatt alone to serve as Kari's watchdog. The FBI agent could stake out the barn at night. Alex, on the other hand, planned to be within shouting distance of her twenty-four hours a day until Selby was behind bars.

Having outlined his course of action, Wyatt turned to Kari. "Can you think of anyone trustworthy who would be willing to go along with us on this?"

He'd polished off not one but two cinnamon rolls with apparent relish, and now sat across the table from her, hands wrapped around his coffee mug, looking at her attentively while all but ignoring Alex.

She hesitated for a minute or so, frowning thoughtfully as she toyed with her fork.

"Actually, I can think of three or four current owners who might be willing to help us, but the one I'd trust most completely is Raymond Fairchild. And his horse, or rather his daughter's horse, Dover, has been almost as much of a problem as some of the others Brandon has gotten rid of."

"How is that?" Wyatt asked.

"Mr. Fairchild paid quite a bit for Dover several years ago. His daughter, Melissa, just had to have him, even though he was known to be a difficult mount. She did really well with him, but a couple of years ago she married, then had twins. She's given up riding altogether, and Mr. Fairchild has been trying to sell Dover without much luck. The gelding is too hard to handle for a younger rider and too old and out of shape to interest anyone with more experience. Lately, Mr. Fairchild has been bemoaning the fact that he's stuck with the horse. He's also been griping about the cost of keeping him at the stable."

"So, if he agreed to help Wyatt, Selby wouldn't be suspicious of him?" Alex asked.

"I don't think so. Brandon has always thought of him as a savvy businessman. In fact, now that I think about it, I'm surprised Brandon hasn't approached him with a deal already," Kari admitted.

"For all we know, he might have," Wyatt interjected. "But that could work in our favor. Your Mr. Fairchild could appear to have reconsidered Selby's proposition and changed his mind."

"But wouldn't that start alarm bells ringing in Selby's head?" Alex pressed, his concern for Kari's well-being paramount.

If there was even the slightest chance that being approached by Raymond Fairchild would give Selby pause, then all bets were off.

"Only if Selby made an offer and Fairchild refused him in a way that totally precluded a change of heart. And *that* we'll only be able to determine by talking to him," Wyatt advised.

"He really is our best choice," Kari said, tentatively reaching out and touching Alex's arm. "And if, for some reason, he can't help us, he won't give the game away."

Alex knew she wanted to reassure him, but he still wasn't pleased she was allowing herself to be put in such a dangerous position. Were Selby to get any hint at all that she was setting him up, he'd go after her with a vengeance. And if, by some chance, he managed to catch her alone in some isolated place, there was no telling what the bastard might do to her before Alex could come to her rescue.

But she and Wyatt seemed to have reached a mutual agreement where Raymond Fairchild was concerned, and Alex couldn't think of any reasonable way to dissuade them.

"Then I think the two of us ought to meet with Mr. Fairchild as soon as possible, Kari," Wyatt said, not only confirming Alex's suspicion, but neatly excluding him from the initial foray, as well.

Fine. Let the two of them talk to Fairchild. There was no reason he had to go along on *that* ride.

"And if he agrees?" Alex asked as he stood, crossed to the counter and retrieved the coffeepot.

"Kari returns to Selby Stables and resumes her normal routine. As soon as she's had a chance to scope out the situation and determine that nothing out of the ordinary is going on, I'll have Fairchild approach Selby. Then we watch and wait."

"We *all* watch and wait," Alex amended.

"Now, wait a minute, Payton—" Wyatt began, evidently aware his authority was being challenged.

"No, you wait a minute," Alex cut in, his tone deadly. "You want to spend your nights staking out the barn, be my guest. But I'm going to be there twenty-four hours a day, watching her back. Whether you like it or not."

"I could have you thrown in jail," Wyatt snarled.

"And I'd be out in a couple of hours."

"Not if I—"

"Kevin, please," Kari pleaded.

"I've been waiting years to get my hands on Selby. Now that I'm close, I don't want some *spook* throwing a monkey wrench in the works."

"But *I* want him there," Kari replied, her voice firm. "Otherwise I'm not going back."

Alex stared at her in surprise, as did Kevin Wyatt. He doubted the FBI agent had anticipated such a show of spirit from her. As for himself, Alex couldn't quite believe he'd heard her right. She wanted him with her, and he could think of only one reason why. She trusted him to look out for her. And he would. With every fiber of his being, he vowed, clasping her hand.

Her smile wry, she clung to him as if for dear life.

"All right, then," Wyatt conceded grudgingly. "But how, exactly, do you plan to do that?"

Without ado, Alex relayed his own course of action. Wyatt regarded him with obvious skepticism, but Kari agreed that what he had in mind would work.

"We're always in need of stable hands, and Brandon prefers to hire Hispanics. They're hard workers, usually good with the horses, and if they're also illegal aliens, as many of them tend to be, he can get away with paying them lower-than-average wages."

"Sounds like I ought to alert the INS," Wyatt said.

"I tried that once," Kari admitted. "The Immigration and Naturalization Service responded promptly. They came in, rounded up a few hands and sent them back across the border. Brandon pleaded innocence and paid a small fine. Then, a week or two later, he hired some more."

"You really think he'll buy into your disguise?" Still dubious, Wyatt turned his attention back to Alex.

"Watch and see," he replied enigmatically.

"I've known him for ten years and he scared me spitless at the airport the other day, acting like some kind of weirdo,'' Kari added, obviously attempting to vouch for him.

His curiosity roused, Wyatt studied her, his eyes narrowed thoughtfully.

"Oh, really? Why would he want to do that?"

"So I could kidnap her," Alex answered honestly, smiling to himself as a blush stole across Kari's cheeks.

Looking more disbelieving than ever, Wyatt pushed away from the table and stood.

"Anybody ever tell you you're a real smart ass?"

"A few people, all of whom have lived to regret it," Alex replied, rising, as well.

"Oh, yeah—"

"What time would you like me to be in San Antonio tomorrow, Kevin?" Kari interrupted, again coming between them in her own quiet way.

Aware how badly he was behaving, Alex shoved his hands in the pockets of his shorts and concentrated on keeping his mouth shut.

"Let me contact Raymond Fairchild and make sure tomorrow will be convenient for him. Then I'll call you later tonight and we can work out the details." He favored her with a warm smile that had Alex gritting his teeth, then added offhandedly, "Or, if you'd like, you're more than welcome to ride back to San Antonio with me. I'd be happy to arrange for you to stay at a hotel for as long as necessary, compliments of Uncle Sam."

For several excruciatingly long moments while Kari seemed to consider Wyatt's offer, Alex called upon all the willpower he possessed to keep from throttling the man. He couldn't force Kari to stay with him. Not without making bad matters worse with the FBI agent.

And Kevin Wyatt would look after her. She was not only the key to his catching Selby; she'd attracted his interest, as well. From the information he'd gathered earlier, Alex knew that Wyatt was a decent, trustworthy man. The kind of man she deserved—

"Thanks, but I'd rather stay here," Kari replied, surprising him yet again. She stood and stacked their empty plates and mugs, then glanced at Alex. "Unless you'd prefer not to have to make the drive to San Antonio."

Not only had she made sure he knew that she wanted him with her when she returned to San Antonio; she had also chosen to stay with him tonight. Chosen of her own free will.

"I don't mind at all," he assured her, taking the dishes from her, then carrying them to the sink.

"Well, then, Mr. Wyatt, give me a call tonight and we'll take it from there." With a dismissive air, she led him to the door.

"I'll do that, Ms. Gray," he agreed, sounding slightly mollified.

Hiding a smile, Alex loaded the dishwasher as Kari waved the agent on his way. He had absolutely no right to feel so good. But, by God, he did.

Had he been a true gentleman, he would have insisted she go with Wyatt. After what he'd put her though the past couple of days, she deserved a bit of a respite. Staying here with him against her will hadn't been easy for her. Yet, given the chance to get away, she'd chosen instead to stay, and he had no intention of putting up any argument, even though he probably should.

Having her so close had been wreaking havoc with his self-control. But since she'd been there against her will, keeping his hands off her had been a matter of honor. Now, knowing she *wanted* to be with him, he realized that maintaining the necessary distance between them was going to be much more difficult. All he could do was remind himself over and over that she deserved a better man than him. A man like Kevin Wyatt.

"You don't look very happy," Kari ventured, her voice filled with concern as she joined him at the kitchen counter.

"I'm not," he replied before he could stop himself, his momentary joy fading in the face of reality.

That she wanted to be with him made no more difference now than it ever had. Not in the long run.

"I know you're not all that eager for me to go along with Kevin's plan, but I don't see how I can do otherwise and live with myself." She squared her shoulders and regarded him with grave dignity.

"Yeah, well, I'm the one who has to explain that to your brother," he shot back, knowing he could get away with using his anticipation of Devlin's righteous anger as an understandable excuse for his sour mood, and thus keep the real reason to himself.

"I'll call him and explain the situation myself," she offered, though without much enthusiasm.

She had to know Devlin was going to hit the ceiling. And she hadn't had nearly as much experience as he had calming her brother. More than likely, Devlin would have her in tears, and Alex would still end up bearing the brunt of his friend's ire.

"I'll do it." His tone brooked no argument.

"Fine." Appearing relieved, Kari crossed to the refrigerator. "I'll fix the salad. Then we can eat whenever you're ready." She gestured toward the window above the sink. "Looks like there's a storm brewing, so I guess we'd better eat in here."

Noticing the gray clouds rolling across the sky and the wind whipping up the tree branches, Alex nodded, then headed for the privacy of his office.

He wasn't sure what he might have to say to Devlin, but he was reasonably certain some of it wouldn't be pretty. And he'd just as soon Kari didn't have to hear it.

Devlin reacted to the news of the FBI's involvement much as Alex had expected. He did not want his little sister involved in a sting operation. But just like Alex, he had no idea how to keep her out of it, short of locking her up somewhere. He ranted and raved for almost ten minutes, while Alex glanced through an old newsmagazine. Finally, coming to the conclusion that their hands were tied, Devlin began to wind down.

"You're sure she's not being coerced by that yahoo, Wyatt?" he demanded.

"I'm sure. She wants Selby behind bars and she's willing to do just about anything to help put him there," Alex replied.

"And you're sure you'll be able to protect her once she's back at the stable?"

"I wouldn't let her go back there otherwise. No matter what kind of fit she pitched."

"What about Wyatt? You think he knows what he's doing?"

"Yeah, I think so. He's a straight arrow with an exemplary service record, but he doesn't come across as the type who would sacrifice an innocent woman in the name of duty."

"Been hacking again, huh?"

"Just a little."

"Well, let me know what kind of response Wyatt gets from Fairchild."

"I will."

Back in the kitchen, Alex found Kari setting the table.

"How did it go?" she asked, glancing at him apprehensively.

"He's not exactly thrilled with the situation, but he's going to stay out of the way for the time being. He won't have Wyatt called off unless you want him to."

"I don't," she assured him much too hastily as she positioned knives, forks and spoons around the plates already on the table.

"Then we'll meet with Wyatt again whenever he says."

Though Alex sincerely doubted Kari was anywhere near as enthusiastic about squaring off with Selby as she seemed to want him to believe, he didn't challenge her. She'd only dig in her heels and insist that she was. And she'd be even less apt to let him know if she started to feel she was in over her head. He didn't want pride to stand in the way of her bailing out should push come to shove.

At Kari's direction, he took the spicy chicken-and-tortilla casserole out of the oven and carried it to the table as she stacked slices of her freshly baked bread in a basket. Along with the salad she'd made while he was talking to Devlin, they would make a tasty addition to the meal.

Despite the fact that they'd each indulged in a cinnamon roll less than two hours earlier, they both ate heartily, exchanging only a few comments, and those were limited to the quality of the food. Outside, the wind picked up a little more, rattling tree branches against the far side of the house, while the sky continued to darken with the approach of night as well as the coming storm.

Alex was grateful for the long silences between them. They'd covered a lot of ground since that morning, and he was fairly sure he wasn't the only one feeling the need for some time out. Not only to organize his thoughts, but also to regain some measure of control over his emotions.

No matter how often he warned himself not to dwell on the fact that Kari had chosen to stay with him, he couldn't seem to think of anything else. Yet he couldn't afford to let her know it. He firmly believed she was better off remaining unaware of the depth of his feelings for her. And he knew it was up to him to see that she did.

He would have to work at drawing back into himself and shutting her out. He had done that before quite successfully. With a little willpower, he could damn well do it again.

Unfortunately, every time he looked at her, his determination wavered. Noticeably.

"You're frowning again," she said, her quiet voice laced with concern. "Are you upset with the meal or with me?"

"Neither," he assured her. Making an effort to shake off the dreariness that had settled over him, he smiled slightly and turned the conversation away from himself. "I was just thinking about your Raymond Fairchild. I hope he agrees to Wyatt's proposition."

"I hope so, too. Otherwise we'll be back at square one, trying to decide who else we can ask to help us."

"After we finish cleaning up in here, I'll see what I can find out about him. Just in case he needs a little push in the right direction."

"Alex." She eyed him with exasperation. "You can't just invade people's privacy whenever the whim grabs you."

"I don't. Unless someone's life is on the line," he stated succinctly.

Taken aback, she lowered her gaze and began gathering the dishes.

"I'm sorry. I should have known you'd never abuse your talent."

"Yeah, well, as long as you know now, I won't hold it against you," he replied in a milder tone.

"That's good to find out."

They cleared the table quickly. Then Alex headed back to his office to do some research on Raymond Fairchild, while

Kari settled down on the living-room sofa to zone out—her words—in front of the television.

Two hours later, having discovered that Fairchild was an upstanding citizen who legally ran a profitable company, saved money and paid his taxes, Alex logged off his computer. Lightning had begun to flash and thunder to rumble, and the wind now blew pelting drops of rain against the windows.

Since he had failed to keep up with either radio or television weather reports over the past couple of days, he figured he'd better catch the late local-news broadcast on one of the San Antonio stations that also served the surrounding area. Heavy rains in the Texas Hill Country often spawned flash floods along the many creeks. That, in turn, often forced the closing of various back roads, some of which they'd have to travel on their way to the city.

As he pushed away from his desk, the telephone rang and he answered automatically. Kevin Wyatt responded with an equally terse greeting, hesitated, then instead of asking for Kari, as Alex expected, gave him the necessary information.

Raymond Fairchild had agreed to see them tomorrow. Unless Alex had any objections, Wyatt would meet the two of them at noon at a hotel on the River Walk in San Antonio. Then Wyatt and Kari would have lunch with Fairchild at a restaurant near his downtown office.

Alex had no objections. At least, none that he could voice.

Grumbling about the officiousness of some government employees, he cradled the receiver and went in search of Kari to relay the news.

He found her right where he'd left her earlier, curled up in one corner of the living-room sofa. Her head resting on a throw cushion, her legs tucked up under her, she'd fallen sound asleep. Neither the raucous commercial on the television nor the rolling thunder outside seemed to disturb her.

Settling down on the other side of the sofa, Alex gazed at her for several moments, wanting more than anything to gather her into his arms and hold her close. But he'd be starting something he couldn't finish, and that wouldn't be fair to her. Not when he had led her on in a similar way once already.

With a sigh of regret, he beat back the longing that ate at his soul, reached for the remote control lying on the coffee table and flipped to the channel he favored for state and local news.

The broadcast was already half-over, but according to the news anchor, the weather report was still ahead. Another commercial came on, making him sigh with frustration. He wanted Kari tucked safely away in the back bedroom. But he didn't want to wake her until after he'd heard what the weather was expected to be the following day.

Across from him, she stirred, then stretched, one small, bare foot edging along the empty cushion between them until it came to rest against his hip. He risked a glance at her and saw her blinking at him sleepily.

"What time is it?" she asked.

"Just after ten."

"What are you watching?"

"The local news. I'm waiting for the weather report."

Behind the window blinds, lightning blazed. Almost immediately, a rattling crash of thunder followed and the tempo of the falling rain increased considerably.

"I'd say there's a good chance thunderstorms are in the forecast," she advised, flashing him a grin as she rubbed her foot back and forth along his thigh in a familiar way that brought back memories of good times shared . . . once upon a time.

"Very funny," he growled, wrapping one hand around her slender ankle and holding her foot still. "I meant for tomorrow."

Without releasing her, he turned his attention back to the television as the weatherman took his position in front of a map of Texas. He liked the pressure of her fragile foot against his shorts-clad thigh, and he wasn't quite ready for her to move away yet.

However, just as soon as the newscast was over, he'd send her off to bed. Then he could prowl through the long, lonely night with her safely out of reach. Even if he ended up sitting in the chair beside her bed in the wee hours once again, he wouldn't lay a hand on her.

He had vowed that his bedroom would be her sanctuary for as long as she was there. And though she was there with him now of her own free will, that was one promise he had every intention of keeping.

The rain was supposed to continue into the following day, but not steadily. Instead bands of thunderstorms spawned by a tropical depression in the Gulf of Mexico would be rolling across south Texas off and on for the next forty-eight hours. Flash-flood watches weren't being issued yet and, with luck, wouldn't be until late tomorrow or the next day.

"Looks like we ought to be able to meet your buddy in San Antonio tomorrow as requested," Alex said, giving her ankle a squeeze, then moving his hand away.

"My buddy?"

Obviously not quite as awake as he'd assumed she was, Kari eyed him with confusion.

"Wyatt."

"He called?"

"About thirty minutes ago. He wants us to meet him at noon at the La Palacio Hotel on the River Walk. The two of you have a twelve-thirty luncheon date with Fairchild at a nearby restaurant," he informed her.

"So he agreed to meet with us. Good."

"I suppose."

"He's not my buddy, you know," she added, backpedaling somewhat as she pushed herself into a sitting position and shifted closer to him. "Wyatt, I mean."

"He'd like to be. That and more," Alex replied, feigning nonchalance.

"Well, too bad. The feeling's not mutual."

"Maybe once you get to know him, you'll change your mind."

Alex had no idea why he was pursuing this particular line of dialogue. Taunting himself with the possibility of Kari and Wyatt together made about as much sense as poking at a sore tooth with his tongue. Unfortunately, now that he'd started he couldn't seem to stop himself.

"I doubt it."

"You might be surprised." Using the remote control, he clicked off the television and stood. Enough was enough. He was only twisting himself into knots. Hoping she'd take the hint, he asked, "Do you have everything you need back in the bedroom?"

She stood, too, closing the distance between them.

"Almost," she murmured.

Gazing up at him, a wistful look in her pale-gray eyes, she reached out to trace the line of his jaw with her fingertips.

Lightning streaked and sizzled, casting an eerie glow upon the dimly lit living room. A clap of thunder rocked the house on its foundation. And then, without a flicker of warning, the lights went out, throwing them into darkness.

With a muffled cry, Kari launched herself at him. Instinctively, he wrapped his arms around her and held her close, savoring the warmth of her body as she pressed against him.

"Hey, it's okay," he soothed, bending over her protectively, his lips feathering the curve of her neck. "Just a little thunder."

As if answering a call, another rumble set the windows shaking.

"You're not scared, are you?"

"Just startled," she answered, a hint of rueful laughter in her voice. But she continued to hold on to him as a shiver stole through her.

"I've got some candles in the kitchen." Reluctantly, he started to ease away from her. "You stay here and I'll—"

"No." Her voice husky, she clung to him tighter and tipped her chin up.

"No?"

As lightning flickered again, he looked down at her and felt his body stir. Time suddenly seemed to stand still. All he could think of was how much he wanted her. Here and now. Now and forever.

Ignoring the little voice inside his head that warned him to cease and desist, he bent his head and kissed her, first with the tenderness of enduring love, then with the heat of passion too long denied. She opened her mouth for him, welcoming the thrust of his tongue, rising on her toes so that she fit more snugly against him and threading her fingers through his hair possessively.

The ardor of her response gratified him in such an intensely primal way he wanted to shout. She must not hate him after all. Otherwise how could she kiss him with such obvious abandon?

Still, he had to stop. And he would. But not yet. Not until he had finished—

As if he'd been yanked back on a leash, Alex jerked his head up. His hands on her shoulders, he set her away from him, holding her at arm's length. With a barely audible whimper, she knotted her fingers in the fabric of his shirt and stared at him with seeming confusion.

"Alex?"

"I'm sorry. I shouldn't have done that."

"But I wanted—"

"No," he cut her off rudely.

"But—" she began again.

His eyes now accustomed to the dark, Alex turned her resisting body toward the hallway as gently as he could.

"It's late. We have a long drive ahead of us in the morning." He marched her to the bedroom doorway, ignoring her sputtered protests.

"Just tell me why," she demanded, whirling to face him the moment he released her.

He could barely see her. Standing just inside the bedroom, she was no more than a shadow among shadows. But he sensed her mounting fury. And with regret, he chose to use it to his advantage.

"Why what?" he asked levelly, acting as if he neither knew nor cared what she was talking about.

"Why did you kiss me like that, then push me away?"

"I said I was sorry."

"Sorry isn't good enough, Alex," she shot back. "You owe me an explanation."

"Well, I don't have one to give." Wearily, he turned and walked away from her.

"You bastard."

"Go to bed, Kari."

"And *you* go to hell." As punctuation, she slammed the bedroom door on his retreating back.

Moving through the darkness that so aptly matched his mood, Alex made his way back to the living room and slumped on the sofa. He ought to be proud of himself. He'd not only put her off; he'd done so in a manner guaranteed to destroy whatever fond feelings she had seemed to have left for him. But all he could feel was pain. The same grinding, aching, empty pain he'd experienced only once before in his life. And this time there would be no second chance for him. He had just used that up.

Never again would she look upon him with warmth or tenderness. Never again would she welcome his kisses or caresses. And that was as it should be. As it had to be for her own good.

More than likely, she would choose to stay with Wyatt tomorrow. That was just as well, too. He would look after her in his own way.

Of course, he himself would still look after her, as well. Even if she insisted that he keep his distance. He owed her that much, and he always paid whatever debts he could. No matter what it cost him.

Chapter 8

"I have to admit I was beginning to wonder if we were wasting our time with Fairchild," Kevin said. "He seemed awfully uncertain when we presented our plan over lunch. I was sure he was going to turn us down. But instead he suggested we meet with him again at his office, and luckily for us, he was much more amenable by then."

"He just needed a chance to think about it and come to a decision on his own," Kari replied. "As I told you, he's a savvy businessman. I'm sure he wanted to consider all his options before making a commitment."

Sitting in the passenger seat of the FBI agent's sedan, she gazed out the window at the falling rain as he maneuvered the vehicle through the early-evening traffic filling the downtown streets of San Antonio.

"Well, you certainly helped to convince him," Kevin stated, his admiration evident. "The man obviously thinks a lot of you."

"I suppose."

Still much too devastated by her confrontation with Alex, she couldn't take pleasure in Kevin's praise. And she was much too weary to pretend otherwise.

She had barely slept at all last night, tossing and turning in the bed one minute, then pacing the confines of the room the next as she tried, unsuccessfully, to sort out her thoughts and feelings.

For the life of her, she still couldn't say why she'd thrown herself at Alex. She really should have known better. Yet various events during the day had seemed to lead inevitably to that moment when she'd stopped thinking sensibly and started acting on instinct.

First Alex had told her she was the most desirable woman he'd ever known. Then Kevin Wyatt had come to call, and Alex had hovered over her protectively, refusing to allow the FBI agent to take advantage of her. And most important, at least to her way of thinking, he hadn't sent her away when he'd had the opportunity.

She had waited, sure that Alex would tell her to go back to San Antonio with Kevin. When he didn't, when he seemed inclined to let her decide whether or not to stay, she had stupidly taken it as a sign that he'd wanted her with him after all.

Having that erotic dream while sleeping on the sofa hadn't helped much, either. Nor had waking to find Alex there with her, looking so sad and so alone. She'd wanted the impossible. And for several long, sweet, sensuous moments, she'd thought that maybe, just maybe, this time—

"You seem unhappy," Kevin said.

His deep voice cut across her thoughts. "Oh, no, not at all," she hastened to assure him.

"I thought maybe Payton had done something to upset you."

''Alex can be rather disagreeable when he chooses. But he's an old friend. I'm used to his moodiness.''

''I have a feeling he thinks of himself as more than that. Unless I'm mistaken, he's also in love with you.''

At the FBI agent's simple statement, Kari glanced away. Her face warming under the heat of a blush, she shook her head, refusing to consider the possibility that Kevin Wyatt knew what he was talking about.

''He's not,'' she denied. ''He's just a friend.''

''I'm just a friend. Or I hope I am. He's in love with you. And, much as it pains me to admit it, I believe you're in love with him, too.''

''No.'' Again she shook her head.

''I realize I haven't spent much time with you and Alex, but I consider myself fairly perceptive. I think I can recognize when two people care deeply for each other. I've even had some experience at it myself.'' He hesitated a moment, then continued somberly. ''Amanda Holcomb and I were going to announce our engagement just before her accident. After that, she wanted to wait.

''I was just starting out at the Bureau, working twelve- and fourteen-hour days. I told myself she just needed time to heal, because that was the easiest thing for me to do. I didn't push her, even though I sensed something was seriously wrong. If I had, she might still be alive today.''

''Oh, Kevin, I'm so sorry,'' Kari murmured, regarding him with heartfelt compassion.

She didn't know him well, but what she knew of him, she liked a lot. And she did indeed consider him a friend.

''It's over and done now. Too late to go back and do things differently. But it's not too late for you and Alex. No matter what's keeping you apart, you can work it out.''

Kari knew that revealing the true nature of his relationship with Amanda Holcomb hadn't been easy for Kevin. But he'd done it to save her from suffering the same grief he had. Unfortunately, she was afraid that the chasm between her and Alex had already widened impossibly.

More than anything, she wanted to believe they still might have a future together. But how many times could she try to breach the hard, cold wall Alex hid behind whenever they got too close? How many times could she let him knock her to her knees emotionally before she crawled away in defeat?

Unless she found out why Alex refused to give in to his feelings for her, feelings she wanted to believe he'd always had, she didn't have a chance of getting past the guard he'd erected around his heart. And after last night, when he'd calmly turned away from her, claiming he didn't have an explanation to give, she had little hope that she ever would.

He had been polite, yet distant, when she'd joined him in the kitchen early that morning, treating her with uncommon reserve. As if they were two strangers sharing space by accident—an unfortunate accident, at that.

Unwilling to reveal just how much he'd hurt her the night before, she'd given as good as she got. She'd helped herself to juice and coffee, as well as a cinnamon roll she didn't want but ate with all the relish she could muster, just to show him that she, too, considered the kiss they'd shared no more than a momentary aberration.

The drive to San Antonio in the steady rain had been interminable. Alex had focused on the road with total concentration, while Kari had gladly sat in silence. Staring out the side window, she'd told herself it was best not to distract him with the angry questions whirling inside her head.

At the hotel, he'd turned her car over to one of the valet parking attendants, wordlessly tucking the ticket into the back pocket of his jeans as he led the way to the lobby.

She'd wondered what he was planning to do while she and Kevin met with Raymond Fairchild, but she wasn't about to show her interest by asking. Better to let him think she couldn't care less how he spent his time.

Kevin had been waiting for them as promised. The two men exchanged wary looks, grudging handshakes and a few muttered words that could only barely be considered cordial. Then Kevin had taken her by the arm as if she were a lost child. With no more than a brief nod in her direction, Alex had stood aside so Kevin could lead her away.

Though deeply hurt by the callous way he'd let her go, Kari had straightened her shoulders, determinedly matching her pace to Kevin's. But halfway out the door, she hadn't been able to stop herself from glancing over her shoulder.

She'd fully expected Alex to have disappeared. Only he hadn't. He stood right where they'd left him, looking dangerous in his black T-shirt, jeans and boots, hands shoved in his pockets, his shaggy curls mussed, his eyes narrowed. Dangerous, yet oddly forlorn.

In that instant, she'd wanted to run back to him, put her arms around him and promise him that everything would be all right. But then they were out in the parking garage, the door closing behind them.

It was too late, she'd thought then as she thought now. Too late for them. No matter what Kevin Wyatt said.

"I don't think—" she began.

"Sometimes not thinking can be a really good idea," Kevin interrupted. "Sometimes it's better to act on impulse, instead. Especially when you're already convinced you don't have a lot to lose."

"Maybe," she murmured without much conviction.

"Trust me." He reached out and gave her hand a gentle squeeze, then deftly changed the subject as he pulled under the canopy outside the front door of the hotel. "Now, about tomorrow..."

"You're meeting with Brandon at the stable, posing as a parent needing a place to board your eight-year-old daughter's horse. You're also interested in having her take lessons. You want to have a look at the facility, a *good* look." As she glanced at Kevin, he nodded approvingly. "You've got the profile of a horse-crazy, eight-year-old girl and the list of questions I wrote up for you?"

"Right here." He patted one of his pockets. "I'll have the information memorized by morning."

They had agreed that the safest way for Kevin to get the lay of the land at Selby Stables was to do so as an owner in need of a place to board a horse.

"Don't worry about looking dumb. Most doting daddies aren't all that familiar with the equestrian world unless they ride, too. But they do insist on seeing exactly what they're getting for their money. By the time you leave, you should have a good idea of how the house, the main barn, the riding arenas and the other outlying buildings are set up. If you want a better look at one area or another, tell Brandon and he'll oblige you. As long as you come across as a big spender where your little darling is concerned, he'll take you just about anywhere you want to go—several times, if necessary."

"What about you? Are you still agreeable to going back on Saturday?" Kevin asked.

"Yes. I'll call Brandon tomorrow afternoon, tell him to expect me sometime Saturday evening, then show up at the stable as if I'd just flown in from Virginia."

"Unless you say otherwise, I'll put Fairchild in motion next Wednesday or Thursday," Kevin said. "What about Alex? Any idea when he plans to make an appearance?"

"No idea at all," she admitted. "I'm not even certain he's still in San Antonio. Not that it matters to me."

"He's here," Kevin said, directing a knowing look her way. "And it does matter to you."

"You sound awfully sure."

"If I weren't, I wouldn't let you go in there alone. I'd offer to buy you a drink, then find a way to lure you back to my place for dinner."

Surprised by his honesty, and flattered in spite of herself, Kari could only stare at him in silence. He met her gaze for a moment longer, then let himself out of the car and walked around to open her door.

"I'll call you tomorrow night and let you know how the interview with Selby went. You'll be at Payton's place, won't you?"

"I'm not really sure."

After the way she'd behaved last night, he probably didn't want her there anymore. But she didn't want Kevin to know that. He was a very nice man, and she really did like him. However, she didn't want him to feel obligated to look after her if Alex had abandoned her. She'd much rather nurse her wounded heart alone.

"You're not sure you'll be staying there?" Kevin asked, regarding her with concern.

"We might stay here, depending on what Alex has to do," she improvised.

"Well, you've got my card. If you're still in San Antonio tomorrow night, call me at home."

"I will."

"Take care, then." He took her hand, drew her close for a moment and kissed her cheek, then let her go again.

"You, too, Kevin."

Shivering as a gust of wind spattered her with raindrops, Kari turned and hurried toward the door, then shivered again as a blast of cold air greeted her entry into the hotel lobby. At that early-evening hour, most of the guests had already checked in, but the dinnertime hustle and bustle hadn't yet begun.

Rubbing her hands over her arms in a futile effort to warm herself, Kari eyed the various groupings of chairs and sofas scattered around the lobby, but saw no sign of Alex.

Off to her right, an arched doorway led into a dimly lit bar. Beyond that, if she remembered correctly, there was an elegantly appointed restaurant. And to her left, down a short hallway, she saw a sign advertising the Terrace Grill Coffee Shop.

Somehow she couldn't imagine Alex sitting in the bar. Nor, for that matter, could she see him passing any amount of time in the hotel dining room or the coffee shop. But he had to be around there somewhere. He had to be.

To satisfy herself, she glanced into the bar. Except for the bartender, who was watching the local news on a television mounted on the wall, the place was empty. The dining room was empty, as well. And although several people were seated in the coffee shop, none of them happened to be Alex.

Suddenly anxious and uncertain, Kari crossed to the reception desk and asked the lone clerk if there were any messages for her. The woman checked her computer, then answered in the negative, her tone apologetic. An instant later, her gaze shifted beyond Kari, her eyes widening with feminine interest and her smile warming considerably.

Curious about what had caused the clerk's sudden change in manner, Kari glanced over her shoulder and saw Alex striding toward them. He met her gaze for a moment, his expression cool and aloof, then turned his attention to the woman behind the desk.

"Ms. Gray is with me," he stated without inflection.

"Oh, of course, Mr. Payton," the clerk replied, making no effort at all to hide her disappointment as she regarded Kari with a critical eye. "Enjoy your stay with us."

Your stay with us?

Looking from one to the other, Kari wondered what was going on. Intent on finding out, she started to speak. But before she could get a word out, Alex took her upper arm in a firm grip, turned her toward the elevators and marched her across the lobby. Angered by his high-handed behavior, she tried to pull away, but he kept ahold of her easily enough.

"What are you doing?" she demanded as one of the elevator doors opened and he drew her inside the empty car.

"Taking you up to our room," he replied, pushing the button for the top floor.

"*Our* room?"

"Don't worry. The suite has two bedrooms. You can have your choice."

"But why—"

"Parts of the road out to the ranch are underwater."

"Oh."

The elevator glided to a stop and the doors slid open again. Still holding her by the arm, he led her down the quiet hallway to their *two-bedroom* suite.

Wouldn't want to risk having her throw herself at him again, would he? she thought bitterly as he slid the magnetic card into the slot and unlocked the door.

Inside, he finally released her and she moved away quickly, crossing to the bank of windows lining the wall as he switched on a couple of brass lamps. Beyond the glass, she could see a long, narrow balcony furnished with wrought-iron chairs and a small table, all wet with the rain.

Familiar with the hotel, she knew the room overlooked a secluded section of the River Walk. Had the night been clear, the view would have been lovely. As it was, she found it rather dreary. But that suited her mood just fine.

"Are you hungry?" Alex asked, pausing beside her.

She shrugged noncommittally.

"We can eat in the hotel dining room or the coffee shop, or just order room service if you'd prefer."

He was being so polite, so *damned* polite she wanted to scream. Instead she shrugged again, taking pleasure in the flicker of annoyance that crossed his face.

"Just let me know what you want to do."

Tie you to the bed and threaten to have my wicked way with you unless you tell me why you cut and run every time we come close to making love.

Stunned by that thought, Kari looked away as a blush warmed her cheeks. Hadn't he shot her down twice already? So why was she even contemplating setting herself up for another fall?

Granted, there was an old saying about the third time being the charm, but she had no reason to believe that meant it always proved true. And just because Kevin Wyatt had said Alex loved her didn't mean she could risk acting accordingly.

Kevin might consider himself observant, but he'd spent only a few hours with Alex. And Alex had always been a master at hiding his innermost thoughts.

Still, she couldn't quite rid herself of the feeling that if she tried one more time she might finally get the answers she needed, and maybe, just maybe, the response she wanted from him, as well. They had been apart for so long; yet somewhere deep in her heart she'd never stopped believing they belonged together. And, as Kevin had so accurately guessed, she didn't really have anything to lose by going after what she wanted.

"How did your meeting with Raymond Fairchild go?" Alex asked.

He moved away from her so quickly she wondered if he'd read her thoughts.

"Just fine." Turning, she watched as he slouched onto the gold-and-white-striped love seat, his back to her.

What would he do if she set about seducing him? Not boldly, but with a subtle sensuality that would surely catch him unawares. He'd kissed her last night at her invitation, but only because his guard had been down. As she remembered those moments now with a clearer head, she knew that once he'd started, he hadn't found it easy to stop.

Unfortunately, she had no experience luring a man into her bed. None whatsoever. Had the lights not gone out last night, she would never have thrown herself into his arms. That action had been purely instinctual. And she doubted he would let her get away with it again tonight, no matter how the storm worsened.

Feeling utterly dejected, Kari looked out the window once more.

"'Just fine'? What's that supposed to mean?" Alex asked, a thread of impatience obvious in his voice. "Did Fairchild agree to Wyatt's plan or what?"

"Eventually," she replied. "Kevin explained the situation to him over lunch. Then we went back to his office and waited while he came to a decision. Knowing Mr. Fairchild, he probably wanted to consult with his lawyer...at the very least."

Tired of standing, Kari moved away from the window. But instead of sitting in one of the floral-patterned armchairs across from Alex, she sat beside him on the love seat, leaving only a few inches between them. When he glanced at her warily, she regarded him with a "why not?" look in her eyes.

"So that's what took you so long."

"What did you think we were doing?" she asked, irritated by his snide tone. Then she added before she could stop herself, "Having sex in the back seat of Kevin's car?"

"Well, that would explain the tender little scene I witnessed outside the hotel when he dropped you off," Alex drawled, evidently unfazed by her attempt to bait him.

"What tender little—" she began, then remembered the chaste kiss Kevin had given her in farewell. "He kissed me on the *cheek.*"

"Obviously he prefers to be discreet in public. But for your sake, I hope he's not quite so mannerly in private. I wouldn't think you'd be satisfied—"

"Shut up, Alex. Just . . . shut . . . up."

Angrily, she stood, hands clenched at her sides, and glared at him. How could he talk with such total detachment about her and Kevin having sex? Surely he had to be bothered by the idea. But he didn't seem to care at all.

"You didn't have to come back here, you know," Alex said.

He was rubbing salt in her wounds—whether knowingly or unknowingly, she wasn't quite sure.

"You could have left a message for me saying you'd decided to stay with him."

"I didn't want to *stay* with him. I wasn't even *with* him in the first place. At least not the way you mean. I wanted to come back here. I wanted to be with *you.*"

To her dismay, tears stung her eyes, blurring her vision. Refusing to let him see her weep, she spun around and started forward, only to stumble into a low table. Off balance, she began to fall forward, but in an instant Alex was on his feet. With a muttered curse, he caught her behind her knees and at her shoulders, lifted her deftly into his arms and sat down again.

"Let me go," she demanded, her voice quavering.

"So you can land flat on your pretty face? I don't think so."

"You're a real bastard, you know," she whispered, then leaned against his chest with a deep, shuddering sigh and, forfeiting what little pride she had left, began to sob.

"Yeah, I know."

With a sigh of his own, he tightened his hold on her, one hand stroking her hair with a gentleness that made her cry even harder.

After what seemed like a very long time, she slowly regained control. Aware of the spectacle she'd made of herself, she wanted nothing more than to crawl off and hide, but she couldn't seem to find the strength to move away from Alex. And he seemed perfectly content to go on holding her.

Shifting slightly, he pulled a fresh handkerchief from his pocket and pressed it into her hand. She accepted it gratefully, wiped away the last of her tears and blew her nose.

"Better?" he asked.

"Not really," she replied, unable to be anything but honest with him.

"I had no right saying what I did to you. I'm sorry, Kari. Truly sorry."

"Did you really think—"

"I wasn't sure what to think. You were gone much longer than I expected you'd be. And then when I saw you with Wyatt outside the hotel..." She felt him shrug. "He's a good man. The kind of man you deserve."

"And you're not?" she asked, tilting her head up to meet his gaze.

He probably didn't realize it, but he had finally given her an idea why he'd walked out on her all those years ago. And she had every intention of using what he'd said to her advantage.

"No," he stated simply. "I'm not."

"But how can you say that?" she demanded. "You're as good and decent as—"

"Take my word for it, Kari. I'm not what you think I am. I never have been, and I never will be."

"I can't do that. I know you and I—"

"You know *nothing* about me," he shot back. "Nothing that really matters in the long run."

"Then tell me. Tell me what you believe will really matter to me in the long run." She reached up and touched his cheek, willing him to look at her. "Tell me what it is that's keeping us apart."

"Hasn't it occurred to you that maybe I'm just not interested? That sexually you leave me cold?"

His cruel words stung. But only for a moment. She was aware of what he was trying to do, and she wasn't about to be deterred. She was too close to getting the truth out of him, and she wasn't going to blow it by letting him make her mad.

"That thought has crossed my mind," she said softly, threading her fingers through the shaggy curls at his nape as she feathered her lips along his jaw. "But I've dismissed it as a silly notion."

Smiling at the way his pulse quickened, she pressed her open mouth to the hollow at the base of his throat and licked at him with the tip of her tongue.

With a groan, Alex tried to ease her away, but she settled her bottom more firmly in his lap, rubbing against him as her lips played along the side of his neck.

"So, I leave you sexually cold, huh?" she murmured. "Alex, you lie."

She was making him crazy, and any minute now he was going to... going to...

She wriggled against him again, this time with a barely audible whimper, and he realized that somehow his hand had moved to her breast. As if of their own volition, his fingers played over her nipple, and he felt it harden beneath the fabric of her clothing.

Too much clothing. Clothing he wanted out of the way. As did she, he thought, aware of her hands on his belt buckle.

He had to stop her. Otherwise he wasn't going to be able to stop himself. He'd wanted her for ten years, ten long, lonely years. And seeing her with Wyatt that afternoon— seeing him draw her close and kiss her—had been almost more than he could bear. Now the urge to take her, to make her his and his alone, was surging beyond his control.

Only if she pulled away in horror and disgust, only if she warded off his advances as she would those of a beastly creature, only then would he be able to let her go. As willful and wanting as she was now, she'd do that only if she knew the truth about him.

With what little willpower he had left, Alex put his hands on her shoulders and held her away. When she gazed up at him, her eyes bleary with confusion, he spoke to her harshly.

"Listen to me, Kari. Listen to me and listen good."

She stared at him, her tear-stained face pale. But her calm, quiet voice was filled with determination as she answered him.

"It won't make any difference, Alex. No matter what, it won't make any difference to me at all."

"You say that now. But you don't know what I am. Or what I could become."

Her faith in him seeming not to waver in the least, she continued to meet his gaze as she waited wordlessly for him

to say his piece. Years ago, she had looked up to him in the
same way she had looked up to Devlin. As if he were some
kind of hero. And despite what he'd done to her, he realized that she still did.

Now, destroying that image once and for all seemed to
him the only way to end what he never should have begun.
Knowing that he couldn't risk having the kind of permanent relationship with her that she not only wanted but deserved, he'd tried to keep his hands off her. Tried and failed,
not once or twice, but three times.

Heaven help him, he was only human, and he wanted her
more than life itself. But taking her without telling her the
truth about himself would be dishonest. And once the truth
had been told...

Just do it, damn it. Do it and get it over with.

Wanting to hold her a few moments longer, yet needing
to put some distance between them, he lifted her off his lap
and set her on the love seat. Then, ignoring her murmured
protest, he stood and crossed to one of the chairs. Halting
behind it, he faced her again.

"Just after my eighth birthday, I stood by the front window of the house where I lived in Philadelphia, watched my
parents drive away, and as I'd done every time they left me,
I wished with all my heart that they'd never come back.
That afternoon my wish finally came true. They were killed
in an automobile accident.

"When the police came to the house and gave the news to
the housekeeper, for just a moment I was...overjoyed. But
only for a moment. They were my parents. I was supposed
to love them, not hate them. Not want them dead. Yet I
knew that now they could never hurt me again. Of course I
considered the possibility that someone else might pick up
where they left off. But I also believed that maybe, just
maybe, I might finally be safe."

From where she sat, hands clenched together in her lap, Kari stared at him, her eyes wide with confusion, seeming unable to comprehend what he was telling her.

"But I don't—"

"Understand?" He spoke for her, hearing the hard edge rimming his voice. "Well, then, let me enlighten you."

Gripping the back of the chair, he smiled bitterly as he continued.

"My father was a so-called self-made man, a nouveau riche social climber who rightly equated money with power. My mother was fifteen years younger, an aging fashion model with a taste for the good life. They enjoyed playing brutal, abusive, humiliating games with each other and, eventually, with me.

"Why they brought me into the world I'll never know. Perhaps out of boredom. Until I was about three or four, my mother kept me away from my father as much as possible. But then she must have needed something to keep him interested, and I happened to be it.

"They were careful never to leave any marks on me, any *visible* marks. And they made sure I understood nobody would believe me if I spoke of what was done to me in the privacy of their bedroom. They employed nannies and housekeepers, but upon being hired, the women were always told that I lied to get attention. Since they were let go after six months, they were never around long enough to learn differently.

"When I started school—an exclusive private school—my teachers were told the same thing. I never even thought of going to one of them. But my second-grade teacher took a special interest in me. She was young and sweet and so approachable. She was worried because I always looked so sad. She kept asking questions. So many questions. One day, I finally broke down and told her how my parents hurt me.

"I just knew she would believe me, and I thought that she would find a way to help me. But within a few days she was gone. My parents made my life even more of a living hell after that. So of course I never talked about what they did to me again. Until now."

Unable to bear the look of horror dawning in Kari's eyes, Alex turned and walked to the window.

"As I said, I was glad when they were killed. Luckily, the state found a distant cousin willing to take me in. She was in her sixties and had never been married, but she welcomed me into her solitary life and was good to me in her own way. She wasn't openly affectionate, but she saw to it that I had the best of everything my parents' money could buy."

He paused again, leaning his forearm against the glass, and watched the rain fall. Somehow he had thought that talking about his past would be more painful. But so much time had passed since he'd been that small, frightened, helpless little boy that it almost seemed as if he were speaking of someone else. And though he hated the thought of Kari recoiling from him in distaste—as she must surely be doing—he felt oddly relieved at having finally come clean with her.

"Alex, I . . . I don't know what to say," she murmured.

"Not a pretty story, is it?" Still not quite ready to face her again, he continued to gaze out the window.

"No, not very pretty at all."

There was an odd catch in her voice, as if she might cry again.

He didn't want her to do that. Didn't want her weeping for him. Her tears wouldn't change anything.

"It happened a long time ago. But you must realize that considering my background, I could end up being just as abusive as my father under certain circumstances." He hesitated, searching for the words that would ultimately drive the final wedge between them, then added, "You must see now that I'm not someone with whom you ought to be on intimate terms. I'm damaged goods, Kari, and nothing will ever change that."

"Is that why you walked out on me six years ago? Because you were afraid that one day you'd turn into your father?" she asked with surprising calm.

"You talked about marriage and children. I knew that's what you wanted, what you deserved. But not with someone like me. I couldn't lead you on. I couldn't let you think there was a chance of any permanency between us. Not when there was a possibility that I might hurt you one day, physically as well as emotionally."

Behind him, he heard movement. Looking up, he saw Kari's reflection beside his own in the glass. An instant later he felt her arm slip around his waist and her head rest upon his shoulder. Stunned, he gazed down at her, but she seemed content to stare out the window.

"Alex, have you ever in your life intentionally hurt anyone, either physically or emotionally, just for the fun of it?"

"No." He tried to ease away from her, but she held on tight.

"Considering the kind of work you do, that's saying something, isn't it?" She hesitated only a moment. Then, giving him no time to respond, she continued in a fiercer tone. "You're one of the most decent, honorable men I've ever known, and nothing you can say will make me think otherwise.

"I've seen you with my brother. I've seen your genuine affection for him as well as your camaraderie. I know you offered to go after the man responsible for killing his first wife and child so he could stay with Laura and keep her safe. Offered even though you could hardly walk straight and probably wouldn't have come back alive.

"And over the weekend, I saw you with Laura and Timmy and Andrew. They made you smile with honest, heartfelt joy. You were so gentle with them, so loving. And you held our godson with such reverence I wanted to weep.

"As for me, I can't recall a time that you've ever treated me with anything less than kindness and consideration, even when I've behaved like a real brat. Granted, you broke my heart six years ago, but now I understand why. You weren't being intentionally callous or cruel. In your own way of thinking, you were actually protecting me. Just as you've been trying to do tonight.

"But it wasn't necessary then, and it isn't necessary now. You are *not* damaged goods. You never have been. And you will never turn into your father. Believe me, Alex. If you can't just yet, let me believe for both of us."

Finally, she tilted her head up and met his gaze, her eyes shimmering with tears. And somewhere deep inside him, a tiny nudge of hope stirred in the darkest reaches of his soul.

"How can you be so sure?" he asked, almost afraid to let himself trust in her certainty.

"I don't know." She smiled impishly as a single tear trickled down her cheek. "But I am. Surer than I've ever been of anything in my life."

He traced the track of her tear with a fingertip, his eyes searching hers.

"I'm making you cry again."

"Only because you're supposed to kiss me now, and you haven't."

"Ah, and if I do, no more tears?"

"No more tears."

"I'm not certain I'll be able to stop with one kiss."

"Actually, that's what I was hoping." Her smile widening, she slid her other arm around him and moved against him provocatively.

He had never imagined she would respond to his revelation with such sympathy and understanding. He'd thought that she would run from him in horror. Instead she'd honored him with her unqualified trust. And now she stood willingly within the circle of his arms, her desire for him undiminished.

"Are you sure?" he asked, still hesitant.

He felt as if he'd been waiting for her all his life, and in a way, he supposed he had. Now he wanted nothing so much as to bind her to him in the most intimate way possible. But only if she wanted it, as well.

"Very, very sure." Tangling her fingers in his curls, she pulled his head down and kissed him, her lips moving over his invitingly.

With a groan, he lifted her into his arms and strode toward one of the bedrooms as she clung to him, nuzzling his neck.

"You won't stop this time, will you?" she asked, a pleading note in her voice. "I couldn't bear it if you did."

"Only if you ask me to."

"I won't," she assured him, smiling up at him as he stood her beside the bed and switched on the lamp.

Moving away from her for a moment, he pulled his wallet from his back pocket, opened it, removed a couple of foil packets and tossed them on the nightstand. At the quizzical look in her eyes, he smoothed a hand over her hair.

"I haven't been with anyone in a very long time. But old habits—especially those taught by your beloved brother—die hard."

"I haven't been with anyone, either." She hesitated, a blush staining her cheeks, then added softly, "Not…ever."

As he realized what she was saying, Alex went still, his eyes holding hers. That she hadn't turned to someone else during all the years they'd been apart was more than he deserved. She was so basically *good*, so sweet and so damned innocent. No matter what she said, he knew he'd never be truly worthy of her love.

But she stood before him now, her arms wrapped around his waist, wanting him as he wanted her. As he'd always wanted her. And he was only human. One day soon she'd come to her senses. But tonight…tonight she would be his.

"Then I'll take special care of you, love. Very special care," he promised.

Drawing her into his arms, he kissed her deeply, using his tongue until she melted against him, kissing him back with equal fervor, her momentary shyness gone. Ever so gently, he caressed her, skimming his hands over her breasts, her back, then down over her hips and her belly, delving between her legs for only an instant. Then, trailing one slow, openmouthed kiss after another along her neck, across her shoulders and over the swell of her breasts, he undressed her.

With soft sighs and whispers of delight, she tugged at his T-shirt, fumbled with his belt buckle and tore at his zipper until it opened. Unabashedly, she slid her hands inside the waistband of his briefs and cupped the throbbing length of him in her palms.

Startled by her boldness, Alex caught his breath, then shifted his hips shamelessly, lifting himself into her hands more fully as a harsh moan escaped his lips.

Immediately, she pulled away.

"I'm sorry," she murmured. "Did I hurt you?"

"Not at all," he assured her.

Bringing her hands to his mouth, he pressed a kiss into each palm, then scooped her up and laid her on the bed. He shucked his clothes, stretched out beside her and drew her close.

She came to him eagerly, matching him kiss for kiss and caress for caress.

Wanting her first time to be as pleasurable for her as possible, Alex moved down her body, kissing her breasts and her belly. Finally, he put his mouth between her legs, using his lips, his teeth, his tongue until she writhed under his ministrations, hot and wet and ready.

Moving away from her just long enough to dispense with the condom, he settled himself between her thighs. Her eyes holding his, she reached for him, wrapping her arms and legs around him, urging him closer, then closer still.

"Please, Alex, now..." she whispered, arching up.

Unable to hold back, he entered her, breaking the fragile barrier of her innocence with one swift, sure stroke.

She uttered a soft cry and went still, her eyes widening with surprise. Nestled deep inside her, he smiled down at her, smoothing her damp hair away from her face, giving her time to adjust to his intimate invasion.

Slowly, she smiled back and began to relax. With a growl of masculine triumph, he teased at her ear with his tongue, then trailed a line of kisses along her jaw. At last, he took her mouth again as he began to thrust into her.

She moved with him, her body slick with sweat, her hands clutching his back, her legs wound around his waist. She whimpered, undulating against him frantically. Then, with another cry of surprise, she came apart in his arms.

Calling her name, Alex reared back, taking his pleasure in her pleasure and feeling, if only for a moment, as if he'd finally been redeemed.

Chapter 9

Lying on her side in the hotel bed, Kari stared into the darkness, listening to the steady beat of rain against the window. Curled around her protectively, Alex slept soundly, one hand loosely splayed across her belly.

She should have been able to sleep, too. With his body warm against hers and his slow, even breathing ruffling her hair, she was filled with a sense of contentment. Yet she couldn't seem to stop her thoughts from spinning uncontrollably.

Their lovemaking had been so wonderfully *right*. As Alex had promised, he'd taken special care of her. Granted, there had been a moment of pain. But ultimately, his tender ministrations had bathed her in boundless ecstasy.

She had never felt quite as alive as she had coming apart in his arms. Nor had she ever felt as cherished as when he'd tended to her afterward.

He had held her close as she slowly regained her composure, then washed away the slight soreness between her legs with a warm washcloth. And finally, as if sensing how much she needed to have him near, he'd held her again, speaking softly, reassuringly, as he used his hands and his mouth on her with a gentleness that had stolen her breath away.

Within a very short time, he'd had her wanting again. Eschewing his own satisfaction rather than risk causing her more discomfort, he'd brought her to completion with his mouth. Her hands buried in his hair, she had held him to her shamelessly as she cried out his name.

Stunned by the response he'd so artfully evoked from her, she'd drifted on a haze of sensation for what seemed like a very long time. But then, having finally gathered her wits about her again, she'd turned to him, intent on reciprocating in kind, despite his protests.

Aware that words alone weren't enough to convince him yet, she'd shown him as best she could—with her limited experience—just how much she loved him, savoring the taste and texture of him until he could no longer hold back.

His breathing labored, he'd hauled her into his arms again. And in the instant before he'd claimed her mouth in a deep, drugging kiss, she had thought she'd seen tears shimmering in his eyes.

When he'd finally raised his head, he'd turned her so that she lay against him, back to front. Then he'd reached up and switched off the lamp. She'd murmured his name questioningly and asked if he was all right. His voice husky, he'd teased her about that being *his* line. She'd persisted, but to no avail. He'd simply nuzzled her neck and told her, rather firmly, to go to sleep.

She'd tried. Really, she had. And she was still trying. But she had too much on her mind.

As she remembered all that Alex had told her about his childhood, her heart ached for the tormented boy he had been as well as for the cold, distant man he'd forced himself to become. And as she'd told him, she understood, at last, why he had walked out on her, even though she couldn't agree with his reasoning.

She had meant it when she'd said she believed he was a decent and honorable man. Meant it with all her heart. She had enough faith in him for the both of them.

Still, she knew better than to think she had convinced him completely.

Because he had wanted her as much as she had wanted him, and because he'd also been off balance, she'd been able to lure him into making love to her. But the years he'd spent believing he had the potential to become cruel and abusive—years he'd also spent thinking of himself as "damaged goods"—couldn't be wiped away within a few hours or even a few days.

Sooner or later, she was afraid, he would begin to doubt himself once more. If she wasn't there to ease his fears, he could very well take off again, and she might never find a way to coax him to come back to her.

As long as he thought that Brandon posed a threat to her, Kari knew he wouldn't leave her. But after that . . .

Would he just disappear? Working for McConnell, he could do that quite easily. And even if Devlin were able to help her find him, he wouldn't.

Not that it would do her any good to track Alex down. She could force herself on him for only so long. Unless he was eventually able to trust in his own basic goodness, he would never be truly happy with her. As if he were living under a cloud of impending doom, he would constantly be waiting for the other shoe to drop, and that waiting would drive him away from her, if not physically, then emotionally.

Having him shut her out that way would be more difficult to bear than never seeing him again. Especially knowing, as she now did, that he loved her enough to set aside his
own wants and needs rather than risk hurting her.

The mere thought of losing him sent of wave of desola-
tion rolling over her. Still, she would prefer to let him go
than make him miserable. But not without a fight.

Alex had sworn he would look after her until Brandon
was behind bars, and Kari had every intention of using the
time that would take to her advantage. They would be together for at least a week, maybe two. And maybe, with a
little luck, she might find a way to make him see himself as
she did.

Her weariness getting the better of her, Kari finally slept,
only to awaken several hours later alone in the bed. In a mild
state of panic, she sat up and called Alex's name, afraid that
he'd left her even sooner than she'd anticipated.

But then, as the dregs of sleep cleared away, she realized
that along with the falling rain she could also hear the
shower running in the bathroom. With a sigh of relief, she
scrambled out of bed and went to join him.

Though she took him by surprise, he welcomed her with
open arms, easing her fear that he'd already begun to have
second thoughts. After much teasing and tormenting with
soapy hands, they ended up back in bed, where Alex made
incredibly slow, devastatingly sweet love to her.

Momentarily sated, they slept again for about an hour,
then awakened hungry for each other all over again. Unfortunately, their growling stomachs testified to their need
for another kind of sustenance, as well.

Kari would have gladly gone without food rather than
chance breaking the wondrous spell that seemed to have
settled over them. As long as they were alone together, living in the moment, she knew she could hold at bay any lin-

gering doubts he might have. But once they rejoined the real world, once he had time to think again and reconsider, the possibility that he would retreat from her as he had in the past increased dramatically.

Of course, she had known that moment would inevitably come. But she had hoped to postpone it for at least a little while longer.

Alex, however, appeared to have other ideas. With reluctance he got up, gathered his clothes off the floor and began to dress. Feeling contrary, she refused to budge, until he reminded her they'd used the last of his condoms. Grudgingly, she finally agreed to his suggestion that they go down to the coffee shop for a late breakfast. But only when he also promised to stop at the hotel gift shop to buy more supplies.

According to their waitress, the rain had already let up to the north and west of the city, while clearing skies by late afternoon were in the forecast for San Antonio itself.

"So, I guess that means we'll be going back to your place after we eat," Kari said, glumly cradling her mug of coffee in her hands.

No matter how hard she tried, she couldn't seem to dispel the nagging feeling that Alex wasn't truly at ease with the sudden change in their relationship. His lovemaking had left no doubt in her mind that he both wanted her and needed her. But for all the pleasure he had given her and taken for himself, she still sensed a certain holding back in him. As if he wasn't quite sure yet that what he was doing was right.

The long drive to his ranch would give him the perfect opportunity to start distancing himself from her. And once they were back at his house, he'd be reminded of the solitary life he'd chosen to live. Chosen for what he'd always believed were very good reasons.

"You don't sound very happy about it."

She shrugged noncommittally, unwilling to voice her concerns.

"I thought you liked it there."

"I did."

"But?" he prodded.

"I like being here with you, too. The way we were last night," she admitted.

"So do I." Smiling, he reached across the table and clasped her hand in his. "But we can be together that way there, too."

"Promise?"

"Promise."

He squeezed her hand reassuringly, then let her go as their waitress appeared with the eggs, pancakes, sausage and hash browns they'd ordered.

Feeling foolish for having tied herself into knots over nothing, Kari dug into her food. Unless she stopped replaying worst-case scenarios in her head, her greatest fear was going to be realized. She had to trust Alex—really, truly trust him—not just say that she did. Otherwise she'd never be able to banish whatever doubts about himself he might continue to have.

"Before we got sidetracked last night, you said that Fairchild finally agreed to cooperate with Wyatt, didn't you?" Alex asked as he poured maple syrup over his pancakes, picking up where last night's conversation had left off.

"Yes, I did."

"How does Wyatt plan to proceed?"

In between bites of her breakfast, Kari told Alex about Kevin's proposed plan of action, mentioning his visit to the stable that day as well as her own scheduled return the next. Alex listened attentively, his expression revealing little of what he was thinking.

"Have you confirmed that there's a flight coming in from Virginia tomorrow evening, just in case Selby is suspicious enough to check it out?" he asked when she'd finished.

"There is. It's due at six-thirty. Kevin is also having my name added to the manifest as an added precaution."

Alex nodded, obviously satisfied, then signaled to their waitress for more coffee. She refilled their mugs, collected their empty plates and set their bill on the table.

"I'm supposed to call Brandon and let him know when to expect me," she continued when they were alone again. "I thought I'd wait until about three o'clock. He has a lesson then, so I won't have to talk to him. I can just leave a message for him on his answering machine."

Sitting back in his chair, Alex regarded her steadily, a frown creasing his forehead. "You really are afraid of him, aren't you?"

She considered denying it outright, but she knew he'd see right through her.

"Sometimes he makes me uneasy," she conceded.

"Are you absolutely sure you want to go back there?"

"As long as you'll be nearby."

"I will be," he vowed. "Within shouting distance, twenty-four hours a day until Selby is behind bars."

Knowing she could count on him to keep his word, Kari nodded gratefully. Then, giving in to her curiosity, she asked, "What did you do yesterday?"

"Picked up a few things I needed to complete my disguise, then took another look around Selby Stables. With the rain, not much was going on." He paused, a disgusted expression on his face. "You know, the security around that place is virtually nonexistent. Anybody could get into your cottage anytime he wanted. First thing tomorrow night, I'm changing the locks on your doors and adding them to your windows."

"*Another* look?" she prodded, ignoring everything else he'd said. "You've been there before?"

"I stopped there about a year ago on my way to Mexico," he replied, matter-of-factly.

"You did?" Thoroughly bemused, she stared at him. "Why?"

"To see you."

"But you didn't...I didn't..." At a loss, she looked away for a moment, then turned back to him indignantly. "Why didn't you let me know that you were there?"

"I didn't think you'd be pleased to see me."

"You're right. I probably wouldn't have been," she admitted ruefully. Then, feeling the need to be equally honest with him, she added, "I almost came to see you when you were in the hospital. But I didn't think you would be pleased to see me, either."

"Probably not," he said as he reached out for her hand anew. "But it's nice to know now that you were thinking of me then."

Weaving her fingers through his, Kari regretted all the time they'd wasted. Still, in spite of themselves, they'd found each other again. And nothing else really mattered now.

They finished their coffee, then Alex paid the bill, leaving a generous tip for the waitress. After a stop in the gift shop as promised, they returned to the room so Alex could make a couple of telephone calls—one to check on the road conditions, which turned out to be good, and another to Devlin so he and Laura would be prepared should Brandon call to talk to Kari after getting her message.

Just after noon they were on the road once more, headed back to Alex's house in her car.

"Seems a shame to drive all this distance only to have to turn around and drive back again tomorrow," she mused.

"We would have had to do it one way or the other. All your stuff is there, and Selby would wonder if you turned up without any luggage."

"You're right," she agreed. "Although I could have pretended the airline lost it."

"That would have just given you another lie to keep track of."

"I suppose."

"We'll be there soon enough," he assured her. "And we'll have tonight and most of tomorrow before we have to leave again."

"You're anxious to get back, aren't you?"

"Yeah, I am. I like being there." He glanced at her, brushing the back of his hand against her cheek. "And I especially like being there with you."

Warmed by his words as well as by the tenderness of his touch, Kari smiled at him, then retorted lightly, "The fact that I baked cinnamon rolls for you wouldn't have anything to do with that, would it?"

"Let's just say it didn't hurt." He turned his attention back to the road. "What about you? You meant it when you said you liked the place, didn't you?"

"Oh, yes, I liked it a lot," she assured him, then added impishly, "even though I resented the hell out of being stuck there with you."

"Gosh, I would have never guessed," he teased back.

"I still can't believe you kidnapped me."

"For your own good," he reminded her gently.

"So you keep saying."

"Because it's the truth. And I'm not holding you against your will now, am I?"

"No."

"Well, then, cut me some slack, will you?"

"All right."

"Have you thought about what you'll do after this business with Selby is over?"

"Not really," she admitted. "But I suppose I should. I'll definitely be out of a job, and I'll also have to find another place to live."

"You're welcome to stay at my place while you look around for something else," he offered in an offhand manner.

Not stay with *him*, she thought, stay at *his place*. And not permanently. Just until she found something else. She knew she should be grateful that he'd thought to suggest it. But in all honesty, she had hoped for more. Especially after last night.

Of course, she hadn't taken into account his job. A job that just the other day he'd said he found quite gratifying. A job that required him not only to spend most of his time out of the country, but also to remain single.

McConnell no longer allowed his married agents to take on assignments that involved a high degree of physical risk. The kind of risk that was always a part of the covert operations Alex had professed to love. The kind of risk that would be missing should he accept a desk job as Devlin had done. Which was something he'd already said he'd never do.

And why should he? He had made no promises of happily ever after, she reminded herself firmly. He had simply taken what she'd so willingly offered and given back what he could in return. He had acknowledged his awareness of her desire for marriage and a family, but he hadn't said he wanted either for himself. And, she now realized, there was a good chance that he never would.

"Thanks, I'll keep that in mind," she answered as lightly as she could, flashing a bright smile his way despite the sadness settling in her soul.

"I have a couple who look after the house and grounds for me, so it wouldn't be a lot of work for you," he added, as if that would somehow seal the deal.

"As I said, I'll think about it."

Avoiding his sudden, searching glance, Kari focused on the view outside the car window. She couldn't imagine anything that would depress her more than living in Alex's house alone. In fact, just the thought of it made her want to weep.

But there would be time enough for that later. All she wanted now was to make the most of whatever moments they had left together.

No more regretting the past or worrying about the future, she ordered herself sternly. She'd done enough of that already, and all to no avail. For as long as Alex stayed with her, she wasn't going to think of anything but loving him. If he still chose to leave her one day, then so be it.

Determined to keep her vow, Kari did her best to remain lighthearted throughout the rest of the afternoon and evening as well as the following day.

With the sun shining once again, the temperature rose accordingly, sending waves of heat and humidity shimmering off the wet ground. By the time they arrived at Alex's house, spending the rest of the day indoors seemed like a good idea. And with only a little coaxing on Kari's part, they eventually ended up in bed, where they stayed for most of the next twenty-four hours. Except for one truly decadent foray out to the hot tub sometime after midnight.

Kari made her telephone call to Brandon and left a message on his answering machine as planned. And that evening, she and Alex talked to Kevin Wyatt.

His visit to Selby Stables had gone off without a hitch, and he seemed satisfied that he would be able to keep the barn area under surveillance at night without being detected. He also indicated that he still wanted Kari to return Saturday evening as scheduled unless she had any qualms. Anxious to put their plan into action, she assured him that she was more than ready to go back.

Although Alex considered Kevin Wyatt a capable man and trusted that he would do his best to look out for Kari, he continued to be anything but enthusiastic about letting her return to the stable. In fact, had he been able to think of a way to keep her away from there altogether without upsetting her, he would have, and Kevin Wyatt be damned.

But Alex knew that Kari felt duty-bound to play her part in Selby's downfall, and she would be furious if he tried to prevent her from doing it.

If anything happened to her, he would never forgive himself. But then, that was why he was going to be right there with her. To see that she was safe.

And to savor—for a little longer—the love she offered him.

He was still surprised each time he reached for her and she came to him willingly, seeming just as insatiable as he. He kept expecting her to snap to her senses, to realize that trusting him so completely might not be very wise considering the kind of background he had. But her initial faith in him not only endured, it appeared to grow stronger.

When they had first arrived back at his house, he'd had some serious second thoughts. Reminded of all the years he'd stayed away from her and why, he had begun to think that maybe he'd been right all along.

But no matter how he'd tried, Kari hadn't allowed him to distance himself from her. She had whispered to him teasingly and touched him tormentingly, until he'd thrown her over his shoulder and carried her to his bedroom, turning the room he'd sworn would be her sanctuary into their own special haven. A haven of the heart he'd found himself more and more loath to leave.

Inexorably, however, Friday had turned into Saturday, and now the clock on the nightstand read three p.m. Much as he hated to wake her from much-needed sleep, they would have to leave within the hour. Otherwise they would never make it back to the San Antonio airport in time for Kari to coordinate her movements with the arrival of the flight from Virginia.

As they had agreed after talking to Wyatt, she would wait near the appropriate gate for the plane to land, keeping an eye out in the unlikely event Selby had come to meet her, while Alex picked up the car he'd rented on Monday and went on to the stable ahead of her. That way he would be on the grounds when she got there, and would be able to look out for her if she happened to cross paths with Selby on the way to her cottage.

Since the bastard was still awaiting her response to his proposal of marriage, Selby shouldn't pose too serious a threat to her yet. But Alex wasn't taking any chances. He planned to spend nights in her cottage and days, starting Monday, working around the stable, close to wherever she was.

Tomorrow would be tricky, however. Kari was scheduled to show horses for several owners at upcoming events, and even though it was Sunday, Brandon would expect her to put in some time riding to make up for all the days she'd been away.

Because Alex had managed to skulk around in broad daylight a year ago without being seen, he was fairly certain he could do so again. Still, he would feel more at ease when he could move about freely, disguised as a stable hand—hiding in plain sight, so to speak.

Unable to put off rousing her any longer, Alex reluctantly sat beside her on the bed.

"Time to rise and shine," he murmured, running a hand over the curve of her hip, now modestly covered by a light cotton blanket.

She sighed and stretched, muttering unintelligibly, then rolled onto her back and eyed him sleepily for several seconds.

"You're up and you're *dressed,*" she said at last, her tone mildly reproving.

Neither of them had bothered much with clothes for the past twenty-four hours.

"You should be, too," he replied, tugging the blanket up over her bare breasts with an inner sigh of regret, then gently smoothing her hair from her face. "We have to be on the road by four o'clock and it's already after three."

"It can't be," she grumbled as she pushed up on her elbows and glanced at the clock. A moment later, she fell back on her pillow, adding ruefully, "But it is, isn't it?"

"Hop in the shower while I fix you something to eat."

Breakfast, lunch and dinner had gone by the wayside, as well.

"I have to pack, too."

"All done," he assured her. "I left underwear, your skirt and a T-shirt in the bathroom for you. Okay?"

"Okay."

She smiled at him with such obvious affection that he had to stand and move away from her before the urge to shove the blanket aside and lay claim to her yet again got the better of him.

"You have thirty minutes max," he ordered sternly.

"Or what? You'll leave without me?" she teased, not the least bit intimidated.

"I would if I thought you'd stay put. But you'd just hitchhike all the way to San Antonio on your own, endangering yourself even more, wouldn't you?"

"I have to go back," she replied quietly, her determination to move ahead as planned unwavering. "I have to go back and do what I can to stop Brandon."

"I know. But I don't like it. Not one damn bit."

"I'm going to be all right," she insisted.

"You'd better be."

His mindfulness of all that could go wrong darkening his mood considerably, Alex left Kari to shower and dress while he put together a late lunch they'd now have to eat on the road.

The drive to San Antonio seemed much shorter than it actually was. In an effort to ease his sense of impending doom, Alex quizzed Kari unrelentingly on what she should and shouldn't do once she was back at the stable. She went along with him for a while, then became increasingly testy herself.

He wanted her to give Selby as wide a berth as possible, even though it wasn't really feasible. As she pointed out, she still worked for the man, and she had to show him the same common courtesy she had in the past. Which happened to include stopping by his house to let him know she had returned as she'd said she would.

"Just call him from the cottage," Alex snapped. "Tell him you're still not feeling well. While you're at it, tell you won't be able to ride Sunday, either," he added, wondering why he hadn't thought of that sooner.

"Oh, he'll really buy *that*," she retorted sarcastically. "I don't look the least bit ill."

"He won't have to see you."

"If I don't stop at the house, he'll come to the cottage. Is *that* what you want?"

"No."

Pulling into a space on the airport parking lot, Alex slammed the gearshift into park and switched off the engine. She was right, of course. And, if necessary, he could get inside Selby's house. He'd done it a year ago and again Friday afternoon. Still...

"I'm not stupid, Alex," she chided softly. "And I'm not about to take any unnecessary risks. But I know Brandon. I know what he expects of me. To suddenly change my behavior would make him start to wonder."

"All right, then. Stop at the house. But if he lays a hand on you—"

"I'll plant my knee in his groin," she interrupted, flashing Alex a teasing grin.

He wasn't sure if he wanted to laugh or cry. So he settled for hauling her across the seat and kissing her, long and slow and deep. Then he eased away from her, opened the car door and got out.

"I'll see you at the cottage," he said.

"At the cottage," she repeated. "Be careful."

"You, too."

Not at all happy, he pulled his backpack from the back seat and started across the lot, hoping against hope that he was doing the right thing.

Kari stayed where she was, watching as Alex wove his way among the lines of parked cars. She had wondered if he would actually stick with the plan. For a while there, it had definitely been touch and go. But in the end, she'd gotten her way by standing firm, even though she would have just as soon never come face-to-face with Brandon Selby again.

Had Alex absolutely refused to let her go back to the stable, as she suspected he'd been on the verge of doing, she probably would have given in. She wasn't nearly as brave as she'd wanted him to believe. But running away of her own volition was one thing she just couldn't countenance.

With Alex nearby, she wouldn't be in any real danger. At least not as long as she avoided being alone with Brandon. She would be just fine. She would be.

Glancing at her watch, Kari saw that it was time for her to head inside the terminal. Since Brandon knew she had her car at the airport, she doubted he would be there to meet her, and luckily, as she scanned the gate area, she saw that he wasn't.

The plane landed a few minutes late, and she easily blended into the crowd of disembarking passengers, walking with them to the baggage-claim area just as she had done on Monday. Standing off to one side, she recalled how completely she had been fooled—and frightened—by Alex's bizarre disguise.

Now even a momentary glimpse of him—weird glasses, stringy black hair and all—would have been reassuring. She had gotten so used to having him around over the past few days that she felt rather lost without him.

As the first pieces of luggage tumbled onto the carousel, she turned and walked to the exit, her departure paced exactly as Alex had instructed. Outside she noticed that the sun had dipped toward the horizon. By the time she arrived at the stable, it would be almost dark.

But Alex would be there waiting for her, she reminded herself. Within shouting distance, he'd said. Even if she couldn't actually see him. Just as he had been a year ago.

She paid the parking attendant, then pulled onto the roadway, smiling to herself. Alex had come close to dying, and then he'd come to see her. Whether or not he ever said the words aloud, that was enough to prove to her that he really did care for her. Now all she had to do was convince him the feeling was mutual.

She hadn't yet told him that she loved him. Not in so many words. She wasn't sure he was ready to believe her yet. But she'd had a lot of fun showing him, and unless she was mistaken, so had he.

He'd grown less and less hesitant with her, and though she realized he was still holding a part of himself back, she couldn't help but believe that she had put at least some of his doubts to rest.

All too soon, the sign for the turnoff to Selby Stables appeared. Following the road, Kari remembered the times, now long past, when she had looked forward to returning there. Now she could only wonder how she'd been so naive.

Awed by Brandon's accomplishments as a rider and a trainer, she had made allowances for his querulous nature, often letting him treat her like dirt. But not anymore. She'd lost all respect for him. Unfortunately, she couldn't afford to let him know it. Not yet. But one day soon...

As Brandon's two-story, white clapboard house came into view, Kari noticed the lights were on in several rooms. Half a dozen cars were also parked along the curve of the drive-way in front.

What in the world was going on? she wondered.

Then, with a sinking feeling in the pit of her stomach, she remembered the dinner party Brandon had decided to give in honor of a fellow ex-Olympian in town for a week-long dressage clinic. He had asked her to act as his hostess and she had agreed, then promptly forgotten all about it.

He'd probably expected her to take an earlier flight in order to get back in time. But she'd been so preoccupied, she hadn't given it a thought. Nor had she mentioned it in the message she'd left on his answering machine. No wonder he hadn't tried to reach her at Devlin's last night. He must have been furious. More than likely, he still was.

She would have liked to slink off to her cottage, but she knew that would only make bad matters worse. An apology was in order, and one offered within his guests' hearing might pacify him somewhat. He loved having his employees grovel at his feet in front of an audience. She only hoped he wouldn't be too obnoxious about it. She didn't want Alex going off in her defense like a loaded gun. Then the jig would most certainly be up.

She stood on the front porch, rang the bell and waited like the supplicant she had to pretend to be. Not surprisingly, Brandon took his time answering the door, and as she fully expected, several of his guests were crowded into the entryway expectantly when he finally did.

"Ah, you're back. Better late than never, I suppose," he drawled, his smile slight as he eyed her angrily.

Dressed in tailored slacks and a silk shirt, he looked as elegant as ever. And as insidious as she now knew him to be.

"I'm really sorry, Brandon," she apologized hastily. "I completely forgot about the party. Otherwise I would have tried to catch an earlier flight."

"Considering how ill your sister-in-law insisted you were, that's understandable," he replied, his seeming beneficence not for her benefit, but for that of his guests. "Although you look well enough now."

"I'm feeling much better, thank you."

"I'd invite you to join us, but I imagine you're rather tired after your long journey. And, of course, you are rather rumpled," he sneered. "We'll have to make our announcement another time, won't we?"

"Yes," she agreed, barely resisting the urge to cower ignobly.

"I assume you'll be up to a workout in the morning, though. Say seven o'clock?"

"Of course."

"Don't be late."

"I won't," she muttered to the door quietly closed in her face.

Her cheeks burning with embarrassment, Kari walked back to her car. She had forgotten how adept Brandon was at making her feel insignificant. But he certainly hadn't wasted any time reminding her.

Shaking with anger and humiliation, she drove the mile to her cottage. Set back from the road in a small grove of trees, the little place called to her in a welcoming way.

Switching on lights, she walked through the tiny rooms, feeling at home. She'd painted and papered the walls to her taste, hung curtains on the windows and added furniture she'd bought and paid for herself.

Calming down considerably, she tossed her bags on the bedroom floor. Sure that a cup of hot tea would settle her nerves even more, she turned to go back to the kitchen and found Alex standing in the doorway. She stared at him for several seconds, the grim look on his face and the rigid lay of his shoulders leaving no doubt in her mind that he'd overheard her exchange with Brandon. Then, with a soft cry, she flew across the room and into his open arms.

"It's all right," he soothed. "I'm here now."

"Yes," she murmured, clinging to him. "Yes."

"Not as easy as you thought it would be, was it?"

She wanted to say she hadn't thought it would be easy at all. But that wasn't completely true. She had been sure she could handle whatever Brandon chose to dish out. Now she knew she had been wrong.

"No." She sighed and rubbed her cheek against Alex's chest, taking comfort in the warmth of his body, the steady beating of his heart, the gentle caress of his hands on her back.

"Want to call it quits? Just say the word, and we're out of here."

She was tempted, so very tempted, to say yes.

After working for Brandon only a few weeks, she had realized that she never wanted him as an enemy. He had let her know that he could ruin her career with a few casual comments if he chose, and there would be nothing she could say or do to stop him.

He had been so sure of himself, and with good reason. Riding on past accomplishments—literally as well as figuratively—he had set himself up in a position of power, and no one, including her, had ever dared to challenge him.

Now she finally had a chance to prove he was nothing more than a common criminal. A once-in-a-lifetime chance she had to take for her own peace of mind.

"No." She sighed again.

"Well, then, I'd better change the locks on your doors."

Putting his hands on her shoulders, Alex eased away from her. He met her gaze for a moment, bent and kissed her cheek, then picked up his backpack.

"I was just going to make some hot tea. Want a cup, too?"

"Sounds good," he agreed.

She ended up making grilled cheese sandwiches, also, using the half loaf of bread she found in the freezer and the block of cheddar cheese in the refrigerator. They ate after Alex finished installing the new locks. Then they went to bed, but not to sleep. Not for a very long, very loving time.

Chapter 10

Late Tuesday afternoon, Alex stood in the shadows just outside the barn at Selby Stables, watching as the filly Kari rode circled the perimeter of the outdoor arena yet again. Under Selby's critical eye, she had been working the skittish young horse for well over an hour, coaxing her to take progressively higher jumps despite the animal's tendency to balk when first presented with something new.

Alex realized that Selby was pushing both Kari and the horse, but there was nothing he could do about it. Since Sunday, he'd had to stand by silently while Kari willingly submitted to her employer's ceaseless demands.

Just doing her job as she'd always done, she had insisted when he'd voiced his concern. And if Selby expected more than usual from her, it was only right, since she had been away for a week.

Alex wasn't so sure about that. The more he saw Selby in action, the more he began to think the man was driving Kari so hard because he wanted to see her get hurt. She had forgotten his little dinner party, and Alex was afraid that to Brandon's way of thinking, she deserved to be punished.

She had put in twelve-hour days Sunday and Monday, and was already well on her way to doing the same today. Granted, she was strong and healthy, but she wouldn't be able to keep up with such a punitive schedule indefinitely. Which was why Alex had called Kevin Wyatt earlier that afternoon with an ultimatum—either Raymond Fairchild met with Selby within the next twenty-four hours or all bets were off.

Wyatt hadn't been enthusiastic about changing his original timetable. But after Alex reminded him of what had happened to Amanda Holcomb, he had finally agreed to push forward.

Out in the arena, Kari was guiding the horse to the first of a series of five jumps. She rode with a grace and confidence that made Alex smile with pride as well as pleasure. She was good, really good. Not only with the horses, but also with the kids she taught so patiently, and with their parents, as well. She would have no trouble at all finding another job. Any stable owner in his right mind would hire her in a minute.

Or she could easily start her own business. He had the perfect place—a place he would gladly allow her to use with no strings attached. He could also loan her the money she would need to fill the barn with horses. Knowing she was there, making a life for herself, would be almost as satisfying for him as if they were there, making a life together.

Much as he wanted to believe that would be possible, he knew better. Once Selby was behind bars, she would be able to think straight again, and what he had told her about himself would finally begin to sink in. Then, wisely, she wouldn't want anything more to do with him, and he wouldn't blame her. He'd go away and stay away, as he had known all along he would have to do eventually.

The filly took all five jumps without hesitation. Unfortunately, however, she knocked down the top pole on the last of them. Slapping his boot with his riding crop, Selby strode toward Kari. Still mounted, she watched him approach, her shoulders slumping as he stopped to replace the pole.

Though too far away to hear all of what he had to say, Alex caught enough to know Brandon was berating her for her lack of concentration as well as her sloppy riding. Wordlessly, she heard him out, then nodded when he ordered her to go around again.

Straightening in her saddle despite her all-too-obvious exhaustion, Kari urged the horse into a canter. Hands clenched at his sides, Alex held his breath, willing her to hang on. To his relief, the filly jumped flawlessly. That should have been a good way to end the session as far as Alex was concerned. But for Kari's reward, Selby raised the poles another foot and instructed her to ride on.

She obeyed, and as had happened twice already, the filly balked at the added height. This time, however, Kari flew out of the saddle, sailing head over heels and landing flat on her back.

Alex had seen her fall often enough in the past, but never quite so hard. When she lay still, making no attempt to get up, panic zinged through him. Without thinking, he ran toward the arena, slipped under the fence and knelt beside her.

"What the hell do you think you're doing, you greasy little bastard?" Selby bellowed from where he lounged against a railing. "Get away from her."

Ignoring him, Alex touched Kari on the shoulder, whispering her name. She opened her eyes and stared at him in momentary confusion, then pushed up on her elbows.

"Do what he says," she muttered.

"Not until I'm sure you're all right."

"I'm fine," she assured him, though she didn't look it. Her face was deadly white, her eyes shadowed with pain. "I just had the wind knocked out of me. Now, get away from me or he'll fire you."

Reluctantly, Alex stood and crossed to the horse, gentling it with a few words as Kari got to her feet and brushed the dirt off her riding pants.

"Give Ms. Gray the reins and go back to work," Selby said. Then he turned to Kari with a sneer. "Try to pay attention to what you're doing, will you? Otherwise we're going to be out here all night."

With a brief, cautioning glance at Alex, Kari took the reins and swung into the saddle, a barely audible groan the only indication of how much she must be hurting.

"Please, do as he says, Alex," she murmured as she edged the filly past him.

He was on the verge of going after her, ready to haul her off the horse forcibly if need be, when the sound of a car coming up the driveway caught everyone's attention. A shiny silver Mercedes pulled to a stop near the house, and a dapper man dressed in a tailored suit stepped out and started toward them.

"Ah, Selby," he said. "Just the man I need to see. I hope you'll be able to fit me into your busy schedule."

"Of course, Mr. Fairchild. I'll be right with you," Selby replied. Turning to Kari, he waved a hand dismissively. "I suppose that will have to be all for today. But I want you on her again first thing in the morning."

As the two men walked toward the house, Alex moved to the filly's side, glancing up at Kari. "I'll put her up for you," he offered.

"Not yet." Gathering the reins, she urged the horse into a trot. All too aware what she had in mind, Alex started after her. She looked back at him, her chin tipped up at a reckless angle, and added, "Stay out of my way."

Heeding her warning, Alex stood off to one side as the filly relaxed into a steady canter. Her mouth set in a grim line, Kari took the horse over first one jump, then another and another, until they'd cleared all five without a single mishap. Then she trotted over to him, slid out of the saddle and tossed him the reins as if he really were a stable hand.

"Cool her down for me, will you?"

"Sí, Señorita," he growled as she limped off.

What he really wanted to do was shake her for scaring him half to death. But on the off chance that their employer was watching, he led the filly back to the barn and set about doing as he'd been told.

He understood why Kari had taken the horse over the jumps. He also knew that under normal circumstances he would have had no right to try to stop her. But she was in the midst of a dangerous situation. And until Brandon Selby was completely out of the picture, she was going to have to realize that the minor risks she was used to taking on a daily basis could easily become much more deadly.

By the time he finished with the horse and did his share of the evening chores it was almost dark, and Raymond Fairchild was gone. He had stayed almost two hours. Out in one of the paddocks when he'd left, Alex had glimpsed him exchanging a businesslike handshake with Selby before he'd climbed into his car. Alex could only hope that meant Selby had taken the bait.

As he had the previous night, Alex went to the bunkhouse—actually a long, low shack divided into six small, airless rooms furnished with little more than cots—where he and the other three stable hands were allowed to live rent free. He hung around for a while, keeping to himself, while the others took turns using the one shabby bathroom and the tiny kitchen. Then, as they settled into their rooms for the night, he drifted off into the shadows.

He made his way to Kari's cottage via a path he'd come across in the woods. She'd left the light burning above the kitchen sink, but otherwise the place was dark. Worried that she might be more badly hurt than she'd let on, he went in search of her. He found her in the bedroom, wrapped in a light cotton robe, lying still and silent on her bed.

"Alex?" She stirred as he sat down beside her, the mattress shifting under his weight.

"Sí, Señorita."

"I'm sorry I was such a witch."

"De nada," he assured her, using the Spanish words for "it's nothing." Then he added, "How are you feeling?"

"Not too good. I soaked in the tub for a while, but I'm so sore. I haven't been tossed like that in a long time."

"Got any liniment around?"

"I thought you'd never ask." She pushed up on one elbow, switched on the lamp and gestured toward the nightstand. "Right there," she said, then flopped down again with a groan.

"Ah, the good stuff." He eyed the bottle with approval, knowing from experience that the concoction it contained would ease her aches considerably. "Just let me get cleaned up and I'll give you a rubdown like you've never had before."

In the bathroom he peeled off the black wig and scraggly beard, removed his contact lenses, shucked his dirty jeans and chambray shirt, then showered quickly. Dressed in khaki shorts and a white T-shirt, he returned to the bedroom to find Kari dozing. He hated to disturb her, but unless he worked some of the soreness out of her muscles now, she'd be in bad shape in the morning.

"Come on, love, slip out of your robe and roll onto your stomach," he said, sitting down beside her again.

Used to being around him without any clothes on, she did as he asked, displaying not the slightest shyness. Stretched out on the bed, she looked so damned inviting that he couldn't stop himself from bending over and nuzzling her neck. She sighed and murmured his name, shifted toward him, then winced.

Mentally cursing himself for even thinking of making love to her when she was so obviously in pain, he sat back and reached for the liniment.

"Where do you want me to start?" he asked, pouring a generous measure of the menthol-scented lotion into the palm of his hand.

"Shoulders," she instructed. "Then down the backs of my legs."

Working slowly from her shoulders to her ankles, Alex massaged the liniment into her muscles as she lay quietly, her face buried in a pillow.

When he finally finished, she turned to look at him, an odd light in her sleepy eyes. "You have magic hands."

"Does that mean you're feeling better?"

"Much better." Smiling, she sat up. "Thanks."

"You're welcome." He held out her robe so she could slip into it more easily. "Now, about that little stunt you pulled out in the arena—"

"What little stunt?" she demanded, interrupting him indignantly.

"Taking those last jumps when you were not only in pain, but also on the edge of exhaustion, for no other reason than to ease your hurt pride. I know all about getting back in the saddle after a fall, but Selby has been running you ragged for three days now. If you keep playing into his hands by letting him get to you with his criticism, you're going to end up like Amanda Holcomb."

She looked as if she was about to argue with him, then seemed to think better of it. Twisting her hands together in her lap, she lowered her gaze.

"You're right," she admitted after several moments of silence. "It was a dumb thing to do. But he made me so mad."

"I know. But you can't afford to let your emotions get the better of you. Not if you want to stay alive. We're dealing with a ruthless bastard who knows he has a hell of a lot to lose if he's found out. And there's a good chance he suspects you're aware of what he's been doing."

Alex wished there were some way he could take the sting out of his words. Yet he had to get his point across. Otherwise she could end up saying or doing something without thinking, and endanger herself even more.

"I'll try to do better," she vowed in a small voice.

"Has he said anything more to you about his marriage proposal?"

"Not since he made that comment Saturday night about postponing our announcement." She crossed her arms over her chest and shivered as if she'd caught a sudden chill. "But that suits me just fine. He'd send me packing if I said no, and I don't think I could force myself to say yes even if it meant he'd end up getting away with murder." Looking away, she shivered again. "The thought of having him put his hands on me the way he would if I agreed to marry him makes me sick."

Shifting so that he sat with his back against the headboard, as she did, Alex drew her into his arms. Though he understood exactly how she felt, he was concerned that Selby hadn't brought the subject up again.

He might not have mentioned it as part of her punishment, thus hoping to keep her off balance and uncertain. Or, more disturbing, he could have abandoned his plan to tighten his supposed hold on her through marriage in favor of simply getting rid her as he could very well have done to Amanda Holcomb.

"With luck, we won't have to worry about that happening," Alex said, trying to reassure himself as much as her. "There's a good chance your Mr. Fairchild gave him something else to think about this evening."

"You mean arranging for his daughter's horse to have an accident?" Kari asked.

"I saw Selby and Fairchild shaking hands as if they'd agreed on something. My guess is that's it."

"I didn't think Mr. Fairchild was supposed to approach Brandon until Wednesday or Thursday."

"I called Wyatt early this afternoon and told him things were getting kind of dicey around here," Alex explained. "He agreed we'd better step up our timetable a bit."

"I'm surprised he hasn't called—"

The ring of the telephone on the nightstand cut off Kari's comment. Obviously on edge, she flinched, then tensed against him.

"That's probably Wyatt now, but you'd better answer it, just in case it's your boss."

She lifted the receiver and murmured a tentative greeting, then relaxed noticeably as she listened to whatever the caller had to say.

"He's right here," she said at last, a smile lighting her face. "I'll put him on." She offered Alex the receiver, adding, "It's Kevin."

"Yeah, Wyatt, what's going on?"

"Selby agreed to take care of the problem with Fairchild's horse for a nice, hefty fee," the agent replied.

"You got it on tape?"

"We did. Fairchild was wearing a wire. But Selby was careful about how he worded his offer. He didn't say anything about destroying the animal. And we couldn't have Fairchild come right out and ask him to do it. Selby could claim entrapment. All Fairchild could do was bemoan the fact that he hadn't been able to sell the horse, then ask Selby if he had any alternatives in mind."

"So you have to catch him in the act."

"I'm starting our stakeout of the barn tonight. In fact, my partner should be in place already. I sent him on ahead so we'd be ready if Selby played along as we hoped he would."

"What about you?"

"We're rotating shifts. I'll be there tomorrow night."

"Well, watch your back," Alex advised. "Selby is a sly son of a bitch. If he suspects he's been set up, he's going to be on the alert. And he's going to be out for blood."

"Then that will make two of us," Wyatt replied matter-of-factly.

Kari had told him about the true nature of Kevin Wyatt's relationship with Amanda Holcomb, so Alex understood exactly where the FBI agent was coming from.

"We'll try to maintain the status quo around here as long as we can," Alex said. "But the sooner you get what you need to put Selby away, the better."

"How's your lady holding up?" Wyatt asked.

"As well as can be expected."

"You're a lucky man."

"I know," Alex agreed.

"Stay in touch," Wyatt said by way of farewell.

"Will do."

As Alex cradled the receiver, Kari looked up at him questioningly.

"Did Brandon agree to get rid of Dover?"

"Yes."

She sighed and rubbed her cheek against his shoulder. "Just like we thought he would."

"Yes."

"So, it's almost over."

"Almost."

"I'll be so glad when it is." She slipped her hand under his T-shirt and stroked his belly teasingly with her fingertips.

"Me, too," he agreed. She would want to be done with him then. But he would gladly pay that price if it meant she would finally be safe.

She slid her hand down to the waistband of his shorts and popped the snap.

"Kari—" He caught her hand as she reached for his zipper.

"Yes, Alex?" she asked innocently, her eyes filled with mischief.

"It's almost midnight. It you don't get some rest, you're not going to be worth a damn tomorrow morning."

"All right, then," she murmured, gliding one smooth, bare leg between his until her knee nudged him in a way he found impossible to ignore. "Rock me to sleep."

He knew he should at least *try* to exhibit some self-control, especially after the fall she had taken. But he wanted her as much as she seemed to want him. And he doubted that would be the case much longer.

As if sensing he was on the verge of capitulating, she slipped off her robe, tossed it aside and stretched out on her side invitingly.

Groaning inwardly, Alex stripped out of his clothes, switched off the lamp and gathered her into his arms. She sighed quietly as she fit herself to him. Then, her hands tangled in his hair, she offered her mouth for him to kiss.

He feathered his lips over hers, tasting her as if for the first time. Then, ever so slowly, ever so gently, he did as she'd asked, soothing her with an ageless, intimate rhythm. The rhythm of a man loving his woman. Loving her deeply and completely. For now and for the always he knew better than to believe they would have.

The insistent, irritating buzz of the alarm clock on the nightstand brought Kari out of a deep, seemingly dreamless sleep at six Wednesday morning. With a weary sigh, she reached out and shut it off, then rolled tentatively onto her back.

She was alone in her bed, as she'd expected she would be. Though she had been too sound asleep to hear Alex stirring, she knew that he'd left her sometime in the wee hours before dawn. Disguised once again, he'd gone back to the bunkhouse to resume his position as low man on the stablehand totem pole.

As she had anticipated, Brandon had hired him with only the slightest urging from her since they were shorthanded as usual. And Alex, now posing as Manuel Ortega, had fit in with amazing ease, his demeanor that of a poor illegal immigrant willing to work hard for slave wages.

He hadn't seemed to have any trouble getting his work done while at the same time staying close to her. But Kari was seriously concerned that he'd drawn undue attention to himself by coming to her rescue yesterday afternoon.

Brandon hadn't liked his interference. Not at all. However, as Alex had said, he would more than likely have his mind on other, more important, things today.

As for her, she'd better get moving or she'd never make it to the barn by seven o'clock. She was already starting out the day with at least one black mark against her. Rousing Brandon's ire even more by being late would be downright foolhardy. She couldn't afford to ask for any more trouble. She was having a hard enough time keeping her emotions under control as it was.

She also had a full day ahead of her, so the sooner she got started, the better. She'd have to begin by riding Miss Molly under Brandon's harsh tutelage. Then she had two group lessons and three private lessons scheduled at various times from midmorning through late afternoon. After that, she could only imagine what Brandon might have in store for her. Probably another session on Miss Molly.

He was determined to start showing the filly in the fall, even though Kari doubted she would be ready for her owner to ride by then. But it wasn't her call. Of course, there was a good chance it wouldn't be Brandon's call, either, she reminded herself. Not if he was in jail. For the time being, however, she had no choice but to go along with whatever he dictated.

No longer able to put off getting out of bed, Kari eased herself into a sitting position, moving gingerly in deference to her aching muscles. She was stiff and sore, but thanks to Alex's tender ministrations, not debilitatingly so. A hot shower would help, and once she got moving, she knew she would loosen up even more.

Even taking time for the hearty breakfast she knew she'd need to keep her going, she managed to arrive at the barn a few minutes early. And a good thing, too. Brandon was already there, as well, exchanging greetings with several owners preparing for morning workouts themselves. She spoke to a couple of them on her way to the tack room to fetch her saddle. Then, catching a glimpse of Alex at the opposite end of the barn, busily filling a wheelbarrow with manure, she headed for Miss Molly's stall.

"Ah, Kari, darling," Brandon called out, starting toward her, a falsely cheerful smile on his face. "You certainly don't look any the worse for wear this morning."

"Just a little stiff," she acknowledged as she waited for him to join her.

"Well, you'll work that out once you're up and riding."

"Yes, of course," she agreed, forcing herself to return his smile. "I'll have Miss Molly ready to go in a few minutes."

"Actually, I'd rather you start working with Dover today," he said.

"Dover?" She regarded him with bewilderment. "Melissa Fairchild's horse?"

"Yes, Melissa Fairchild's horse. Her father came to see me yesterday. He wants the animal sold as soon as possible, but he's refusing to back off on his asking price. I thought we might garner some interest in him by showing him at a few Class A shows starting Saturday in Dallas."

"Saturday in Dallas?" She realized how dim-witted she must sound, yet she couldn't seem to help herself. Sending Dover to a Class A horse show on the spur of the moment made no sense at all. "But surely it's too late to enter him, isn't it?"

"I took care of that last night. A good friend of mine is on the committee. He was more than happy to add you to the roster for the advanced hunter-jumper class. I know the horse is a bit rusty. But you'll have several days to work with him."

She had *three* days, to be exact. Three days to get one of the most recalcitrant mounts she had ever come across ready to exhibit. She couldn't believe Brandon was serious. But evidently he was. Which left her more confused than ever.

Was showing Dover in Dallas what he'd had in mind when he told Raymond Fairchild he'd take care of his problem? Did he really believe someone would be so impressed with the gelding's performance that the person would offer to buy him on the spot? Or did he have something else in mind? Something much more nefarious?

Preparing the horse for a show might be some kind of cover, but for what? Kari could only hope Alex would have some idea, because she honestly did not have a clue.

"I'd better get busy, then," she replied, hoping she didn't sound as disconcerted as she felt.

"Yes, you'd better," Brandon agreed. Then he added smoothly, "Before you try to ride him, you might want to work him on the lunge line for a while to settle him down a bit."

Kari had a feeling it was going to take a lot more than a workout on the lunge line to remind the gelding of his manners. But she knew better than to say as much to Brandon.

After nodding her acquiescence, she turned and walked back to the tack room. Thankfully, Brandon hadn't indicated that he intended to supervise her sessions with the horse personally. For that at least she could be grateful. For the rest of it, however—

"What's going on?" Alex growled, joining her in the tack room.

"I'm not sure." She glanced at him warily. "Did Brandon see you come in here?"

"He's on his way back to the house."

"Good." She slung her saddle onto the rack, then selected a bridle, lunge line and buggy whip. "He wants me to ride Dover in a horse show in Dallas on Saturday."

"Did he say why?"

As Kari repeated what Brandon had told her, Alex listened, a frown furrowing his forehead.

"Does that make sense to you?" he asked when she'd finished.

"It's possible that someone might offer to buy the horse after seeing him at the show, but it's also highly improbable."

"That's what I would think," he agreed, then added, "I don't like it."

"Neither do I, but I don't see that I can do anything but go along with him and find out where it takes us. Either he's serious about trying to sell the horse, or he's using the show as a means to another kind of end," she said. "Though I can't imagine he'd attempt to do any fatal damage to the horse anywhere but here."

"I can't, either," Alex admitted. "Too many factors would be out of his control."

"Maybe Kevin will have an idea what he's up to."

"Maybe. I'll try to get in touch with him later and see what he thinks." He reached out and brushed her cheek with the back of his hand. "In the meantime, you be careful, okay? That horse is a real handful."

"You noticed that, huh?"

"Noticed, hell. He tried to kick my head in the other day."

"Don't worry. I can handle him. He likes women much better than men."

"For your sake, I certainly hope so," he said as he moved toward the open doorway. "See you later."

"Yes, later." She followed after him, keeping a discreet distance in case anyone should see them. "Think you'll be up to giving me another rubdown?"

"Want to make a habit of that, do you?"

"Oh, yes, definitely."

Wednesday, Thursday and Friday passed in a blur of frantic activity for Kari. Along with teaching her riding classes, she worked with Dover every spare chance she had, just as if she really was preparing for a horse show.

She simply couldn't believe that Brandon really intended for her to go Dallas. But neither could she or Alex or Kevin come up with another reason for his seeming charade.

Not only was he in a relatively good mood; he also seemed more than happy to allow her to work with Dover on her own, offering only occasional bits and pieces of advice. And he wasn't planning on going to Dallas with her, either.

Since the show wasn't scheduled to start until early Saturday evening, he had decided she could leave that morning. Driving the stable's Blazer, with one of the double-horse trailers in tow, she would arrive in more than enough time to be ready to ride in her class. Rather than make the return trip late that night, she would then stay at a motel, while Dover would be boarded at a local stable belonging to one of Brandon's associates.

She had traveled similarly to other shows, so there was nothing out of the ordinary about the arrangements he'd made for her. And the stable where Dover would stay was among the most reputable in the country. She doubted the horse would be in any danger there.

Still, Kari grew more and more uneasy with each passing day. Something about the whole situation just didn't feel right to her. But she couldn't for the life of her put her finger on what it was. Along with Alex and Kevin, she kept waiting—in vain—for Brandon to give himself away by some odd word or unexpected deed. But he remained annoyingly cool and composed.

By Friday night, when Alex finally joined her at the cottage, she had all but reached the end of her rope. Unless Brandon made some move to do away with Dover during the night, she would be heading for Dallas at seven the next morning.

Only the fact that Alex would be with her, albeit unknown to Brandon, kept her from panicking completely. He probably wouldn't have a job as a stable hand anymore after he turned up missing tomorrow. But he had absolutely refused to let her go to Dallas alone, vowing to find another way to stay close to her without arousing attention if Brandon hadn't made a move to destroy the horse by the time she returned on Sunday.

"All packed and ready to go?" he asked, sitting on the side of her bed and pulling off his boots.

He looked as worn-out as she felt, and with good reason. He had been working twelve- and fourteen-hour days at the stable, and although he'd gone to sleep at the same time she did each night, he'd been up again long before her alarm went off at six o'clock.

"Just about." She hung her formal riding habit in her garment bag, then sat beside him.

At first she had found having Manuel Ortega in her bedroom somewhat disconcerting. But she had gotten used to seeing Alex in disguise over the past few days.

"Good."

"What about you?"

"I've got most of my stuff together." Removing the black wig, he ran a hand through his matted hair, then stood and headed for the bathroom. "Something smells good."

"I found a carton of beef stew in the freezer. We can eat whenever you're ready."

He joined her in the kitchen not quite fifteen minutes later, looking like himself again, his blond curls damp from the shower. She glanced at him and smiled, then shifted the pot of stew from the oven to a trivet on the counter.

He came up behind her, wrapped his arms around her waist and pulled her back against him. "I've got an idea," he muttered, nibbling on her earlobe.

"After we eat," she admonished with a laugh, her stomach growling as she lifted the lid on the pot. "Much as I love you, right now I'm more interested in food."

When he went still, she realized what she'd said. Realized, too, that she was glad she finally had, even though the moment wasn't as romantic as she would have liked.

"Actually, I had something besides lovemaking in mind myself," he admitted.

"Oh, really? And what might that be?" she asked, turning to face him.

"I thought maybe we could hop in your car, drive down to Mexico, find a nice, quiet beach and drop out for a while," he replied all too seriously.

"Oh, Alex." She sighed and shook her head. "I can't."

"I know, but it was worth a try." He hugged her close for a moment, then stepped back. "I met up with Wyatt in the woods. He's going to have a man at the horse show as well as a man at the motel, and he'll be at the stable where Dover is supposed to stay. Just in case Selby tries something."

"Do you really think he will?"

"I don't know what I think anymore. But I can't quite believe that all he intends is for you to ride in that show tomorrow night."

"Neither can I."

"I checked to make sure the Blazer and the horse trailer were in good working order before I left the stable yard, and Wyatt is going to keep an eye on them tonight to make sure nobody tampers with them. However, there's no telling what we might run into once we leave here, so we're going to have be on the alert."

"Guess that means we'd better make an early night of it," she said, ladling beef stew into a bowl for him.

"Right," he agreed. "Dinner and then bed."

"Mmm, I like the sound of that."

"To sleep," he added sternly.

"Eventually..." Smiling, she sat down at the table and started to eat.

"Has anyone ever told you you're incorrigible?"

"Not that I can recall. But then, you do know how to bring out the best in me," she teased.

"And you know how to bring out the best in me, too," he said, his tone suddenly solemn as he reached for her hand.

"Yes, I do," she replied, clasping his hand as she met his gaze. "And don't you dare forget it."

"I won't."

She could only hope he meant it. Otherwise...

Otherwise she was afraid she would lose him to the demons of his past. Demons that still seemed to haunt his soul, no matter how she tried to banish them.

Chapter 11

The nights Alex had spent lying beside Kari in one bed or another, with the length of her body curled trustingly close to his, he had slept better than at any other time of his life that he could remember. But as Friday faded into Saturday, he found himself wide-awake, staring into the shadows, his thoughts racing as he tried to determine exactly what Brandon Selby had up his sleeve.

Alex had no doubt that Kari's trip to Dallas for the horse show was an elaborate ruse. Somehow, somewhere along the way, she was going to run into trouble. But from what quarter? Had Selby hired someone to ambush her? Or was he planning to waylay her on his own?

Alex would have thought he'd stick to what had worked for him before. But even Selby must have begun to realize he'd had more than the usual number of horses die while being boarded at his stable. Maybe he had decided it was worth the risk to take care of Fairchild's supposed problem somewhere far away from Selby Stables. And at the same time take care of his personal problem with Kari.

But how, damn it? How the hell was he planning to do it?

Alex was trained to expect the unexpected and be prepared to deal with the situation accordingly. But never before had he been faced with the possibility that a miscalculation on his part would cost the woman he loved her life.

Too restless to lie still any longer, Alex eased away from Kari, tucking the blanket up around her shoulders. He wanted her to get as much rest as possible. Which wasn't going to be as much as she would have gotten if he hadn't let her seduce him again with her tantalizing hands and her teasing mouth. He had no more willpower left where she was concerned. At least not when she was within touching distance.

He crossed to his backpack, pulled out jeans, a black T-shirt, running shoes and his nine-millimeter automatic pistol, then slipped into the bathroom to dress. Back in the bedroom again, he glanced at the clock on the nightstand; it was almost five o'clock.

He would have time to check in with Wyatt and take another look around the stable, but then he'd have to get back. He wanted to be with her when her alarm went off at six. That way he could choreograph his movements with hers to guarantee her ultimate safekeeping.

Tucking the automatic into the waistband of his jeans, he moved down the hallway, into the kitchen and out the back door. Following the path through the woods, he walked swiftly, yet silently toward the stable. He emerged near the bunkhouse, which was still bathed in darkness at that early hour, though the stable hands would probably be stirring within the next thirty minutes or so.

As he headed for the barn, he heard what sounded like an engine turning over, then the muted squish of tires moving slowly over grass. Realizing someone must be moving the Blazer and the horse trailer hooked to it, Alex broke into a run, rounded the side of the barn, then skidded to a halt in the shadows.

Several hundred yards away, the Blazer, lights out, eased onto the drive and continued toward the road, still moving very slowly. Though he couldn't be sure, he thought he'd glimpsed a horse's rump through the open upper half of the trailer door before it swung out of his range of vision. A dappled-gray rump that could only be Dover's.

Cursing under his breath, he sidled into the barn, intent on finding out what the hell was going on.

"Wyatt? Where are you?" he whispered, moving down the line of stalls. Around him, the horses shifted and snorted, acknowledging his presence, but he heard no response at all from the FBI agent. As he came to Dover's stall and saw that it was empty, he raised his voice and ordered, "Damn it, Wyatt, answer me now."

From the tack room came what sounded like a muffled groan. Drawing his weapon, Alex edged closer, halting just outside the doorway.

"Wyatt?" he said again.

"In here," the agent replied, his voice barely audible.

As Alex stepped into the tack room, he caught sight of Kevin Wyatt curled up on the floor. "Ah, hell," he muttered, kneeling beside him.

"The son of a bitch shot me...twice...in the back and...left me for dead," Wyatt said. "Lucky for me... wearing my vest."

"Damn lucky," Alex agreed with inexpressible relief as he eyed the bullet holes in the agent's shirt. "I'm guessing he was the one pulling away in the Blazer a few moments ago, too. I'm also guessing he has Dover in the trailer, since the horse's stall is empty."

"Don't know," Wyatt replied. "He was on me before I realized what was happening." He tried to sit up, then fell back with a moan. "Hurts like hell."

"Yeah, I know," Alex sympathized. "But you'll live." Standing again, he turned toward the doorway. "What do you think he's doing?"

"Beats me. Unless—"

"What?" Alex demanded.

"He could be setting up an accident, planning to run the Blazer off the road with the trailer in tow. But unless the police find someone dead in the driver's seat they're not going to buy it."

"Not *someone*. Kari," Alex stated, fear for her slicing through him.

He should have known. An accident before dawn, probably on some back road, orchestrated to look as if Kari had been driving. All Selby would have to do is knock her out, take her to that old river bridge a few miles away, put her in the driver's seat and send the Blazer careering down the embankment.

"There's a phone on the desk in the corner," Alex advised. "Think you can drag yourself over there and call for backup?"

"Yeah, sure."

"Tell them to ditch the lights and sirens," he said. "I don't want Selby spooked."

"Will do."

Breaking into a run, Alex shot out of the barn, headed for the woods and his shortcut to the cottage. Surely Selby would want to make it look as if Kari had left for the horse show just as she should have, only earlier. Which meant that he'd have to wait while she dressed.

As long as they were still at the cottage, Alex knew he'd be able to stop Selby with a minimum of risk to Kari. He could drop the bastard with a single shot from several hundred yards away if necessary. But once Selby had her in the Blazer, she would be in a hell of a lot more danger.

There was no telling how desperate he would be if he found himself cornered. And any kind of chase could, and probably would, all too easily end in a nasty crash that Kari might not survive.

"Take your time, love," he muttered as he swerved between the trees. "Please take your time."

Frowning, Kari sat up in bed, switched on the lamp and eyed her alarm clock quizzically. Five-fifteen. And if she wasn't mistaken, someone was knocking on her front door.

"Who on earth . . ." she grumbled, slipping into her robe and knotting the sash.

And where was Alex? she wondered as the knocking continued more insistently. Not in the cottage. Otherwise he would have already answered the door himself or come to advise her what to do.

Knowing him, he had probably gone to check on things one last time before they set out for Dallas. But surely he wasn't the one knocking at her door. He had a key, for heaven's sake.

She padded down the hallway, barefoot, paused to turn on the lamps in the living room as well as the porch light, then peered out the peephole in the door. Her heartbeat accelerated as she caught a glimpse of Brandon. What was he doing here at five-fifteen in the morning, immaculately dressed in slacks and a polo shirt, hands tucked casually in his pockets?

Actually, she wasn't sure she wanted to know. But she couldn't pretend she wasn't there. She'd just turned on all the lights. She'd played her part all week, acting just like the conscientious employee she'd always been. To do otherwise now would surely start alarm bells ringing in his head. And after all the groundwork they'd laid to catch him in a criminal act, she didn't want to do anything now that might ultimately arouse his suspicions.

His patience seeming to wear thin, Brandon raised his hand to knock yet again. Hoping she was doing the right thing, Kari turned the lock and opened the door.

"Brandon?" She met his gaze questioningly, then glanced past him and saw the Blazer with the trailer attached parked on the road in front of the cottage. "I thought we agreed I'd leave at seven o'clock and travel on my own."

"There's been a slight change of plan."

He took a step toward her, but instinctively she stood her ground. She didn't want him in her cottage. Not at all.

"What kind of change?" she asked, wishing she hadn't opened the door quite so wide.

"Why don't we go inside and I'll explain," he suggested.

Something in his tone made the hairs on the back of her neck stand up. "I'd rather you just tell me here."

"Well, that's too bad, Kari, darling. I'd prefer to tell you inside. So please, move out of my way," he ordered, drawing his hand from his pocket and pointing the deadly looking .38 he held at her chest. *"Now."*

For one long moment, Kari stared at the gun he held, then slowly she backed up, allowing him to enter.

"Brandon, what—"

"All in good time, my dear." He closed the door and locked it, then gestured toward the hallway. "I believe your bedroom is that way, isn't it?"

A sick feeling in the pit of her stomach, she nodded.

"Lead on, then. Lead on."

This couldn't be happening. Brandon with a gun, ordering her into her bedroom. What could he possibly mean to do to her? Rape her first, then kill her? And where on earth was Alex? Already lying dead somewhere, a bullet from Brandon's gun buried in his body? He would have never let Brandon get this close to her if there had been any way he could stop him. And Kevin—had Brandon killed him, too?

As she walked down the hallway, despair ate at her soul. He wouldn't get away with it. Wouldn't get away with killing them. Too many people were wise to him now. But that wouldn't bring Alex and Kevin back. If they really were dead, she reminded herself, realizing she was on the verge of hysterics.

She halted just inside the doorway, refusing to go anywhere near the bed unless forced to do so. Arms crossed over her chest, she turned to face him, eyeing him challengingly despite the fine trembling of her body.

"Now what?" she asked.

"Now you get dressed just as you planned for your little trip to Dallas."

He lounged against the door frame, holding the gun on her, an amused look on his face. The bastard was enjoying himself and wanted her to know it.

"All right." She picked up the underwear, jeans and shirt she'd left on the chair the night before and started toward the bathroom.

"Oh, no, not in there. Here—where I can keep an eye on you."

Slowly Kari moved back to the chair, then tossed her clothes down. Turning so that she faced away from him, she fumbled with the knot she'd tied in the sash of her robe. She was almost grateful for the way her hands shook. The more time she managed to take getting dressed, the longer they would be in the cottage. And the longer they were in the cottage, the more chance there was that someone would come to her rescue.

Alex, oh, Alex, please hurry...

She could not, *would not,* believe that he was dead. Otherwise—

"Stop dawdling," Brandon commanded in an irritable tone.

"I'm not," she retorted, finally loosening the sash.

She opened her robe, but left it on as she stepped into her underwear. Then, refusing to show any more of herself to him than was absolutely necessary, she reached for her jeans.

She had no doubt that he intended to kill her. But as she balanced first on one leg, then the other to slip on her jeans, she realized that he couldn't afford to do so here in her cottage. Otherwise he would have done so already.

Whatever he had planned for her—and for Dover, she thought, remembering that she'd seen the Blazer and trailer parked out front—would occur somewhere else. Somewhere that Brandon could make her demise as well as the horse's appear to be an accident.

She could almost hear him now, blaming her for leaving early, then driving recklessly in her supposed haste to get to Dallas for some reason she had no doubt he'd already manufactured.

The bastard. He thought he was so clever, and so far, he had been. But this time he would be caught. He would be.

Finally forced to shed her robe so she could put on her bra and white sleeveless shirt, Kari took a deep breath, then let the garment slide off her shoulders. All he would be able to see from where he stood was her bare back, but that was still too much for her peace of mind.

As she reached for her bra, she heard him shift behind her. Glancing over her shoulder, she saw that he'd moved a little farther into the bedroom and was now watching her with a lascivious glint in his dark eyes.

"Too bad you couldn't mind your own business, Kari, darling. I believe you could have been a satisfyingly submissive wife once I taught you to come to heel. But you had to let your curiosity get the better of you after Moonwalker's unfortunate...accident. And then you had to dally over accepting my proposal."

Kari wanted to deny his accusations, but she knew it was much too late for that. Even if she hadn't been aware of what he'd been doing, he had made sure she knew now. There was no way he could back off, even if he wanted to. Not after holding her at gunpoint while all but admitting he had arranged for Moonwalker to suffer an irreparable injury.

All she could do was take it from there and maybe buy herself a little more time by playing up to his ego.

"So Moonwalker *was* destroyed intentionally," she said. Surprised at how calm she sounded, she finished fastening the buttons on her shirt and tucked it into her jeans. "But why, Brandon?" Feigning puzzlement, she sat on the chair and unrolled a pair of socks.

"For the same reason I destroyed all the others—my benefit. A cut of the insurance money in some cases, and as a means to maintain my reputation in others."

"What did you do to Moonwalker?"

"Smashed his foreleg with a crowbar, then turned him loose so it would look as if he'd fallen," he stated with a vicious kind of pride.

Feeling ill, Kari stared at the socks she held, then bent to slip them on her feet.

"What about the other horses?" she asked. "I thought they all died of colic. How did you manage that?"

"They only looked as if they had," Brandon said, gloating. "In reality, they were electrocuted."

"Electrocuted?" She stared at him askance. "But how?"

"Quite simply, my dear. I used an industrial-size extension cord and a pair of alligator clips. I attached one clip to the horse's ear and another to his anus, plugged in the cord, and *voilà*. The poor things dropped dead so fast I doubt they felt any pain at all. There weren't any telltale signs, either. In fact, from all appearances, they looked like they'd died of colic, at least enough to convince the veterinarians who were called to the stable afterward to verify their deaths."

Now truly sickened, Kari swallowed hard as she reached for her sneakers. He was deranged. He had to be. Otherwise how could he boast with such equanimity about killing all those horses?

"And now you're going to get rid of Dover and me," she murmured.

"Yes, indeed I am," he replied. "Two for the price of one, so to speak. Fairchild was tired of paying for the horse's upkeep. He offered me a... bonus if I found a way to take the animal off his hands. I suppose he finally heard about my little service from one of the other owners I've helped. And as I said, you became something of a liability when you made such a fuss about Moonwalker.

"You're a smart woman, Kari. Too smart for your own good. Just like Amanda Holcomb. And too cautious. You should have accepted my proposal when you had the chance, instead of running like a scared rabbit. You would have saved us both a lot of trouble. Now it's too late." He glanced at his watch, then waved the gun at her. "Finish tying your shoes, gather up your things and let's go. I want to be gone before the stable hands find your friend in the barn."

"My friend?" Sure that her worst fear was about to be realized, she stared at him, her heart pounding as she waited for him to elaborate.

"Well, I'm only *supposing* the man I found trespassing in the barn was a friend of yours. Someone you asked to spy on me, I presume. Unfortunately, I had to shoot him, but there was no time to move his body. So the stable hands will find him and the police will be called, but I'll be gone. Off to watch my protégée ride at the show in Dallas. Too bad she won't make it there after all. And too bad about that fellow in the barn. Of course, the police will investigate, but I imagine we'll never know how he came to be there with two bullets in his back." He glanced at his watch again. "Come along, now. Time's a-wasting."

Moving woodenly, Kari stood, crossed to the closet door and took down her garment bag.

"All right, I'm ready to go."

"Get your purse, too," Brandon instructed, gesturing toward her dresser with his gun. "We wouldn't want anyone to wonder why you drove off without it."

Trying to assimilate what he'd just told her, Kari did as he said. He had shot a man in the barn and left him for dead. *One* man. Which meant that either Alex or Kevin could be nearby. Maybe hiding somewhere outside, waiting for them to leave the cottage.

Oh, please . . . oh, please . . . oh, please . . .

She didn't want to believe that either of them was dead. Did not want to believe that at all. Nor did she want to die herself. Not at the hands of Brandon Selby. But time was running out for her, she admitted as she walked down the hallway. Once Brandon got her to the Blazer, he would probably knock her out. Then she would be completely at his mercy.

Her last hope was to try to get away from him as they crossed the front yard. She could make a run for it and pray that he didn't shoot her.

Could except for the fact that he grasped her by the upper arm, his fingers biting cruelly into her flesh, as they entered the living room.

"Open the door and walk down to the Blazer," he ordered. "And don't try to fight me or I'll hit you . . . hard."

"You're going to do that anyway, aren't you?" she retorted.

"Yes, of course, but when I do it will be entirely up to you."

Nudging up against her, he shoved her forward, pulling the door shut as they stepped onto the front porch.

The bastard was so close to her. So damned close. But he had his .38 lowered to his side. Even if he pulled the trigger as a reflex, the bullet wouldn't hit Kari. Which meant it was now or never, Alex thought as he crept through the shadows thrown by the overgrown shrubbery planted haphazardly around the cottage.

He couldn't allow Selby to move her out of the glow of the porch light into the darkness of the front yard. Unless he could see both of them clearly, as he was able to at that moment, he couldn't risk taking a shot.

But now...now...

Using both hands to hold his automatic steady, he rose fluidly from his crouch and took aim.

"Going somewhere, Selby?" he asked, his voice cracking across the lawn like a whip.

Startled, Brandon turned and pointed his .38 at him as Alex had intended. At the same instant, Kari jerked free of his hold on her. His line of fire unimpeded, Alex squeezed the trigger.

Selby grunted. Then, his eyes widening in surprise, he stumbled backward, his .38 falling to the porch as he pawed ineffectually at the red stain blossoming across the upper left side of his chest. A moment later he collapsed in a heap and lay still.

As if frozen where she stood, Kari stared at Selby and whimpered, her garment bag and purse sliding out of her hands.

Though keeping his eyes on Selby, Alex lowered his weapon and moved toward her slowly.

"It's all right, love," he soothed. "It's all over now."

She jerked again, then turned her head and stared at him, a bewildered look on her face.

"Alex?" she murmured as he stepped onto the porch and slid an arm around her waist. "He...he didn't shoot you?"

"No," he assured her.

"But then, Kevin..." she began, her voice filled with anguish. "Kevin is—"

"Going to be awfully sore for a while, but otherwise he's just fine. He was wearing his vest."

"Oh." She blinked once, sighed softly, then fainted dead away.

Lifting her into his arms, Alex spared a last glance at Brandon Selby, then started down the steps. In the distance, he heard the sound of a car creeping up the road. The police, more than likely. Just in time to mop up.

He hoped there would be an ambulance not far behind, as well. Before anyone started asking questions, both Kari and Kevin Wyatt were going to need medical attention. And Alex intended to see that they got it.

As for Selby...it was too late for him. Though Alex took no pleasure in having killed the man, he had to admit he was relieved that Brandon Selby would never pose a threat to Kari or anyone else again.

By the time Kari and Kevin were released from the hospital, and the local police as well as Kevin's superiors at the FBI had finished taking everyone's statement, it was early evening. Kevin gladly accepted a ride home from a fellow agent, leaving Alex and Kari alone at last.

"Now what?" she asked as they walked to her car.

"Now we go back to my place. Unless you don't feel up to the drive." Though she looked exhausted, he didn't really want to take her to a hotel tonight. He wanted to take her home.

"I don't mind the drive. But maybe we ought to stop by the stable first. I'd really like to check on the horses."

"All taken care of," he assured her as he opened the car door for her. "The police have notified all the owners of Selby's death, and a member of the mounted patrol will be on hand to look after the horses until other arrangements can be made."

"That's good to know." With a weary sigh, she slid into the passenger seat and fastened her seat belt.

As he walked around to the driver's side, Alex couldn't think of another person—except maybe Laura—who would be as conscientious as Kari. After going through the kind of trauma she had that day, anyone else would have walked away from Selby Stables without a backward glance.

His heart swelling with love for her, Alex climbed behind the wheel and started the engine. She was such a good person. Too good for the likes of him.

"What did my brother say when you called him?" she asked, turning to look at him as he pulled onto the street.

"A lot of things I'd really rather not repeat," he admitted, smiling as he glanced at her. "Suffice it to say, he was glad to hear you weren't hurt. Laura, too." He hesitated, focusing his attention on the road again, then added, "She wants us to come for a visit as soon as possible. She says she wants to see for herself that we're both all right."

"Mmm, I'd like that," Kari said, not batting an eye at his use of the word *us,* as if it were natural for them to be coupled so. "But I think I'm going to need a few days to recuperate first."

"Yeah, I think so, too," he agreed as she tipped her head against the headrest and closed her eyes.

Though she seemed to have bounced back from the emotional turmoil she'd suffered that morning, Alex knew she was still in a mild state of shock. She had been threatened with death, then she had watched a man die. As if that hadn't been enough for one day, she had spent the past twelve hours recounting the experience over and over again for one law-enforcement official after another. That she hadn't indulged in a bout of the screaming meemies was a testament to her strength and courage.

Gradually, over the next few days, the horror of all that she had witnessed would begin to fade. And while she would probably never forget what had happened that morning, the knowledge that she had survived, relatively unharmed, would aid in her recovery. She was safe now. Safe at last. Once she realized that, she'd be just fine.

But then, of course, she wouldn't need him anymore. At least not in the way she had during the past two weeks when her life had been in danger. Perhaps not in any way at all.

She had seen for herself what he was capable of doing. He had killed a man before her very eyes. That he had done so to save her life might be hard for her to keep in mind when she had a chance to think dispassionately about the kind of past he'd had.

Her loving acceptance of him had taught him to believe in his own basic decency. But now he wondered if she would still be able to believe in it herself.

Kari dozed off twice during the long drive, starting awake with a soft cry both times. After that, she seemed content to stare out the window in silence, which was also fine with Alex. At one point, however, she reached out and clasped his hand. Glad she could still turn to him for comfort, he wove his fingers through hers. He didn't let go until he was forced to get out and open the gate at the entrance to his property.

At the house he tried to get her to eat something, but she only nibbled on the grilled cheese sandwich and sipped the tomato soup he set in front of her. Not trusting her to stay upright in the shower on her own, he joined her under the steaming spray, then quickly toweled her dry and carried her to his bed.

He would have left her then, but she clung to him with surprising strength, and when she awoke screaming a short time later, he was glad that he'd stayed. He gave her one of the sleeping pills the doctor at the hospital had prescribed for her, and held her as she drifted off again, leaving only

when he was sure she was too deeply asleep to be disturbed
by another frightening dream.

Having come to a decision, he returned to the kitchen,
found paper and a pen and sat down at the table to write a
letter. After that, he dozed for a while on the living-room
sofa, getting up occasionally to make sure Kari was still
sleeping peacefully.

Just after dawn he called his housekeeper, Estella, and
when she arrived at the house an hour later, he did what he'd
known all along he would have to do. He called a taxi to take
him back to San Antonio.

He had to give Kari some time to think, and he had to
take a little time away from her to do the same himself. He
had meant it when he told her she brought out the best in
him, and he now knew in his heart that would never change.
More than anything, he wanted to spend the rest of his life
with her. But until he had given her a chance to consider all
that he'd told her, he couldn't, in good conscience, ask her
to be his wife.

He couldn't bear it if she agreed only because she was still
held in thrall by the sexual hunger he'd awakened in her over
the past two weeks. Weeks she had more or less been forced
to spend in his company because she'd had no other safe
place to go. Weeks when he hadn't been able to stop himself from taking all she had seemed so willing to give.

The sound of the taxi pulling up outside the house drew
him from his reverie.

"You'll look after her for me, Estella?" he asked as he
slung his backpack over his shoulder.

"Of course, Señor Payton."

"And you have the number where I can be reached if
there are any problems?"

"Right here." Smiling indulgently, she patted the pocket of her apron. "Along with the letter you're leaving for the señorita."

"Good."

"When will you be back?" she asked, following him to the door.

"I'm not sure."

"Soon, I hope."

"Me, too."

"You should spend more time here, señor," she scolded. "This place is good for you."

"You're right, Estella. It is."

Especially with Kari here, too.

Maybe, just maybe, he could finally begin to live the life he'd always wanted. A life he had thought would always be just out of his reach.

But only time would tell.

Chapter 12

Lured by the aroma of freshly brewed coffee—and, if she wasn't mistaken, homemade banana-nut bread—Kari made her way down the hallway, across the living room and into Alex's kitchen, a smile tugging at the corners of her mouth.

Thanks to the sleeping pill he had given her, she had slept deeply well into the afternoon. Although it had taken her a while to awaken completely, by the time she had showered and dressed in her jeans and one of Alex's shirts, she'd felt almost like herself again.

The events of the previous day were still fresh in her mind, but not disturbingly so. She was too glad to be alive and well and here with Alex, who was also alive and well. When she considered what could have happened yesterday, what *had* happened paled in comparison. And while she wasn't happy that Brandon was dead—she would have much preferred to see him rot in prison—she was relieved that he would never be able to do anyone else any harm

"I'm sorry I was such a slug," she began as she stepped into the kitchen, fully expecting to see Alex there.

Instead her gaze fell upon an elderly Hispanic woman, neatly dressed in a black skirt, plain white blouse and brightly colored, flowered apron, her salt-and-pepper hair pulled back in a tidy bun, her brown eyes warm and inquisitive.

"Good afternoon, señorita. I am Estella, Señor Payton's housekeeper." She nodded toward the table, set with a single place mat and napkin. "Sit down and let me get you some coffee," she added. "And perhaps a slice of my banana-nut bread?"

"Yes, of course. Thank you," Kari murmured, her smile fading. "Where's Alex?"

Not anywhere there. She knew that instinctively. But she couldn't quite believe he had left her already. She knew he still had two weeks before he was supposed to report to McConnell. And somehow she had foolishly believed they'd spend that time together. Time she had been counting on. Time in which to strengthen the fragile bonds that had only just begun to grow out of their love for each other.

"He left early this morning. He didn't say where he was going, but he gave me a telephone number where he could be reached in an emergency."

The housekeeper handed Kari a slip of paper. The number on it was one she recognized, having used it in the past to get in touch with Devlin. You called the number, left a message, and the person you were trying to contact called you back whenever he could.

"Also, he asked me to give you this," Estella added.

As Kari looked up, the woman pulled a plain white envelope from her apron pocket and offered it to her. Hesitantly, she took it. Her name was written on the front, and from the feel of the envelope, there couldn't be more than one sheet of stationery inside. She turned it over and over several times, then set it aside as Estella placed a mug of coffee and a plate of banana-nut bread in front of her.

She would read the letter sometime later when she was alone and hopefully prepared for what would more than likely be his final farewell. Right now, it would be all she could do to drink her coffee and eat a few bites of the housekeeper's homemade bread without bursting into tears.

She should have been better prepared for this moment. She also should have known it would come sooner rather than later. Alex hadn't made any promises except to keep her safe, which he'd done with flying colors. Now that he no longer deemed his presence necessary for her well-being, of course he would want to be on his way.

He'd never been one to linger once he had decided on a course of action. And where she was concerned, he had obviously decided—yet again—not to allow her any say in the matter.

"You must be very special to Señor Payton, señorita," Estella said, joining her at the table companionably, her own mug of coffee in hand.

"Why do you say that?" Kari asked, wishing she could really believe it was true.

But then, he wouldn't have left her, would he? Unless he still thought of himself as damaged goods.

"He's never brought anyone here before. Anyone at all."

"He didn't have much of a choice with me," she hedged. "I needed a place to stay temporarily, and my brother asked him to look after me."

"Ah, don't fool yourself. The one thing Alexander Payton makes sure he always has is a choice," Estella replied in a kindly tone. "And he didn't want to leave you. I know tha for a fact. I saw the sadness in his eyes, and I've never seen sadness in his eyes before.''

''But he did leave,'' Kari said, unable to hide her grief any longer. Swiping at the single tear that trickled down her cheek, she added, ''Without even saying goodbye.''

''Maybe he says that in his letter.''

''Maybe.''

''You should read it, señorita.''

''I will. Later.''

With a *tsk*ing sound, Estella rose to refill their mugs. As she set the coffeepot back on the burner, the telephone rang and she went to answer it.

For an instant Kari thought it might be Alex, then admitted that in the highly unlikely event it was, he probably wouldn't ask to speak to her anyway.

''For you, señorita,'' the housekeeper said, stretching the telephone cord so Kari could take the receiver without getting out of her chair. ''A Mr. Kevin Wyatt.''

''Hello, Kevin,'' she said, trying to sound more cheerful than she felt. ''How are you feeling?''

''Like a herd of buffalo just took turns tap-dancing across my back,'' he replied with a rueful laugh.

''That good, huh?'' Her spirits lifting, she smiled. Of them all, he had come closest to losing his life, but he seemed to be taking it in stride.

''Yeah, that good. How about you?''

''Just fine,'' she replied—too quickly, she realized.

''Nice try,'' Kevin chided. ''How are you really?''

''Alex is gone,'' she blurted before she could stop herself.

''I know. He called me from the airport this morning and asked me to do a couple of things for you. I just wanted to let you know I've taken care of everything as requested.''

"What do you mean by *everything?*" she asked, truly puzzled.

"I had your furniture packed and put into storage. I also had your clothes and other personal belongings packed and sent to Alex's place. Several boxes should be delivered to you later in the afternoon or early in the evening." Kevin paused, then added, "You did know about this, didn't you?"

"Not until just now," Kari admitted. "But thanks for taking care of it."

She hadn't thought about retrieving her belongings and closing up the cottage. Probably because she had no real desire to go back there. As Alex had obviously guessed. He, along with Kevin, had saved her a lot of anguish, for which she was deeply grateful.

"I don't suppose you have any idea where he went?" Kevin asked.

"None at all." Fingering the envelope on the table, she wondered if it held any clues. More than likely not. "He did leave a telephone number where he can be reached, though. Would you like me to give it to you?"

"Yes, please."

Kari repeated it from memory so he could write it down.

"Do you think you might be up to coming into San Antonio on Monday?" Kevin continued. "We'd like to go over Selby's records with you and see if we can nail the owners who paid him off for destroying their horses."

"Sure. What time would you like me to be there?"

"How about ten-thirty?"

She agreed to meet him at his office then, politely refused his offer to provide transportation, told him to take care and said goodbye.

She told Estella she was expecting a delivery later in the day, then added that she would be going to San Antonio on Monday, probably just for a day, maybe two. After that, she wasn't sure what she'd do. But she knew she had to start thinking about it. She felt odd staying in Alex's house without him. Yet she wasn't all that eager to leave, either.

Suddenly feeling as if she couldn't breathe, she tucked his letter into the back pocket of her jeans, excused herself and went out to the deck. The sky was clear, the sun hot, the air still. Pulling one of the chairs into a patch of shade, she sat down and eyed the big old barn standing empty on the far side of the lawn.

A long time later, a van arrived and two men unloaded half a dozen cardboard boxes under Estella's strict supervision. A short while after that, the housekeeper advised her there was a casserole warming in the oven. Then she showed her how to operate the security system and, promising to return the next morning, left for the day.

Alone on the deck, Kari watched the evening shadows creep across the lawn, no more sure where she was going to go or what she was going to do than when she'd first come out there. With a sigh of resignation, she dug Alex's letter from her pocket. Knowing she had put it off long enough, she lifted the flap, pulled out the single sheet of paper, unfolded it and began to read:

Dear Kari,
First let me say that more than anything, I wish I could be there with you now. But that wouldn't be fair to you. For the past two weeks we've been more or less forced into each other's company, and I realize that hasn't made it easy for you to think straight. Maybe our spending some time apart will give you a chance to sort

out how you really feel about everything that's happened.

I'll be traveling around until the end of month. Then I thought I would take Laura up on her offer and visit our godson for a few days. The invitation was for both of us. I hope you'll be there, too. But if not, I'll understand.

Alex

Clutching the letter to her chest, Kari blinked back the hot tears stinging her eyes. Damn him and his chivalrous soul for tying her up in knots. Of course, he had probably assumed she would read his letter as soon as Estella gave it to her. But still—

He hadn't left her. Not for good. Just for the time he thought she needed to change her mind about loving him. Well, he was in for a big surprise two weeks from now, because she wasn't about to change her mind. Not now. Not ever.

She was going to be waiting for him in Virginia. And she was going to tell him—once and for all and in no uncertain terms—exactly how she felt about him. How she would feel about him as long as she had breath in her body.

And if he still didn't believe her, she would tell him again and again until he finally did.

For several minutes after the taxi pulled away from the curb, Alex stood on the sidewalk in front of Devlin's house, backpack over his shoulder, hands tucked in the pockets of his jeans. Around him, the sounds of a midmorning Saturday in suburbia drifted on the summer breeze. Lawn mowers roared, dogs barked, kids on bicycles called out to one another and birds chirped high up in the trees.

He had spent most of the past two weeks on a quiet beach in the Florida Keys, walking in the sand and watching the waves roll in, missing Kari more with each day that passed. The temptation to go back to her and do whatever was necessary to bind her to him permanently had been all but overwhelming. Yet he had stayed away, knowing that he owed her the time he had promised her.

A couple of days ago, he had finally left the little house hidden in the dunes. He had intended to go straight to Devlin's, but at the Miami airport, he had booked a flight to Philadelphia, instead.

He hadn't been back there in twenty-five years, hadn't wanted to go back. But suddenly he had seemed to be drawn there. Not so much to the city as to the elegant old house in the posh neighborhood where he had lived in fear and self-loathing so very long ago.

He hadn't been able to go inside, of course. Wasn't sure he would have if, by some fluke, the opportunity had presented itself. But standing at the edge of the manicured lawn, gazing at the place that still sometimes haunted his dreams, he finally felt a kind of letting go deep inside himself.

He couldn't change what had been done to him there, but he did have the power to determine how *he* behaved now as well as in the future. Yes, he had been subjected to unspeakable horrors once. But he had not only survived, he had gone on to make something worthwhile, something decent and honorable, of himself. And having done that, he no longer had any reason to allow his past either to rule his life or ruin it.

When he had finally turned back to the taxi waiting for him on the street, he had done so with a sense of autonomy he'd never experienced before. And then, his heart filled with hope, he had headed for the airport and a flight to Virginia.

Now he was there, trying to build up the courage to approach the front door, ring the bell and find out if Kari was waiting for him. Leaving the way he had, he'd given her every reason to be furious with him. But he vowed that if she had found it in her heart to give him another chance, he would spend the rest of his life making it up to her.

So, just do it, he ordered himself, putting one foot in front of the other. He had told her he would understand if she wasn't there, and he would. But actually facing the possibility of having to go on without her was more than he could contemplate.

Both Laura and Devlin answered the door. Standing side by side, they eyed him critically for several seconds. Then Laura smiled and stepped forward, hugging him with warmth and affection.

"Finally," she murmured. "We were beginning to wonder if you'd gotten lost."

As she moved back, Devlin offered his hand in greeting.

"Good to see you again, buddy."

"Good to see you, too," Alex replied. Then, unable to help himself, he glanced past them, seeking but not finding the woman he loved.

Her smile widening, Laura took him by the arm and drew him into the house.

"Kari is out in the yard with the boys," she said as if reading his mind.

With an overwhelming sense of relief, Alex dropped his backpack on the floor and started toward the hallway. Then, realizing he had completely forgotten his manners, he paused and turned back to his friends.

"I just thought I would go out and . . . say hello."

Slipping her arm around her husband's waist, Laura gazed at Alex reproachfully. "Actually, we were hoping you would do more than that. A lot more," she added meaningfully.

"Well, then, I guess I had better not disappoint you."

He made his way to the kitchen and out the back door, halting on the patio as he caught sight of Kari over by Devlin's rose garden. She stood with her back to him, holding Andrew up against her shoulder, listening carefully as Timmy pointed to one blossom, then another, naming them for her.

For the space of several heartbeats he stayed where he was, drinking in the sight of her as if she were water and he a man lost much too long in the desert. Then Timmy spotted him and tugged at the hem of her shorts excitedly.

"Aunt Kari, Aunt Kari," he cried. "Uncle Alex is here. *Finally!*"

The boy took off running toward him. Alex met him halfway, catching him in his arms and giving him a fierce hug. Kari followed more slowly, her eyes holding his as she rubbed her hand gently over the baby's back.

One day, he thought, one day—God willing—she would hold *his* child that way.

"I'm glad you came," he said as she halted a few paces from him.

"I'm glad I did, too." She smiled slightly. "I missed you."

"I missed you, too." Suddenly ill at ease, he shoved his hands in his pockets.

"All right, boys, time to go inside," Laura said, walking past him to take Andrew from Kari, then resting a motherly hand on Timmy's shoulder and herding him toward the house.

"But, Mom—" he protested.

"No buts, young man," she interrupted. Then she glanced up at Alex and, as if reading his mind, added more softly, "Just say what's in your heart."

As the back door closed, leaving them alone, Kari took another step toward him, then another, slowly closing the distance between them as her eyes searched his.

Just say what's in your heart.

"I love you," he murmured. "Have for as long as I can remember and will until the day I die."

"And I love you, Alex. With all my heart for always," she replied as he put his arms around her and held her close, so very close, at last.

Epilogue

Hanging up the telephone, Alex crossed the kitchen and headed out the back door of the house. Waylaid on the deck by Maxie, their exuberant Australian shepherd, he paused to scratch the dog's floppy ears, his gaze roving over what was now known as Gray-Payton Farms.

Half a dozen horses grazed in the far pasture, while in the arena he had built almost three years ago as a wedding gift for his wife, four young riders practiced taking their horses over low jumps under the direction of Kari's recently hired assistant, Jennifer Hayden.

Kari herself, holding their two-year-old son, Seth, by the hand, stood near the barn, supervising the unloading of a mare sent to them for training. Having recently found out she was pregnant again, she had been taking it a little easier lately. But she still insisted on putting in full days working hard to make their stable even more well-known than it had already become.

Alex had had no second thoughts at all about giving up the work he had done for Uncle Sam. He'd resigned the Monday after he'd returned to Virginia, and a week later, he and Kari were married at her brother's house. They had come back to Texas immediately and had opened Gray-Payton Farms for business one month later. He had loved every minute of it just as he had loved her, and then their son, and now their new baby-to-be.

Remembering the call he had just taken, he continued on his way to the barn, the dog racing along ahead of him.

Kari and Seth greeted him with identical smiles, warming his heart as they always did. Swinging his son onto his shoulders, Alex bent and kissed his wife.

"Kevin called to say he's running late," he said.

"But he's still coming?"

"Yes, he's still coming."

"And Jennifer has agreed to stay for dinner."

"Are you sure it's wise to push them together?" Alex asked, putting an arm around her waist and drawing her close to his side.

"I can't think of anyone else who might be able to help her," Kari replied, her concern for her new friend evident. Then, on a lighter note, she added, "And we'll be following an old family tradition started by Laura and Devlin. So, what could it hurt?"

"What old family tradition is that?"

"Making sure two people who ought to be together have a chance to actually be together," she advised with a mischievous smile.

"You know, I like that tradition, love. I like it a lot."

"So do I," Kari agreed, resting her head on his shoulder. "So do I."

* * * * *

FORTUNE'S *Children*™

Bestselling Author
LISA
JACKSON

Continues the twelve-book series—FORTUNE'S CHILDREN
in August 1996 with Book Two

THE MILLIONAIRE AND THE COWGIRL

When playboy millionaire Kyle Fortune inherited a Wyoming
ranch from his grandmother, he never expected to come
face-to-face with Samantha Rawlings, the willful woman
he'd never forgotten...and the daughter he'd never known.
Although Kyle enjoyed his jet-setting life-style, Samantha and
Caitlyn made him yearn for hearth and home.

MEET THE FORTUNES—a family whose legacy is greater than
riches. Because where there's a will...there's a *wedding!*

A CASTING CALL TO
ALL FORTUNE'S CHILDREN FANS!
If you are truly one of the fortunate
few, you may win a trip to
Los Angeles to audition for
Wheel of Fortune®. Look for
details in all retail Fortune's Children titles!

There's nothing quite like a family

REUNION

HANNAH • MICHAEL • KATE

The new miniseries by
Pat Warren

Three siblings are about to be reunited.
And each finds love along the way....

HANNAH
Her life is about to change now that she's met
the irresistible Joel Merrick in HOME FOR HANNAH
(Special Edition #1048, August 1996).

MICHAEL
He's been on his own all his life. Now he's
going to take a risk on love...and
take part in the reunion he's been
waiting for in MICHAEL'S HOUSE
(Intimate Moments #737, September 1996).

KATE
A job as a nanny leads her to Aaron Carver,
his adorable baby daughter and the
fulfillment of her dreams in KEEPING KATE
(Special Edition #1060, October 1996).

Meet these three siblings from

Silhouette SPECIAL EDITION®
and

∇ INTIMATE MOMENTS®
™ Silhouette

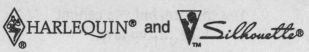

HARLEQUIN® and **Silhouette®**

are proud to present...

HERE COME THE GROOMS™

Four marriage-minded stories written by top
Harlequin and Silhouette authors!

Next month, you'll find:

A Practical Marriage	by Dallas Schulze
Marry Sunshine	by Anne McAllister
The Cowboy and the Chauffeur	by Elizabeth August
McConnell's Bride	by Naomi Horton

ADDED BONUS! In every edition of
Here Come the Grooms you'll find $5.00 worth
of coupons good for Harlequin and Silhouette
products.

On sale at your favorite Harlequin and Silhouette
retail outlet.

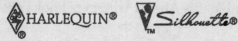

HARLEQUIN®   **Silhouette®**

HCTG896

You can run, but you cannot
hide...from love.

OUTLAWS
and
Lovers

This August, experience danger, excitement and
love on the run with three couples thrown
together by life-threatening circumstances.

Enjoy three complete stories by some of your
favorite authors—all in one special collection!

THE PRINCESS AND THE PEA
by Kathleen Korbel

IN SAFEKEEPING
by Naomi Horton

FUGITIVE
by Emilie Richards

Available this August wherever books are sold.

Silhouette®
™